last kiss of summer

last kiss of summer

Jessica M. Felleman

G. P. Putnam's Sons

G. P. Putnam's Sons
An imprint of Penguin Random House LLC
1745 Broadway, New York, NY 10019
penguinrandomhouse.com

Produced by Alloy Entertainment LLC

Design by Nicole Rheingans
Text set in Milo Serif Pro

Library of Congress Cataloging-in-Publication Data is available.

First published in the United States of America by G. P. Putnam's Sons, 2026

Manufactured in the United States of America

LSCC

ISBN 9798217001910
1st Printing

The authorized representative in the EU for product safety and compliance is Penguin Random House Ireland, Morrison Chambers, 32 Nassau Street, Dublin D02 YH68, Ireland, https://eu-contact.penguin.ie.

For Mom and Dad

And in memory of Lorraine Knapp,
who loved a love story,
and Joan Felleman, who made sure
I learned the language of love

CHAPTER ONE

Sera

There's this moment on the Sagamore Bridge where time stretches out. From way up here, you can glimpse the ocean just beyond the canal. Even through the early-morning fog I can see it—a sliver of blue, promising me a good summer, maybe even a great one. I've been waiting for this. It's been a painful two years since my family came down to Cape Cod, and it's felt like even longer. I fiddle with the beaded bracelet on my wrist—a reminder not to waste the time I have left.

I was born with a heart defect and had a transplant as an infant. My heart came from a girl named Edith B. Eichman, EBE for short, and two summers ago, it started to fail me. But I've been stable since January, and after two years of being stuck in Brookline to be near my doctor, we're finally coming back to our happy place.

As our car creeps slowly over the bridge, I nudge my sister out of the way and snap a photo. I send it off to Maddy with a text to meet me for coffee before her shift. I can't wait to see her. We've planned to spend all summer doing our favorite things—thrift shopping, lying around at Northport Beach, walking the nature paths, eating Maddy's baking concoctions, and going art hunting. I have time to make up for.

"No photos," Abbi groans, and tugs the hood of her oversized sweatshirt over her red curls.

She let her boyfriend, Cam, borrow her car for a gig in Providence, so she got stuck with the early wake-up call like the rest of us.

"The sun is barely up, and it's overcast," I tease, knowing she was out late with her friends from Emerson like she has been almost every night since finals were over. How she maintains a 4.0 GPA with a double major in political communication and journalism, a minor in environmental studies, and such an active social life is some kind of genetic marvel I didn't inherit. "Why are you wearing sunglasses?"

"Because they're *vintage*." Abbi's voice is low, warning. "I wouldn't dare shove them in a tote bag."

"Because you're *tired?*" I toy with the idea of calling her out for being hungover, but I'm too giddy to start a serious round of negging that I'm bound to lose anyway. I count that as emotional growth. Graduating from high school must have anointed me with some new level of maturity. Or maybe it's just self-preservation.

"Look." I point past her face, and she swats my hand away.

"It's the ocean—big deal. I've seen it hundreds of times."

"Abigail," I whine a little, knowing I should be nicer to her after all she's done for me in the last couple years: taking a semester off school in the fall when I had surgery, being my emotional support as things got bad and my friends from school politely faded away. Without her and Maddy, my second-best—no, *best*-best—friend, I think I would've kicked the bucket from sheer boredom instead of heart failure. No volleyball, no school, no art camp, just one day after the next of *Is today the day I die?*

"Seraaaa," Abbi whines back, but there's a smile at the corner of her freckled cheek, so I know she's not mad at me. "Don't forget to make a wish before we're off the bridge," she reminds me, tucking herself back up into a ball. "Maybe that Luke hasn't gotten any cuter."

"Luke's not *that* cute," I mutter.

Abbi snorts, seeing right through me even with her eyes closed.

I sigh, annoyed, and pivot back to my window. The familiar murky blackish green of the canal makes my heart ache as it winds south around a corner into the mist.

I've been trying not to think about Luke, my once-upon-a-time best friend, and Abbi knows it.

Two years ago, as we drove home to Brookline a few days early, my bridge wish was for there to be nothing seriously wrong with my heart. Clearly that didn't work. After weeks of back-to-back appointments and tests and monitoring, I was diagnosed with stage-three hypertrophic cardiomyopathy. I barely had time to think about my crush on Luke and how wrong I'd been to think he liked me back. It wasn't until weeks later that it really hit me. He'd rejected me. And he hadn't even checked in to see why we'd left the Cape so abruptly.

After a year of trial and error, I had minor surgery last

October, and then we finally found a medication that works. EBE will need to be replaced one day, but my doctor says I have about five years before my health starts to decline. I'm feeling good now, and I want to do *all* the things I didn't get to over the last two years. I have a job teaching at my old art camp, and my parents agreed to a gap year for me to think about what's next. I'm not sure what that will be, but I know I want more. More time for fun and travel and as many new things as I can squeeze in before I need a new heart and have to slow down and get through that major surgery. I have plenty to think about without dwelling on Luke and how much of a crap friend he turned out to be, or what could've been between us if I hadn't misread everything.

As we exit the bridge and pick up speed again, I swear the clouds part. We've finally left mainland Massachusetts behind for the next three months, and the summer is wide open. Everything here feels brighter. The trees are a deeper green, and the air is warmer even in the damp misty weather. It feels like the whole place is celebrating our return. I'm not going to let Luke ruin this summer.

I put my headphones back on and choose the playlist Maddy and I have been building together—*Sera and Maddy's Summer of Greatness*.

And then we're there. Scrappy tan and brown baby rabbits peek out of the tall unmowed grasses on the main drag. We all exclaim at the new four-way stop they've put in on our street corner and the new street sign with *Beach Rose Lane* done up in cursive.

"About time," Dad says as a group of kids around my age zip by on their bikes. Fishing rods are strapped to their backs as they head toward the docks. They all lift their hands at us—locals—and we wave back even though we don't know them.

Our cedar-gray Cape house sits snug next to a towering rhododendron that was the perfect hiding spot for hide-and-seek when we were little. A row of beach rose bushes on the left acts as a divider from Luke's house, with its painted blue front. The tires pop over the white crushed-clamshell driveway. Before we're fully stopped, I throw my door open and step out to unlock the garage. Once I punch in the code and the door starts to creak up, I head for the skinny path around the right side of the house.

Dad's been here to do upkeep, but there's something a little abandoned-looking about the backyard patio. The firepit is rusty and full of dead leaves, and the double-seater swing hanging off the pergola is broken, one side resting crookedly on the sandy dirt. At the back of the yard, though, the old playset and tree house both look sturdy. It'd make a good painting, and I can't wait to unpack my watercolors.

I heave open the heavy sliding door that leads into the kitchen just as Abbi and Mom come in from the garage with the first round of bags.

"I'll help," I offer, kicking my sneakers off and hop-sliding across the smooth wooden floor in my socks.

Mom waves me off. "No, no, go get settled in. I know you're dying to see Maddy." She dumps the bags on the dining table and looks around the dark-wooded kitchen. "I'm so glad to be back," she says, reaching out and touching my light brown hair—the same color as hers. I take after her Jewish half. Abbi's red hair and freckles come from Dad's Irish relatives.

"Me too," I say with a smile. "We'll bring back muffins," I promise as Dad comes in with another armful of things.

"Two for me," he says, dropping bags of groceries and turning toward the basement. "I'll turn on the water."

Mom calls out, reminding him to be gentle with the pipes. We don't need another incident like we had when I was eleven and we had to go next door to shower for two weeks. I will be avoiding Luke as long as possible, and needing to use the Tisdales' shower would make that tough. I grab my backpack off the table where Mom left it, and she swats playfully at me when I reach for one of the suitcases.

"Get outta here. I mean it." She lifts a box out of Abbi's hands too. "You too, Abbi. Go air out your rooms and then get out of the house. I bet you could use a coffee. You're moving a little slow."

Abbi shrugs, caught, and I smirk at her before dashing to the corner past the fridge. Hidden in what looks like a tiny cupboard, there's a set of stairs that lead to my room, which is in the older part of the house. Mom and Dad added on the garage and their bedroom above it when they bought the place, but Abbi's and my rooms are in the original upstairs. I make my way up the dark narrow stairwell and step on the creaky first floorboard of my room. I open all three windows, including the one that looks over the rosebushes at the Tisdales' next door. I spy to see if they're awake, but it's barely 8:00 a.m., and the navy-blue curtains of the bedroom facing mine are pulled shut. I catch sight of a *Congrats, Seniors!* sign in their yard next to a couple little-kid bikes and a half-set-up volleyball net that a gray cat is sniffing suspiciously, but no human movement. I feel a twinge of relief, then spot Luke's old black truck in the driveway. It's covered in dew, and I remember leaning out the passenger window as the wind whipped through my hair, the music loud, Luke pulling me closer to whisper something in my ear, his breath shivering down my spine.

I blink away the memory and drop my bag on the window bench. I'm heading to the closet, looking for bedsheets, but Abbi stops me in the hall.

"Are you ready? I need coffee, like, now." She's already changed out of Cam's hoodie and into a pair of black jeans and a white crop top. Her jewelry is layered, the only thing with color besides her hair, and her sunglasses rest on her smoothed-out curls. She's even had time to swipe on some mascara. I look down at my black leggings and old volleyball league sweatshirt.

"Do I need to change?"

Abbi's silence is enough of an answer, so I slip back into my room and pull on a pair of jean shorts and a fresh long-sleeved T-shirt. There's a little knot of anxiety in my chest. I try to ignore it as I run a brush through my hair and steal one more glance out the window.

Abbi appears at my door, giving an unapproving eye to my outfit.

"Let's go." I grab my tote bag and pretend to ignore the look, pushing past her. She catches up to me as I turn left out the driveway, away from the ocean and toward downtown. I send off a quick text to Maddy letting her know we're heading to Lorell's.

Calling it "downtown" might be too generous. Unlike Brookline, the total sum of Northport's center is one street barely a quarter mile long. Sure, there's the back half facing the harbor too, but a lot of those places are abandoned. Northport isn't as fancy as other towns on the Cape. There are tourists, but the strong year-round population can be a little off-putting to outsiders. Locals take being a local very seriously. Thankfully, even though we were only ever here a few months a year, we've always been treated like locals, probably because of how close we are with the Tisdales. I worry our two years away and my rift with Luke have changed that.

Like she can read my mind, Abbi loops her arm through mine as we turn onto Main.

"It's good to be home," she says. "I missed the smell."

I take a deep breath in. The dense salty air calms me. "Me too," I say.

"Ooh, look." Abbi points as we come upon the first of the downtown shops.

The storefronts already have their themed summer art on the windows. I recognize some of the artists' names, both from gallery shows I've been to and even kids I went to camp with down here. Art school is on my maybe list, though the idea of spending more time in school, even art school, grates on me like a sunburn. I just want to move, see the world, *live*. I'm tired of wasting time.

When we reach Nyeman's Antiques & Interior Design, I slow. Luke's grandparents own it, though his parents took over a few years ago, bringing in all the gifty and decor items Cape visitors expect. His mom also started doing interior design consultations, and I guess it's become a big enough part of the business that they got a new sign. I'm happy for her, but I stop completely when I see the art in the window. The painted window is all Luke. Black and white, professional and clean. The two bridges stretch over the canal with the Nyeman's name done in a sharp original font between them. It reminds me of the fake book covers he used to make up when our favorite series author didn't have anything new.

Luke's been working shifts after school and on weekends since we were thirteen. He could be in there prepping to open. I can't walk by. He might see me.

"Sera." Abbi is already past the shop, but I widen my eyes at her to be quiet. She sighs, flips her sunglasses into her hair, and peers inside. "Relax. The lights are off; he's not in there. It's too early."

"Right," I say, catching up to her.

"You still haven't talked to him?" she asks as we step around a family with three little kids who are crowding the tiny brick sidewalk.

"Nope."

"Don't you think you should?"

"Why?"

Abbi sighs and shakes her head but doesn't say more. She and Maddy are the only people who know what happened with Luke, and talking about it with them once was embarrassing enough.

At the bookstore, I stop to stare through the decorated

window at the new releases, hoping for some good science fiction and wondering if Lori, the owner, has shelved any good books in the used section upstairs.

"Oh, Cam's calling me," Abbi says, glancing down at her phone. "You got the Lorell's order, right?"

"You know my summer job hasn't started yet," I reply, raising an eyebrow.

"Well . . . I'm a broke college student, so, not it." She's already walking over to one of the rocking chairs on the bookstore's porch.

I roll my eyes and head toward the bakery three doors down.

Thankfully there's no line yet. I step inside and the heavy tang of coffee mixed with baked goods brings a smile to my face. But as I weave through the tables toward the counter in the back, I see someone sitting by the window, and my heart has a fit, in a nonmedical way.

Luke Tisdale sits there staring at me like I'm a sea monster crawled onto shore. All that worry over him being home next door or in his parents' shop, and he's here. It's like he knew I was coming. Like he was sitting in wait to ambush me about where I've been for the last two years. I start to sweat, and my legs tense, ready to turn and leave. Because it's *Luke*. My ex–best friend and the boy who literally has two pieces of my heart. *Crap.*

CHAPTER TWO

Sera

As I try to get out of there, stat, I end up crashing into a woman and her two kids as they come through the door. I take a few quick steps out of the way, apologizing to her, but that means I'm a few steps closer to Luke. He's still looking at me, and there's no running. He stands and greets me with an awkward hug. At first all I can think about is his last message from just over a year ago—**please don't ghost me again, Sera, I just need to talk to my best friend**—but then I notice how big he is, and I freeze, arms at my side.

Luke and I have always been about the same size. The proof lines the walls of both our houses in pictures from the days after we were both born, broken and in need. That's the reason our families are so close. I got a new heart, and Luke had domino surgery, getting the healthy valves from my otherwise useless original heart. The newspapers loved us, sharing photos of us holding hands in the same crib post-surgery and the story of how our families were brought together by the same near tragedy.

When Luke was discharged and his family returned to the Cape, my mom convinced my dad to rent the place next door to theirs. Our moms became inseparable as we fought our way to being healthy toddlers and then troublemaking terrors. My family loved Northport and the Tisdales so much we would've moved here full-time, but Dad couldn't stop teaching at Emerson, so we became part-timers. My parents bought the house, and we came down as often as we could—weekends, most holiday breaks, and of course, all summer. Northport is where we feel most like ourselves, and the Tisdales were always part of that. It was all family barbecues and group bike rides to the beach. Days spent out on Luke's dad's boat and evenings around our firepit. It was perfect—until it wasn't.

Because suddenly, two summers ago, I found myself looking at Luke differently. I was thinking nonstop about what kissing him would be like. Wondering if he'd be any better at it than my ex-boyfriend, Ethan, who never gave me the intense butterflies I was feeling around Luke. Every time Luke grabbed my hand to get my attention or reached over me to point out something he liked about my painting, my skin would ripple with electricity. I craved these moments of contact. I began to count how often his eyes found mine in a crowd. My stomach flipped every time I made him laugh. It felt like there was an *and then* about to surprise us. Maybe it was nothing. Maybe the way he looked at me when we were alone—like he was thinking that kissing me was worth potentially ruining our friendship—was all in my head. Still, I'd been ready to risk it.

But he didn't feel the same way, I remind myself. Thankfully I'm over it. *I'm over it. I'm over it,* I chant to myself to get through the hug.

Luke smells familiar, like sunscreen and salt water but also something new and lightly spicy that I can't put my finger on. The contact is a little too sudden, so I don't have time to raise my arms, and he only holds me for a second before stepping away like I might be diseased. And, well, I am, but not in a way that's catching.

The heat of his body lingers on mine, the echo of the contact teasing me with the startling fact that he hasn't just gotten *cuter* in the last two years, he's gotten *hot*. He's taller than me now, and that's a feat, since at five ten I'm not used to looking up at many people. I was just as tall as him the last time we were down here. It made it hard not to stare at his bow-shaped lips, swoopy brown hair, and smooth olive-toned skin. I shake my head a little to rid myself of that thought.

I force myself to meet his gaze and finally find my voice, squeaking out a *hey,* or a *hi,* or a *hello.* I'm not sure. I don't hear myself over the blood pounding in my ears.

"Hi," Luke says, dipping his hands back into the front pocket of his dark red hoodie. "It's been a while . . ."

"Yeah," I manage, and try to smile. "It's nice to see you."

He raises both eyebrows at me in a challenge, and I shrug, caught. It's not nice. It's complicated. Luke *did* reach out last year, asking to talk, asking to pick up our friendship. But after what had happened, and with everything going on with my health, I just couldn't do it.

"I'll go," I mutter, turning to leave, feeling my commitment to living every moment in the fullest slipping away. A good wallow sounds great about now.

"You don't want a blueberry muffin?" Luke surprises me by moving through my awkward attempt to end the conversation and gesturing to the counter.

Of course I want a muffin. What I don't want is to linger here with him and the sour feeling of what I thought was my healed-over hurt. I stare at the logo on his sweatshirt for a beat before answering. It's the Northport High School mascot, an osprey, but with a baseball bat in its claws instead of the usual fish, and I finally put two and two together. I wonder if he's a jock now, not just sitting on the bench to please his dad. He's probably popular and well-liked and has no worries beyond which scholarship to accept and which farewell parties to grace with his presence. He looks like the last time he got bad news he was an infant.

"Aren't they your favorite?" he adds, looking at me with a quick gut-wrenching smile that doesn't touch his dark green eyes.

"Only pastry worth having on the whole Cape," I say, trying to regain some sense of normalcy. This is my town too. I can be normal. I get back in line, and for some reason he stays next to me. I order as quick as I can: six muffins, an iced sugary coffee concoction for Abbi, black coffee for my parents and Maddy, per her request, and a chai latte for me.

I force myself to pretend everything is fine. I read the handwritten chalkboard menus over and over as my foot jiggles. I can't keep still. I play with the band of my smartwatch, grateful the medical ID part is on the underside of it. Then I fiddle with the beads on my *EBE* bracelet, the one he made me when we were ten. I've only taken it off once since, two years ago for my last volleyball tournament, right before my life imploded. I tug my sleeve down.

When he still doesn't leave me alone, I step away and turn to face him to give myself some space. "So, how are you?" It feels too rude not to ask the basics.

"Okay." I'm surprised by the short answer when he so clearly wants to talk. "You?"

"Okay." Two can play it close to the chest.

"Are you staying all summer?"

"That's the plan."

"Will you—"

He's interrupted when the cashier hands me a pink paper bag.

"I should go." I pick up one of the drinks, not looking at his face or the confusing expression of hurt there that's plucking at my heart rate.

But I haven't really thought this through. There's too much for me to carry alone. I put the food down. I can feel Luke waiting for me to ask him for help. No thanks. Thankfully someone else calls my name.

"Sera!" Maddy comes rushing up and wraps me in a rib-crushing hug.

"Maddy! You made it," I say, my mood lifting instantly as I squeeze her back.

"Of course. You bought me coffee before work. You're an angel." Maddy's family runs Waterviews. It's mostly a traditional American diner, but since Maddy's mom is Brazilian, they have some South American dishes on the menu too. It's the best restaurant in town, in my opinion.

"Want to go to Frappie's after your shift?"

"They closed," Maddy says with a pout.

"Really? They had the best ice cream on the Cape."

"We'll find you a new favorite," Maddy says as she straightens her oversized wire-frame glasses. "But I can't go out tonight. I have to watch Marissa," she grumbles.

"We have all summer," I remind her.

"Yes, we do!" she sings, and I laugh in relief with how easy it is to be myself with her again. Maddy picks up her coffee and turns to Luke.

"Hey. Are you at the marina or the shop today?" she asks him.

"The marina," he says, his eyes still on me.

"Cool. Remind Georgie he needs to let you off tomorrow night," she says.

Luke smiles and says he already did. Maddy grins, and I feel a slight pang at the ease between them.

Maddy turns back to me. "I'm working tomorrow too, but we'll catch up at the bonfire. You're still coming, right?"

"At Thirds Beach? Yes," I confirm. "Wouldn't miss it."

"You're coming to the bonfire?" Luke shifts on his feet, and Maddy's terrible at hiding the grin she flashes between the two of us. She and Luke have been friends since kindergarten, and she's been trying to get me to mend our friendship so she's not stuck in the middle anymore, but I haven't budged.

"Duh, Sera's a townie at heart. We couldn't have our senior bonfire without her."

Luke is quiet. Obviously I'm not wanted.

"Unless I'm not allowed, for some reason?" I challenge him, not sure why he's acting like he's the one who's hurt.

Luke flushes, stammers that of course I can come. "Just didn't think you cared about Northport stuff anymore."

"Of course I do," I say defensively.

"I gotta run," Maddy says before we can get into it. "I can help you out with these." She grabs a drink tray from a pile I didn't see and fills it for me.

"Thanks. Abbi's at the bookshop," I say, picking the food back up and turning toward the door.

"Bye, Luke," Maddy says as she leaves ahead of me.

I look at him quick, not sure what else to say. Luke stands there staring at me for another beat before he finally goes back to his table, where a familiar paperback sits, spine up, waiting for him to return to a battle we both know front to back. Maddy shoots me an *Are you okay?* look over her shoulder, and I shrug before following her outside.

We find Abbi blowing a kiss to Cam on FaceTime outside of the bookstore. She swoops in to take the drinks from Maddy, who shouts bye to us both and rushes to her car.

"That was not the way I wanted to start this summer," I say, speed-walking back toward home.

"What happened?" Abbi says. "Wait up, your legs are longer than mine!"

I slow down just enough for her to catch up.

"Luke," I say, taking a calming sip of my chai.

Abbi smirks. "I thought you were *fine*, over it, right?"

"Right. I am," I tell her, while telling myself that nothing ever really happened, so there's nothing to be hung up on.

There's a brief silence while we both bask in how I am *so not over it*.

"Maybe you'll meet someone new. Cam's coming down tomorrow with some friends."

"I'm not dating one of Cam's friends." I'm horrified. "I'm not a groupie."

"But you'd make such a cute groupie," she says, hip-checking me.

I stumble, my mind still lingering in the café. Abbi reaches out and grabs my hand, forcing me to stop walking.

"Hey," she says, pulling me to face her. "You were bound to run into him eventually."

I sigh. "I know, but did it have to be right away?"

"Maybe it's better this way," she says, reaching up and brushing my hair behind my shoulder. "It's happened. It's over. This summer is about having fun. Don't let some dumb crush from your past ruin that."

I look into her calm blue eyes. "You're right," I say.

She throws her arm around my shoulder.

"I'm always right," she declares, and I laugh.

Fun, right, I think. That's what this summer is for. No more moping. I'm going to live every minute of every day to the fullest. I can do that.

CHAPTER THREE

Sera

It rains all Sunday, keeping us in and threatening the bonfire. I've been reorganizing my room, unable to sit still. I moved all the furniture around, stacked my unread books by my bed, and sorted through art supplies I want to take with me to teach. I'm scrolling through Instagram artist time-lapse videos when Maddy texts. It's cleared up enough, and everyone's decided the bonfire is still on. I'm both relieved and nervous. Even though I've been okay since January, I finished school from home and haven't been to any parties in almost two years. I rush to get ready, popping into Abbi's room with my hair still wet from the shower to ask if Cam will be here in time to drive us.

"Probably not." She's lying on the floor listening to a science podcast. Something about volcanoes. Her toenails are freshly painted, and the smell is still in the air even with her window propped open. "We'll just take Dad's car, and *you'll* drive us home." She tips her head back and looks me up and down. "Is that what you're wearing?"

I'd slipped on jeans and the Olivia Rodrigo concert T-shirt I dyed myself three years ago.

"Come on." She tugs me back down the hall to my room, shoves me toward my closet, and takes the window seat, peering through the curtains at Luke's house. "Show me something that doesn't also double as painting clothes, workout clothes, or pajamas."

My closet is honestly a little bare. Comfort clothing is all I've been bothering with for the last couple of years, and I haven't done a refresh since I've gotten better. Everything from two summers ago is too small, kind of childish.

"Can I at least keep the jeans?"

"Yes, but then you need a tank top or a cuter shirt and a jacket. Do you still have that green one? And what are you doing with your hair? Makeup?"

I sigh again. My hair has always been a bit lackluster compared with Abbi's, even though I like how long it is. "Probably just letting it dry. No makeup." When Abbi does my makeup, it takes an hour.

"I'll blow it out." Abbi goes out to the bathroom and comes back with some products and the blow-dry brush, which, though old, isn't rusty yet from the Cape humidity. I pick out a few tank tops that still mostly fit, and she points to a cropped orange one. I change my T-shirt out for it and sit on the bench in front of my wicker vanity.

"So"—Abbi moves into interrogation mode—"who are you seeing tonight?"

"Maddy, the volleyball girls, maybe some other friends from camp if they're there."

Abbi nods, her eyes focused. "And the evening's goal?"

"Do I need to have a goal?" I laugh, then cringe as she pulls a little hard.

"Any situation you enter without a goal leaves you two steps behind. Opportunity wasted." Abbi doesn't like to do just one thing at a time. She thinks life is best when you're operating at hyperspeed.

"It's just a party, Abbi. Can't my goal be to catch up with my friends?"

"Sure"—she switches hands and moves to the other side of my head—"but that feels like an easy, low-bar goal."

"Fine, what's your goal for the evening?" I tease her.

"Make sure Cam and my Cape friends hit it off well and experience a true moment of joy."

"How is that different from mine?"

"It comes down to specifics, Sera." Another sheaf of warm, now-straight hair falls against my back. "How are you going to remember tonight?"

"Right." Abbi's exuberance is grating on me, and I just want to be there already, away from these questions.

"Best summer ever," she reminds me as she finishes the last section of my hair. It falls nicely around my shoulders, and I run my fingers through it, relaxing a bit. She's being sisterly, just in her own way.

"Yes." Healthy, happy, here. I can do specifics.

"So?"

I don't hesitate this time. "Make sure Maddy knows how much I've missed her and . . . take a chance at something new."

Abbi spins me around and grabs my shoulders, blue eyes practically glittering. "Yes, perfect."

The bonfire is in full swing when Abbi and I arrive. We haven't hit solstice yet, so sunset is still stretching later every night. We get there just as the last pink in the sky fades away, leaving the five or six bonfires spread down the beach to light our way from the lip of the dune. Thirds Beach is a skinny slip of land between private houses that are too far away across the salt marshes to be bothered by the town's teens blasting music and drinking.

I pause at the edge of the sand to take off my sandals and try to catch sight of Maddy at one of the fires. Abbi is already moving toward the closest one, waving at someone.

"Don't do anything I wouldn't do," she says over her shoulder, just as I see Maddy sprinting up the beach toward me. I squeeze her into a hug, lifting her ever so slightly until she squeals.

"Strong as ever, I see," she says as she leads me toward the fire she came from. I recognize a few kids from town, along with people I don't know. Northport may be small, but the thing about the Cape is that when you throw a party, every teen from Falmouth to Harwich is going to come.

"Yep." I take a deep breath of the smoke-tinged air and pat my chest once. After surgery last fall, my doctor put me into light strength training, saying it'd be good for my heart as it recovered. "All good."

"I'm so glad you're back." Maddy breaks into the circle at the fire and leans down to grab a couple of sodas from a cooler, handing me one. "I know you've already heard my complaints, but last summer sucked without you. No one would come to the film festival with me, and work was a drag without you stopping by. Luke was way too busy to come by on his own very much."

I crack open the soda, then hold it out to toast to her. "Well, I'm so sorry for missing it—I'll commit whatever crimes needed to make up for it." Maddy snorts. "For real"—I lower the can, clicking it against hers—"I wouldn't have made it through the last couple of years without you. Whatever you need this summer, I'm your girl. Need me to watch Marissa so you can go on a date? Rig the Fourth of July pie contest? Count me in."

Maddy laughs and slings an arm over my shoulder. "I may take you up on the pie sabotage, but I'm taking a hiatus from dating."

"Really? No summer romance?"

"Not this year," she says, dropping her voice to a whisper. "The breakup is still fresh. I need some me time. What about you?" Maddy pulls me over to sit on a couple of beach chairs that have just been vacated.

I look around. I haven't seen Luke, but I get the sense he's here. "I don't think so," I say. But in the back of my head I hear my own promise to myself, *something new*. "Though I'm not opposed to something," I admit.

Maddy squeals. "I mean, Luke is still single, mostly. He's never been serious about anyone. I bet you'd be different. I still think what went down between you two had the beginnings of something epically romantic." She pins me with a look. "Talk to him?" Maddy's too sweet to admit that what happened—or really, what *almost* happened—between Luke and me meant nothing to him.

"No, terrible idea. Not Luke. Over that temporary insanity." The lie burns a little in my throat, and I take a quick sip of my soda. "We're not even friends anymore."

"Fine, okay, if you're sure."

"I'm sure."

We settle back into chatting with the rest of the people around the fire. Everyone fills me in on the parties I missed and tells me where they're going to school. Two friends from art camp are going to MassArt, and we exchange numbers so we can hang out in Boston this fall. Maddy's ex, Ella, is going to California, and we all groan and pester her for abandoning the East Coast. Most kids can't wait to get off the Cape once they're done with high school, and I get that. I'm ready for a change too. But I'm still jealous that they got to spend their whole lives out here. When we come down for off-season weekends and February breaks, the quiet is always so peaceful compared to the hum of summer Cape and year-round Brookline and Boston. Maybe I'll find a job and stay here this fall, work on perfecting my landscapes. It's an idea at least, and it sounds better than what my parents want, which is for me to start taking a couple classes next summer before I start college full-time the following fall.

"What about you, Sera?" Ella asks.

"Gap year, like Maddy. I'm not sure what I want to do."

A couple people are walking by while I say it, and one of them does a double take. Luke. Our eyes catch, and I look away, turning back to Maddy, who launches into a list of fairs and events that she wants to cook for or go to. I'm trying to listen, but the group Luke is with has settled at the fire nearest ours and keeps turning up the music, so it's hard to focus on anything else.

"Who *are* those guys?" I complain, trying to sound casual. Maddy looks over at the group.

"The baseball team. They killed it this year. Made it to state and actually won. They're, like, the new football stars." Before I can control it, I feel a quick twinge of pride.

"Northport had football stars?"

"Ouch, well played." Maddy stands up and stretches. "I've gotta get going. I'm opening the diner tomorrow. We're still on for the beach in the afternoon, right?"

"Definitely."

"Great. I'll bring the food!"

"Something edible?" I tease. Maddy's well aware her concoctions don't always work out.

"Bring snacks if you're worried, but not too many, because it'll hurt my feelings."

"Heard, chef!"

After Maddy leaves, I excuse myself for a walk down to the water. I need a break from hearing about everyone's big plans for the future. The ocean at Thirds is usually calm, and now's no exception. The waves are small and quiet against the shoreline. I drop my shoes where it's still dry and carefully make my way closer to the water. The moon is bright and full tonight, lighting my way. The water is ice-cold, but after a minute or two, it feels good. I look around for interesting rocks and pick up a few smooth, flat ones. Another one catches my eye, cracked and heart-shaped. I bend down to get it. When I stand up, I see Luke making his way toward me, picking up rocks of his own. My pulse jumps, anxious, happy to see him and annoyed all at once. I slip the heart-shaped rock into the pocket of my jacket and turn away from him, watching out of the corner of my eye as he approaches. I can just make out the tan line that starts halfway up his calf. His feet practically glow. Any other summer, I would've teased him mercilessly about it. But it's not—*we're* not—like that anymore. I palm one of the flat rocks and then pull my shoulder back and flick the rock out over the water. It skips three times before sinking out of view.

"Not bad," Luke says.

I force a small smile and turn away to look for more rocks. I send two more out, neither making it very far, before he sends one of his own, which skips a dozen times into the darkness and, for all we know, keeps going for miles until it pings against the side of a boat. It's annoying how cool it is. I want to talk. It's like a constant itch in my chest, the natural reaction to being near him, but I don't even know where to start that won't put me right back where I was before. Finally he says something before I can cut him off again.

"Why didn't you tell me you were coming back this summer?"

A few answers tumble through my head. *Because I didn't want to talk to you at all. Because you'd find out anyway. Because I thought you liked me and I'm still embarrassed and hurt that you don't.*

I shrug. "I've been busy."

"Sure." He sounds a little mad, and that just puts me more on the defensive.

"I can be busy."

"Yeah, we're all busy, Sera. Whatever . . . I just thought . . ." His voice trails off. Is he upset with *me*? The rowdy crowd behind us starts calling his name, and he turns back, waves like he's telling them to give him a second. A girl's voice I don't recognize rises above the rest, and I swear he blushes. I think about Maddy's comment, that Luke's never been serious with girls, and how much that clashes with what I know of him. Or knew. There's almost no sign of the nerd I spent half the summer at art camp with every year. Who loved to watch weird movies and dig through the paperback science fiction section at the bookstore and escape the real world with me. Who would always answer my distress calls when I needed to get away from Abbi. Who I shared my biggest fears with: lobsters biting my toes, our hearts failing us again. And my biggest hopes too: that I could paint something so beautiful that people would talk about it after I was dead, and that I'd get to travel somewhere far away, where the world looks so different it could be another planet.

"You've changed a lot," I say as I turn to head back to the beach, hoping he takes that as the answer to his question. He turns back with me, catching my gaze with his eyes and holding me there as we walk.

"A lot has changed," he replies tensely.

I'm about to ask him what the hell that's supposed to mean when a volleyball comes flying our way. Out of instinct I lean down and bump it in the direction it came from.

"Sorry, my bad." A guy I sort of recognize comes running to catch it. Luke tenses as he approaches. "Wait, Sera Watkins?"

I blush, embarrassed that I can't remember him but pleased to be remembered. He's cute, even if he's a little tidier in looks than I'm normally drawn to. He steps closer, holding the ball against his hip. He's tall, and his blue eyes sparkle a little in the dark. I avoid the urge to glance at Luke and share one of our *looks like the rich kids are here* looks.

"Yep," I say, a little more confidently than I feel, trying to channel any of that shared DNA I have with my sister. "The one and only."

"Had to be with a pass like that." He grins. "I'm Jackson."

"Sera," I say. "But you already knew that . . ."

Jackson laughs. "Yeah, you played in a game against my school, Boston Latin. It's been a couple years, but you don't forget plays like that."

"Thanks," I say, feeling a sheepish smile on my lips. "That was a fun game." In my periphery, I see Luke drift away, back to the bonfire. He slides an arm around the girl who called after him. But I can still feel him looking at me. *Let him*. I focus on Jackson. "Do you stay in Northport?"

"Harwich Port. But we have pickup games in Dennis, if you'd like to come by."

"Right. Cool."

"Wanna play?" He gestures back to the few people waiting for him.

I hesitate for a beat, glancing back at Luke. His arm is still around that girl. It's just them and a few of his teammates left at that fire. The party is starting to wind down.

"I'm actually retired," I joke, hoping he doesn't ask me to elaborate. Strength training is one thing, but playing volleyball since my diagnosis freaks me out.

"Oh, no worries. Maybe we can just . . . hang sometime?" he says, his blue eyes hopeful.

My stomach does a somersault. "Yeah," I manage to say. "Sounds great."

I hand him my phone. He adds in his info, sends himself a volleyball emoji, then hands it back.

"Okay, Sera Watkins. See you soon." He grins, a dimple in each cheek, and passes a hand through his hair so I get a good look at the muscles on his arm. I can't help but feel a small thrill as I head back up the beach to find Abbi. *Something new,* I think, *check.*

I find Abbi and Cam snuggled together at the first fire, which is burning low, the wood shimmering orange.

"Ready to go soon?" I ask, waving a small hi to Cam. His topknot bobs as he says hi back to me.

"Yep, I'm beat." Abbi turns, plants a quick light kiss on Cam's mouth, and then gracefully hops up.

"You didn't want to go to Cam's?" I ask as we climb up the

dune. His aunt and uncle have a house in Barnstable with an apartment over the garage that's all his for the next two months, which is cool and all, but his parents are visiting his mom's family in Japan for the summer, and I still can't believe he didn't want to go.

"Not tonight," she says, linking her arm through mine. "Always leave them wanting a little more."

Unless you're like Luke, I think. *Then you just leave and move on to someone else.*

"You have fun? Meet your goals?" Abbi asks.

I look up at the moon-bright sky dotted with stars, the clouds long cleared away. My phone pings in my pocket as we reach the peak of the dune and start to walk down the other side. It's Jackson saying hi and sending me a pin for his volleyball game on Tuesday. I smile.

"Yeah, actually, I did."

CHAPTER FOUR

Sera

Though normally I'm a morning person, I sleep until my alarm rings at nine. I turn it off and spend a few minutes scrolling through Instagram. Jackson followed me last night, and he's already liked a couple of my painting posts. I follow him back and scroll through his profile. He plays lacrosse, and it looks like he's going to Harvard. I'm careful not to like anything, but I watch his stories, which show him already out on a sailboat this morning in a crisp white shirt and expensive-looking sunglasses Abbi would probably be drooling over. I've never been sailing, though I've been out on the ocean plenty with Luke and his dad.

A breeze blows my gauzy white curtains into the room. There's a layer of fog hiding the tops of the trees, and I hope it clears up before Maddy and I go to the beach later. I turn back to my phone and hit the like button on a time-lapse video from an artist I met at a Boston gallery earlier this year. Their work encouraged me to start painting portraits after always preferring landscapes, and I take note that they're going to be showing some work in P-town this summer.

Suddenly I'm craving pancakes. I pull on a pair of leggings and one of Mom's old, oversized law school sweatshirts. Barefoot, I creep carefully down my secret staircase to the kitchen, only touching the stairs where they won't creak too loudly, not sure if anyone is still sleeping.

The kitchen is part of the original house, so the ceiling is a little low, but it's cozy and familiar. I dig the heavy iron griddle out from under the stove and get it warming. Then I pull the pancake mix from the pantry and check the freezer to see if Mom brought home any blueberries yesterday.

"Score." I lift the giant bag out, and I'm just ladling the first pancake onto the over-buttered griddle when Mom comes in.

"Morning," I say as she fusses with the coffeepot and I drop frozen blueberries onto the pancakes until I'm satisfied each one has enough. "Did Dad sleep in too?"

"Of course not. He's out for a run." She gets the coffee brewing and comes to peek over my shoulder. "Got enough blueberries?" she jokes as I put another handful in.

"Is there such a thing as too many?" I laugh, and she agrees.

Her phone pings. "Oh, you have a call with Dr. Lee at ten," she reminds me, watching me peel turkey bacon from the package and lay it in a cold pan the way Maddy taught me.

"Yup, I know. It's just a check-in." Now that I'm eighteen, my parents don't need to be in on my appointments, but they still set calendar reminders.

"And you're feeling okay?"

"Yup." She stares at me for a minute like she's trying to catch me in a lie. "Seriously, Mom, I'm great. Even after all the beer last night," I joke. She narrows her eyes at me, then huffs, knowing I wouldn't dare. The coffee finishes running, and I fill her mug.

She pats my hand as thanks and then falls into her morning routine of coffee and the paper. Abbi appears in a matching pajama set as I slide the second batch of pancakes into the oven to stay warm. She grabs a mug and some coffee, and I ask her to pour me one too.

"What time is your appointment with Dr. Lee? And aren't you supposed to stick to tea?" she asks, holding my Black Dog mug hostage.

"It's not till ten. And I'm fine and allowed to have a little coffee." I grab my mug from her and pour myself half a cup. Abbi may have gone back to school in the spring, but she occasionally gets like this still, worried over nothing. I don't want to see her slip back into a version of herself where my health is at the center of her life. I want us all to just enjoy right now.

"Right, right, sorry," she says. She starts setting the table while I finish the last batch of pancakes and move the bacon to the drip plate.

Dad comes in next, freshly showered, and peels the pages he wants out of Mom's hands. I set the pancakes in the middle of the table with a flourish.

"Wow, what service." Dad forks two onto his plate and waves his mug around until I grab the pot and bring it to the table with me. "Hey, don't you have an appointment soon?" he asks.

"James." Mom warns him to back off even though she and Abbi have already done exactly the same thing. I can't help but laugh. Adjusting to our lives not revolving around my appointment schedule could definitely happen faster for me.

"Yes." I shovel a warm bite into my mouth and sigh in delight. "Damn, I'm good."

"Well, you could always go work for the Waterses if camp counseling doesn't suit you," Dad says.

"I don't think Maddy would let me in the kitchen," I admit.

"Not after that hand pie disaster at the town fair two years ago," Abbi adds.

"It's not my fault salt and sugar look exactly the same," I moan.

Mom laughs and takes another bite. "Well, at least you followed this recipe correctly."

"I'm going to love teaching," I say, even though I've never done it before. "I won't need another job."

"What about you, Abbi? Decided about that offer to coach volleyball?" Dad asks.

"Yeah," Abbi says, blowing on her black coffee. "It's too last-minute, I have research for that scholarship paper, and Cam and I have our Maine trip in August, so I said no."

"All right. Be young. Have no responsibilities. But remember your car payment is on you."

"Dad, I have plenty saved up from the *Globe* internship."

"Okay, okay," Dad says, backing off.

I hide my smile from Abbi and Mom, unable to help enjoying Abbi getting reprimanded, and keep eating until my plate is wiped clean.

After we're all done, Dad starts cleaning up, and I take my iPad to the screened-in porch and log in to my online health chart. As I click on the video link to my appointment with Dr. Lee, I catch a flicker of motion through the bushes between our house and the Tisdales'. I was always jealous that Luke's parents weren't the overprotective type. My health issues turned my parents into total helicopters. But Luke has been pretty much perfectly healthy since the surgery. Plus his mom has his two little brothers to run around after—chaos monsters at six and eight the last time I saw them. My screen chimes as Dr. Lee logs in.

"Hi, Sera."

"Hi, Dr. Lee. How's your Monday?"

"Good so far, thank you. How are you?"

Mom slips onto the wicker love seat next to me, and Abbi and Dad come around behind. In my camera view, I can only see Dad's crossed arms, but Abbi leans down so her curls brush my ear. You'd think we all had heart conditions.

"I'm good too. Feeling great, actually."

"Any of those side effects coming up?"

"Nope."

"Any fatigue? Dizziness?"

"None at all."

"Good, good." Dr. Lee flips through something on her desk and then looks back up. "Your scans from last Thursday showed that the procedure we did last October has reduced more of the thickening of the left ventricle muscle, so I'm happy with that improvement. Your ejection fracture could be better, so I'd like you to get some labs before our check-in next month, to see how you're managing the meds before we increase them. The nurse will send location options to your chart so you can find a place that's convenient. If those look good, we won't have to check in again until probably December." She pauses and fusses with some papers on her desk. "And we did get confirmation from UNOS that you're to remain on the transplant list in tier five unless there's any worsening of your condition."

I nod. It's what we'd been expecting. The fact that I will eventually need a new heart keeps me on the list, but there are so many more people who need them way sooner, like the people in tiers one through four. I'm happy to wait.

"Oh, and please make sure your watch is always charged, and remember to keep your medical alert ID on it at all times, even when swimming."

"Thank you, Dr. Lee," Mom says, leaning into the camera's view. "Should she watch her diet at all?"

"After six months of stability, if you're feeling good, then I don't see the need. I know there's plenty of good ice cream and fried seafood down there, so feel free to enjoy, but not too much caffeine or salt. We want to watch your blood pressure, keep it low, but not too low. With these results, we won't need to see you moved up the transplant list for a few years still."

One of the things I love about Dr. Lee is that she always talks directly to me, even if I'm not the one who asked the question.

"Thanks, Dr. Lee." She nods, and offers up a small smile, making sure she hits each of us with it, even Dad's torso.

"I can't wait to hear what you get up to at our next check-in. We'll talk then."

I log off before Mom or Abbi can jump in and add anything.

"All good?" I ask, waiting for them to object to Dr. Lee's advice, but they all nod.

Dad pats me on the shoulder and says he's going golfing, and Abbi says she wants to get some reading and yoga in and disappears up into her room. Mom and I sit for a few minutes, watching the fog lift off the backyard. I tip my head onto her shoulder, enjoying the quiet.

"Do you want to come to the beach with me and Maddy?" I offer, honestly fine if she says yes. It might be nice to spend some time together again that isn't focused around my doctor's appointments.

"No, that's all right. I don't want to cramp your style, and I'm meeting Paula for lunch anyway. We have the annual blood drive to finish planning, and she's been through a lot recently. I've been a lax friend with all that was going on . . . here . . . We haven't been in touch much."

"Mrs. Tisdale? What happened?" I sit up and look over at their yard. Luke's brothers are definitely back there playing, but there's no sign of him.

"Actually she's gone back to her maiden name. So, when you see her, it's just Paula, or Ms. Nyeman."

I flinch at the unfamiliar name. Even Luke's nana doesn't go by Mrs. Nyeman. "Why?"

"Oh, Luke didn't tell you? Well, they went through a bad divorce last year. It was messy, hard on the boys too, I think, and poor Paula nearly lost the house." Mom was a fancy divorce lawyer before I was born and she dropped to consulting part-time for her old firm. They're always begging her to return, but she says she makes plenty of money as is and doing any more would break her soul, so she must be telling the truth about how rough it was. I'm shocked. The Tisdales always seemed so perfect. They never argued like my parents do sometimes, and they were always so affectionate toward each other. I feel a wave of guilt that I didn't know, and then it hits me—that's probably why Luke reached out last year, and I was too selfish to realize he needed me.

"Wait, this happened last year? Do Abbi and Dad know?" I feel a twist of anger in my gut alongside my guilt.

Mom fiddles anxiously with her wedding band. "Yes. I'm sorry, honey. With your health issues I didn't want to put more stress on you. We thought it best to wait until you were more stable. Though I should've told you before we came down. I really thought Luke would have mentioned it. He didn't?"

"No." Mom knows something's up with us, but she hasn't asked, and I don't want to share.

"Oh, okay. Well, now you know." Mom sighs. "Hopefully it'll be a better summer for all of us, hmm?"

I agree, and she leaves me alone on the porch, staring at Luke's, hoping she's right. Then my phone pings.

Maddy

hey girl sorry I need a rain check

afternoon waitress is out sick

Sera

Nooo we're supposed to have QUALITY TIME

Maddy

I know! hang tonight?

Sera

DUH. I'll pick you up. I'm sorry you have to work!

Maddy

See you at 8pm sharp! Apologies in advance if I smell like the fryer

I toss my phone onto the cushion next to me and groan. I'm antsy. I want to *do* something, but without Maddy my instinct is to look for Luke and ask him if he wants to get into trouble. We used to spend boring days organizing neighborhood capture-the-flag games or helping with odd jobs we'd catch people in the middle of, even if we weren't very helpful. The fence at the Waterses' house is still three different shades of white if you look carefully. I can't just skip next door like everything's fine again, but I also don't want to sit in the house when it's clearly going to be a beautiful day. I bounce myself off the love seat and go pack for the beach.

CHAPTER FIVE

Luke

I trip on Oliver's skateboard as I leave the house, and the guilt at abandoning my mom while Oliver and Adam are in full-on melee mode tugs me back to the kitchen.

"You sure you're okay?" Mom has the day off since the shop is always closed on Mondays, and she's still in her bathrobe, sipping coffee from her favorite mug. She has one eye on her book and one eye out the back door to the yard, where my brothers are a flash of neon bathing suits and tanned skin.

"Yes. Letting them get some energy out and then I'll take them to the skate park. Enjoy your day off. Go to the beach. Have fun." She says the last word like I've never heard of it before.

I sigh in mock defeat just to see her smile, but I'm actually a little bummed. The last couple weeks have been sitting heavy on me. I didn't think I'd miss baseball that much, but not having the physical outlet or school means I'm so up in my head all the time now. There's no avoiding thinking about the bills for the house or the shop, and my fees for community college courses, and the repairs Mom's car needs. And now Sera is back, and still angry at me for some stupid reason she's never explained. I can't stop thinking about how she looked at me last night, like we don't know each other at all anymore.

Part of me wishes I had a shift at the marina or a poster to design for a town event to keep my mind off things, but the beach will have to do. I leave my truck in the drive and walk down Beach Rose Lane until I hit the bike path, moving carefully over the shifting sandy ground. I slow as I get closer to Northport Beach. The fog has dissipated, and the sun is out. The place will be packed with Northport locals getting in beach time before the summer people show up and take over. I shift my backpack with my towel and a beat-up paperback in it. I don't really want to run into any of my friends. In the light of day it'll all feel too real. The end of high school, everyone leaving for their big colleges and new adventures, and me, staying. *Because I want to,* I remind myself. Still, when I catch sight of a gap in the scrappy woods marked by a faded red ribbon on a small tree a few feet in, I decide to change my destination.

I push through the trees onto the almost invisible path. It's badly overgrown. I haven't been down here much in the last two years. Baby oak trees, sassafras mittens, and springy ferns brush against my arms and legs as I make my way to the ocean. The sound of the water grows louder as I get closer, easing the tightness and worry in my chest. Ten minutes later, the path opens up, revealing my favorite place in Northport: the Beach at the End of the Universe. The stretch of sand is barely longer than our house, and it sits between scraggly forest to the west and a huge natural rocky outcrop to the east. The rock on the end juts out far enough so that at a run, you can jump safely into the ocean.

Sera and I found it the summer we were ten, right after we became obsessed with *The Hitchhiker's Guide to the Galaxy.* It was the perfect hideaway with simple rules: *Don't forget your towel, and don't panic.* We would spend hours here, pretending to time travel, making up our own science fiction stories, and generally ignoring the real world, where we both got stared at for our keloid scars and made fun of for being attached at the hip. But we were happiest when it was just the two of us. There were no bossy older sisters or crying baby brothers. When we were at our beach, there were no worries other than making sure we outsmarted any aliens that might show up to kidnap us for studies and torture—and they never caught us because we were too good at jumping universes for them to snag us. To jump universes, we had to sprint off the end of the spaceship rock, jumping as far as we could and shouting out a number before we hit the water. If the number matched how long it took to swim back to shore, then we'd made a successful jump and were no longer on Earth. Nothing serious could get us here. Here we were safe.

So I guess I should've known that I wouldn't be the only one seeking it out today.

Sera's already here. She's pitched a small sun tent on the west side near the woods and is halfway to the spaceship rock, eyes on the ground, looking for treasure. Because no one ever comes here, this is always the best place for rare sea glass and intact seashells. I'm technically here to look for some rocks, since I left my art final unfinished and it's bugging me that it's not done even though the teacher gave me a pass. I could leave. Sera hasn't seen me yet. Northport Beach has plenty of rocks too. But I haven't seen her in so long, and I've missed just spending time with her.

Sera crouches down, and the wind catches at the cover-up she's wearing, revealing a slice of her black bikini. I watch as she stands back up, her hair falling down her back. My heart gallops a few beats. *It's been two years. She doesn't want you, dumbass,* I remind myself, shaking off the sadness that's threatening to build in my chest.

She must sense me, because she suddenly turns around, pinning me with her soft amber eyes. I wonder if she'll ask me to leave, and my hand starts to shake, but then she lifts her free hand and offers me a little wave. Like a truce. I take that as permission to join her, and kick my shoes off by her tent, leaving my phone, book, and towel there as well. I try not to stare as she walks over. She puts a pile of shells down and peels off her cover-up, then stands and stretches her back. I force myself to keep my eyes on the shoreline.

"Hey," she says, quiet but not as dismissive as she was yesterday. "What's up?"

"Just needed to get out of the house for a bit." I wince. "My brothers were in the middle of a *Super Mario Smash Bros. Melee* reenactment."

"Yikes." Sera's mouth quirks into a smile that's gone just as fast. I'd give up a whole paycheck just to see it again. "Sounds dangerous."

"Yeah. The last time I got hit that hard with a pool noodle, I was ten." She laughs, and it feels like some of the awkwardness from last night has melted away. If this were before, I could hug her or mess with her long brown hair, which is getting tangled in the wind. If this were before, she'd ask me to French braid it—I'm good with knots, thanks to gigs at the marina—while she read from one of her library books or told me the latest hilarious but annoying thing Abbi did. I miss that. I miss her. I'm willing to forget that horrible night that I still don't understand if she is. I search for something normal to say. "Hope you didn't take any of the good rocks yet. I was hoping to get a few to finish my art final."

"Isn't school over?" Sera teases. I meet her eyes for a moment and shrug.

"Sure, but I hate leaving things unfinished." I see her shoulders tense a bit as she turns back to the shore. Side by side, we step carefully over the rocky beach to the water. "It just wasn't done," I say quickly. I need to relax. We were best friends for years. We should be able to have one normal conversation even if we're not anymore.

Sera clears her throat. "I'm happy you're still making art, even though you're also a jock now." Her voice is nervous, like she isn't sure how I'll take it. I feel my shoulders drop down my back. It's nice to know we're both feeling a bit out of sorts.

"Well, just don't rat me out for doing kid stuff," I joke back, crouching down to grab a couple flat rocks. After a few more steps I realize she isn't next to me. I turn to face her. She looks upset. Why do I keep fucking this up? "Hey, I didn't mean it." I reach out and nudge her shoulder, risking a small normal gesture. "You're just way more talented than I'll ever be. This is, like, just a hobby for me."

Sera nods but won't meet my eye. "Talented. Right."

In daylight, this close, I can see how the two years have changed her. She's a little taller, thinner, but also softer, curvier in new places. I try my best not to look at her chest, the bright flash of her keloid scar teasing me from between her breasts. There's a row of freckles trailing down her stomach, but I halt my eyes there even if my body doesn't get the message.

"You're talented too." Her voice is a soft whisper that stings. "I saw the window art at the shop. And what about the New School? Didn't you apply?"

I shrug. I haven't spent much time on art since my dad left last spring, and any budget for an out-of-state school, not to mention somewhere as expensive as an out-of-state *art* school, was off the table. The posters are fun, but they don't pay the bills. I need to stay close and help with my brothers and the shop. Maybe part-time classes can turn into full-time in a few years, but college isn't the priority right now.

Sera doesn't push, thankfully. I don't want to get into it because it means talking about my dad, and I try to avoid that. She missed her chance to hear about all of this.

We keep walking toward the rocky outcrop and finally fall into light conversation. Sera asks me about baseball, and I give her the highlights of the last couple seasons—our state championship win, the play my teammate and I made to close it up. I catch her twirling a strand of hair around her fingers as she listens—something she always does when she's concentrating. If she's comfortable enough to just be herself, then I should be the same.

I ask if she's read the new prequel from our favorite series, *The Soul Druid Chronicles*, that just came out in January, and she lights up.

"Of course! I can't believe she tied those two timelines together like that. I feel like I need to go back and reread everything."

"I already am. Lori ordered new copies for me," I admit.

"Really? I'm jealous. All my copies are in the basement down here, and they have a weird smell."

"You can borrow mine," I offer as we reach the rock. "If you want."

"I know where you live." She smiles for real this time, her eyes lingering long enough for me to wonder if I still have it wrong, before she turns and scrambles up the side of the rock ahead of me.

I follow her, using our well-worn hand- and footholds. At the top, she hesitates for a second before offering me a hand up. I take it, even though I don't need it, happy for the small touch. We walk to the edge of the long rock. Sera sits, dangling her feet over the water and watching the ocean slam against the rocks below.

I sit down next to her and lean back as we're sprayed by the mist from another crashing wave. The rock is warm under my palms, the breeze cool. There's a foot or so between us, and that space feels charged, a little dangerous. I want to move closer, but instead I close my eyes and let the sun heat me up, try to ignore the threads in me that feel tied to her.

"I'm sorry about your parents," Sera says suddenly. "My mom just told me this morning. I didn't know."

I freeze.

"I wish I'd replied to your message last year, when you reached out." She clears her throat, not realizing that last year was just the final act. "I wish I'd been there for you—as a friend. You know?"

"Me too." The admission is sour in my stomach, but true. Sera used to be the first person I told anything to. Which girls I was crushing on, whatever crazy idea I had for a new art project, or what prank we should pull. But when I started to fall for her, well, I didn't know how to tell her that. And then my parents started fighting, and I just sort of retreated into myself. Once I held back one thing, it just felt easier to hold back everything.

"Well, I'm here now." She leans over and bumps me with her shoulder, the contact sparking unwanted goose bumps on my skin. "And I'll be here all summer . . . so, like, if you need to catch me up on all the worst shit, I'm happy to listen." She sounds hesitant. I look at her, holding her gaze.

"You mean it?" I ask.

"Yes," she replies. "Friends?" She holds her hand out, and like no time has passed, we immediately move into our secret handshake. We invented it when we were twelve in case we were ever suspicious that the other had been body-swapped. Shake, slap palms, slap the backs of our hands, then touch just the tips of our pointer fingers together.

"Friends," I agree.

"We can even switch up the universe if you need it." She sweeps her arm at the sparkling water in front of us.

"I think I'll stay in this one for now," I admit. "It's gotten a lot better in the last forty-eight hours."

I brace for her to pull away, but she doesn't. Her eyes flick to mine, and I take in her face, her glossy lips, the trail of freckles across her cheeks like a constellation. A heat tingles in my spine as she blushes. She bumps my shoulder again and stays there a minute. I lean back into her.

"It's weird to be in Northport and not going to camp with you. We're so old," she jokes.

"Yeah, I'll miss it," I say. "I missed it last year too."

"You didn't go?"

I shake my head but don't elaborate. We couldn't afford it after the divorce. The lawyer bills were crazy. But I was glad to help Mom, and it would've been too painful to be at camp without Sera anyway. It helps that the work at the marina is physical, grueling, and kind of mindless. Between that, working at the shop, baseball, and the girls who started making it so easy to lose myself, I had plenty to keep me busy.

"I'm actually going to be teaching there a few days a week while Miss Iris is away for a bit," she shares.

"That'll be fun." I try to picture Sera in a teacher's smock and can't help but laugh. "But you're going to be terrible at telling the kids to slow up on using materials."

She laughs too, the sound dancing around us. "What's the camp going to do? Charge them? They're kids." She shakes her head like we aren't, and maybe that's true now. "Did you know the studio is open to staff? And I can bring a guest, so if you need supplies or a space to draw or anything . . ." She avoids my gaze. Is she asking me to come by?

"Oh, thanks." I leave it there. Already this conversation feels like a gift out of time, something she might not repeat again this summer, or ever.

She lies back and rests her hands on her stomach. I have the sudden urge to lean over and smell the crease of her neck, to see if she still smells like lemon sugar and paint. I stand up instead, trying to shake it off. The ocean is calmer, the tide almost peaked with the noon sun. I pick my way to the back of the rock. I take off my shirt and jump around, loosening up my limbs. Then, before I chicken out, I sprint the full length of the rock and leap into the water. The icy chop sucks me right in, blasting all the thoughts from my head. I surface, swipe the hair out of my eyes, and look up to see Sera leaning forward, mouth agape. I wave her in.

"No way!" she shouts. "It's probably freezing!"

"It's bathwater!" I shout back, even as my teeth chatter a little. I turn and start to swim toward the shore, passing through patches of water that briefly feel warmer before the cold stabs up again. When I feel my palm hit sand, I float the rest of the way in, rolling over out of the surf like a seal. I can hear Sera laughing, and I feel lightheaded and giddy, laughing with her. I finally get up and run to the beach tent to grab my towel. I pause as I notice my phone light up. Lila, the junior I hooked up with at the bonfire. I quickly shove my phone in my backpack before jogging back to the rock. I can feel Sera watching me as I climb up, and for a moment I'm embarrassed, but then a little proud. I'm not the skinny kid she grew up with. Baseball training and work have filled me out. My friends are always teasing me about how I'm hot now, and there have been plenty of other girls I've been with who seemed to agree, but there's something about Sera looking at me that makes me feel like it's true. Her gaze snags on the scar on my knee.

"Your turn, Watkins," I say to distract her.

"Nope!" She jumps up and tries to sneak past me, but I stick an arm out to block her way, shaking the wet hair out of my face and grinning when she yelps. She tries to fake me out, but she's too slow and easy to catch. She squeals as I wrap one arm, then the other around her, lifting her easily back toward the edge. She's strong, her muscles tensed against my arms as she leans back and then away, laughing.

"You're freezing!"

I let her go and step away, heart racing.

"It's not bad, I promise." I lie a little. "You get used to it." My eyes flicker to her chest again, that scar to match mine. "I think EBE would love it." I wink and then race off before she can reply, flying through the air and diving into the water. It's still cold, but not unbearable this time. I stay there, treading water, hoping she'll join me, feeling like something hangs in the balance.

"Come on, Sera! It's summer tradition!" My voice carries over the waves. I swim back a little to give her space. I turn around just in time to see her fly off the end, her silhouette slicing through the blue sky. When she surfaces, she lets loose an earsplitting scream that dissolves into gasping laughter. I whistle, echoing her, and then watch as she pivots my way. There's a huge smile on her face, and her eyes are shining. We tread water for a beat, looking at each other. I want to swim to her, wrap my arms around her waist in the water. But she's already turning away from me, swimming back to shore.

CHAPTER SIX

Sera

A couple days later, I bike two miles west to the Blue Honeybee Art Complex to meet Miss Iris. Northport used to be a small haven for artists, and the complex was built in the '70s by a few famous sculptors and mixed-media artists. It sits on a high stretch of land with its own access to Northport Beach. The pathway at the entrance takes you by the ancient red farmhouse that functions as the office, but more important, it goes past the Blue Honeybee.

It's a giant metal sculpture of a ten-foot-tall daffodil with a honeybee sitting in its petals. It's not painted, but the metal was worked in such a way that the bee shines a deep metallic blue that shifts a little depending on the weather. Today is a cloudless day, and the air is cool, but the sun is heating the metal, so even far away it shimmers like ocean water turned to glass. Every year, our opening assignment was to make an homage to the complex's namesake. You could paint, sculpt, or reimagine the bee in whatever way you wanted. One kid once did an interpretive dance and became a legend, so the bar was high. Luke and I used to spend the months between camp messaging back and forth with ideas for our own projects. Then we'd go dead quiet in the week leading up to camp so we could surprise each other and get the other's honest opinion on our final piece.

I stop at the foot of the sculpture and place my palm on the warm stem of the flower, snatching my hand back before it burns me. Camp always made art seem important, larger than life, serious yet fun at the same time. With my future so up in the air, all I had last year was my painting, and so it's a different kind of homecoming to be here again.

I park my bike by the side of the farmhouse and head to the littles' studio, where I told Miss Iris I would meet her. I take the path past the office, the cafeteria, and the theater building, toward the first of the three converted barns that house the studios. The small patches of grass between the buildings are freshly mowed, so the air smells green, sharp, and acidic. From here, you can't see the ocean above the rise of the dunes, but you can catch the tops of sailboats scattered across the horizon. There's a groundskeeper shoveling new mulch shavings down on the walking paths, so I cut across the still-dewy grass. I follow the familiar route around to the side of the first barn, where the garage doors are wide open. Each barn is almost identical, though the littles' is a bit smaller. Light floods in from the outside and through the skylights above, making the space bright and airy. The studio is separated into mediums, but not in such a strict way that you can't mix it up if needed.

I walk through the paints section, looking through the

available canvases and thinking about the last time I was here. The summer when everything between Luke and me first changed. We were in the studio alone while everyone else was up at lunch. I was teasing him about his lack of color use, partly jealous of his talent, and partly because I liked to watch him defend his love of grayscale. Wielding a paintbrush, I reached out and smeared a bright flash of purple across his cheek. He picked up his own brush, dripping with black paint, and pointed it at my forehead.

"You better run, Watkins," he said.

I squealed and sprinted across the room. He followed and got me back with a glob of midnight black. Soon we were racing around the room, tossing paint, laughing. Luke caught me around the waist and we both toppled to the floor. I wrestled my way on top of him, pinning his hips with mine. Our eyes locked, and suddenly we both stopped laughing.

He went so still and just stared up at me, smiling as the heat in my cheeks spread down. I remember thinking how cute he was as he reached up and played with the ends of my hair.

"You're really pretty, Sera," he said. And I went liquid, mesmerized by his voice. Everything tilted sideways, and I felt myself lean down toward him. But just as I did, the door swung open behind us. Miss Iris burst in, arms full of supplies, and we scrambled up to help her.

I blink away the memory, the hope I felt then.

I'm feeling the soft tips of the brushes, wondering if I could assign my class to paint on shells collected from the beach, when I hear footsteps behind me.

"Hello?" I weave around the standing easels toward the entrance of the barn as a woman comes out of the washroom.

"Sera?"

"Miss Iris! Hi!" Miss Iris was always my favorite teacher, more lenient and inspiring than anyone else. I saw her in February at a gallery in Boston after reading in the camp newsletter that some of her paintings were on display. It was my first solo outing since I'd been declared stable in January, and I said yes immediately when she offered me the summer job. She looks the same as always, in her giant earrings and linen pants paired with an oversized knit sweater. Her dark hair is piled in a bun on top of her head.

"Just Iris now, since you're officially a coworker." She swoops in for a quick hug and leaves two little air kisses behind on either side of my face. Then she steps back and does that thing adults do where they exclaim how tall I am and how beautiful and I brush it off.

"So, where should we start?" I ask. "I'm definitely interested in learning how to wrangle the littles."

Iris laughs, her blue eyes twinkling. "Oh, it's impossible to wrangle them. Don't even try. We're here to guide, and inspire, and support."

"Right." I pause. "How?"

She laughs again. "Just keep them busy." She gestures for me to follow her back to the painting area. "It's really great to have you back. We missed you last year. Luke too. It wasn't quite the same without you both here causing trouble," she teases, and I feel myself blush.

"I'm happy to be back too."

"You're taking a gap year, right?" She opens the door to one of the supply closets, and I follow her into the cramped, overstocked space.

"Yup."

"That will be good for you," she says, scanning the shelves to find what she's looking for. "No need to decide too quick if you're not sure."

"Exactly," I say. "I'm not in a rush to get back to school."

"I think you'll thrive as a teacher." She hands me a tray of empty paint containers, their white lids stained rainbow from years of use. "You were always so organized, and so delighted to be here and pitch in with the group projects."

"Thanks." I brace myself as she piles two more trays on top of the one I'm already holding. Then she picks up a couple big buckets of paint and gestures with her chin to one of the wide tables in the studio.

We repeat this process until the table is covered with trays. Then we pour an even amount of color from each of the paint buckets into the containers. Each kid will get their own small set of primary colors to keep in their cubby. I always ran out of yellow first, and Luke was always stealing my black. Iris explains her teaching plan while we work. It sounds like I have flexibility to do basically whatever I want with my group of seven- to nine-year-olds, though she gives me a few examples of projects to start with.

"So, what's this fellowship you're doing?" I ask as we finish putting lids on the little jars.

"Oh, I'm so thrilled." She blows a stray bit of hair out of her eyes and stretches her back after she rests the heavy blue paint bucket back on the ground. "It's six weeks in Paris. The cohort is small, only five other artists, and every week one person leads a group workshop about their particular craft as we work on individual projects on our own time. There's a small gallery funding it, and they run a show before we leave. Galerie Jeanne Fontaine. We get free access to all the museums in the city, French lessons if we need them, and there's even a cooking class, which I'm so excited for. We're all living in our own apartments in this beautiful old town house with a gorgeous garden, and have studios at an artists' cooperative, so we meet local artists too." She pauses for a breath and then puts her hand to her forehead. "Oh gosh, I'm so sorry, listen to me, just going on and on. It seems even at fifty-six you can still get giddy over the things you love." She chuckles.

"Wow." I'm a little stunned by how wonderful it sounds. "That's amazing."

"You know, you don't need a degree to apply," Iris says. "They hold a few spots for artists under twenty-five. You should apply for next year. You could probably get credit for it, too, if you do go to school afterward."

"Really?" It sounds beyond wild, the idea of going off to Paris instead of taking summer classes so I can be "caught up" before I start college.

"Definitely! I'll help you apply. What have you been working on these days? Your watercolor landscapes?"

"Mostly those, yes. Though I've been playing a little with portraits."

"I love that. Show me!"

I pull out my phone and show her the art I've shared on Instagram. She's too nice, *ooh*ing and *aah*ing over the painting of Abbi I've been working on, but it's encouraging. We talk for a little while longer about the work she'll be doing in Paris and what my classmates were up to last year as I help Iris with another few tasks around the studio. By the time we're all set up, I feel comfortable in the room and know at least the first week of plans for what I'll be picking up when Iris leaves.

"Think about the fellowship." Iris nudges me as she locks up and hands me the spare keys. "You could submit a series of portraits—they just need to follow a specific theme."

"I will," I promise.

We walk back along the path to the entrance together. Iris leaves me at my bike. It's getting close to dinner, but I still have a little time before I need to be home to help. I turn back and take a photo of camp, the complex quiet and waiting for students. I want to text it to Luke—he'd understand how weird it is to see the place so vacant. I post it to my IG story instead. Before I can even put my phone away it pings, but it's not Luke, it's Jackson. He's liked the story and sent a thumbs-up, and I can see that he's typing.

Jackson

I'm going to the Northport drive-in movie thing next Wednesday night. See you there?

My stomach flips. I skipped his volleyball game yesterday to go to the beach with Maddy because I wasn't sure he was really interested. But then I remember the way Jackson's mouth quirked up as he looked at me, and my promise to myself that I'll be open to something new. At least it's not confusing. He wants to spend time with me, plus he's hot, and I would like to see him again. Before I can second-guess myself any more, I send a response.

Sera

Yes! I'll be there 😊

*

That night, paint stained onto the tips of my fingers, I fill my family in on the idea of maybe applying for the fellowship. We're cleaning up after dinner, and it seems like everyone is relaxed enough to have this conversation.

"I can work on my submission pieces after camp," I say. "Iris said she could recommend me too. And if I get in, maybe I should wait a little longer before applying to college, like maybe another year? I could just focus on my art and staying healthy."

I can feel them all looking at each other around me and I pretend not to notice as I take another wet plate from Abbi, dry it off. School is important to my parents. Abbi taking a semester off last fall was the worst-case scenario, and it was Dr. Lee's idea to take a gap year, supported by my therapist and the school counselor. I haven't been able to find a way to tell them that the idea of going back into some kind of formal classroom fills me with dread. Unlike other kids my age, I likely won't be getting a job in four years; I could be preparing for a heart transplant and the uncertainty and recovery that comes with that. I don't really know how much time I have to just do what I want, and I don't want to waste it.

I look over at Mom standing at the kitchen island. She swirls her wine and thinks it over. Dad's wiping down the kitchen table. They look at each other, communicating something with their eyes.

"Okay," Mom finally says. "I'm happy you're thinking about the future, Sera. It sounds like the start of a good plan, but let's not cut school applications out entirely yet." Dad nods in agreement. I drop my dish towel and hug them both quickly, then disappear up to my room before they can change their minds.

I flop onto my bed with my laptop and look up the fellowship. As I flick through the photos of the house, and the studio, and a group of artists painting on easels by the Seine, I feel something swelling in my chest that has nothing to do with my heart, physical or emotional. Hope. Purpose. I open the application, read through the requirements, and clock the deadline for next year. August 11. I set a reminder in my phone for August 1.

I've never been out of the country, and I wonder what Paris is like. Cafés for breakfast and picnics by the Eiffel Tower for lunch. Maybe I'd meet a cute French boy and we could tour the city on his moped, drink wine, and talk art and books. I click through a map of the city, looking for the gallery Iris mentioned.

I'm thinking about croissants versus pain au chocolat and downloading a language-learning app on my phone when I get a text from Luke. I deleted his contact info two years ago, but I still know his number by heart.

Jumped universes today without you. Wasn't the same!

There's a rush in my ears and an old familiar feeling of excitement and anticipation that I thought was long dead. I think about the way he looked in the sun. He was practically glowing. I think about how hard it was to keep my eyes off the places on his skin I wanted to touch. I hover my finger over the text. Then I remember what happened two summers ago and the pain is so sharp, my breath catches. Maybe we're friends again, but I need to keep my distance. I quickly close out of his message and go back to the fellowship's website. I click through the photos again, stopping to watch the mixed-media artists from last year present their pieces. I imagine what I would paint in Paris and wonder if the city really does glimmer with lights.

CHAPTER SEVEN

Sera

A couple weeks into our stay in Northport, and we've already fallen into a rhythm. Dad and Abbi get up early and go for a run, while I sleep as late as I can, which is never later than eight, then start the crossword with Dad when he's back. We finish it before everyone splits up for the day, though Mom, Abbi, and I have managed a few full beach days together too. Now that my job has started, things will shift a little on Mondays, Wednesdays, and Fridays. Wednesdays, Dad has scheduled golfing with another professor who spends the summer on the Cape, so he's offered to drive me to work. He drops me off at camp with an iced chai and an egg sandwich from Lorell's after we make a quick pit stop for my lab tests.

"You've got everything you need?" he asks as I get out of the car with my bag.

"Yup." I smooth out the long-sleeved white linen top I stole from Mom's collection of beach cover-ups and straighten my beaded necklace. On the first day, Iris and I taught together, and after the kids did their Bee presentations, we did some beading. I now have a dozen stunningly ridiculous chunky necklaces to choose from. I carefully labeled each one gifted to me to make sure I remember whose is whose. I plan to wear one every day I'm teaching.

"And Abbi is picking you up at four?" I fight the urge to tell him we've been over this three times already. Even though I've been stable for half a year now, any medical test or pharmacy run still makes Dad uneasy.

"Correct."

"Okay." Dad turns back to the wheel but doesn't pull away.

"I'm fine, Dad. Thank you for driving me. Watch out for wild swings from Mr. Price."

He chuckles and the concerned look on his face vanishes. "Have a good day, Sera."

"Love you, Dad."

"Love you!" he calls back, then puts the car into gear and drives off.

It's funny how quickly I've taken to teaching. I'm not even nervous for my first day alone. It helps that the kids in my group are total sweethearts. And there are a few who remind me of myself and Luke: a little more focused, a little intense for their age. I want them to feel how special this place can be, how special they are. I want them to remember me and this short time we have together. Judging by their enthusiasm, we seem to be off to a good start. From the minute they arrive, with hugs and a garble of stories to share about what happened since I met them two days ago, they fill the studio with their energy.

Today, we're working on mixing colors. The kids react like it's magic when we make purple and green and orange. I have them paint little scenes using their mixed colors on flat rocks collected from the beach. The day goes so quickly I don't have time to wonder if I did anything right. Suddenly it's pickup, and I'm holding ten new pictures drawn for me by the kids. Three of the moms tell me how much fun their kids are having, so it must be going fine.

Abbi picks me up a little late, pulling into the dirt parking lot with the windows down, one of Cam's band's EPs blasting.

"Can you turn that down, please?"

Abbi sighs but hits the volume so it's no longer shaking the whole car.

"We're eating dinner at home first, right?" Tonight is the annual drive-in movie fundraiser at the harbor, where I plan to eat my weight in sour candy and popcorn, but I need some real food.

"Yup. Hey, is it cool if Cam comes tonight? His gig got canceled, and he's feeling a little sad."

"Of course. Maddy's got plans for where to park. I'll just make sure we can fit one more. But if you two start making out, I'm kicking you out of the car."

Abbi rolls her eyes but seems placated. "It's a fundraiser. For the broken footbridge at Thirds Beach. There will be no making out."

"I'll believe it when I see it," I say. Abbi bats her eyes at me, feigning innocence.

"Is that rich kid going—the one you've been texting? What's his name? Theodore? Robert? John?"

"*Jackson*," I say.

"That's what I said."

"Yeah, he is."

"Ooooh," Abbi says, making a kissy face at me.

I don't take the bait; instead, I change the song to something sappy I have in her queue.

"Ugh, Sera. You have *the worst* taste in music, and by the way, what even is that monstrosity around your neck?"

I gasp overdramatically. "For your information, this was made by an eight-year-old who has more talent in his pinkie finger than you have in your whole body. And my taste in music is great. Epic. Unheard-of."

"You wouldn't know good music if it bit you in the face." She's trying to keep her face straight, but I can see her about to crack.

"You should know, I guess. You got bit in the face by . . ." I search for an insult but come up short. "An ugly-maker machine."

Abbi bursts into laughter. "I'm wounded!" she says. "Take it back!" She reaches over with one hand and tickles me in the ribs.

"Never!" I reply through a fit of giggles.

By the time we roll into the driveway, we're both laughing so hard it hurts.

Abbi, being Abbi, dresses up a little for the movie night she claims she *won't* be making out at, so I put in some effort too, pulling on a long white flowy skirt and cropped T-shirt. I even pat on some sparkly eye shadow. Abbi's curls are down and perfect, and she helps me out with my half-straight, half-wavy nonsense by giving me a French braid that makes my hair look way thicker than it is.

For the drive-in fundraiser, the town clears the parking lot at the boatyard and projects the films onto the side of a giant garage wall. If you have a dock slip spot, you can watch from your boat. We used to do that with Luke's dad, but from my understanding of what happened, he moved farther up the Cape and isn't around much. It's weird to me because he was from Northport just like Paula and always made a big deal about contributing to his hometown.

The place is already packed, so we have to park on Main, pretty far back from the harbor entrance. We take the alley between the bookstore and the pottery shop and pop out on Harborside, turning right and following the crowd of people looking to find places to sit in front of all the cars. Abbi locates Cam at the donation tent. He rode his moped over. The kissing starts immediately, and I roll my eyes and give them a minute before I clear my throat.

"Strike one," I sing.

"Fine! PDA is finished," Abbi promises.

"I've got a blanket and some snacks in here," Cam says, patting his bag, "if we want to go sit up front?"

"Sera's friends have a spot," Abbi says, falling into step next to him, her arm through his. I text Maddy that we're here, and she texts back that she's in the third row of cars.

As we weave between vehicles, I catch sight of where we're

headed, and my stomach flutters—Luke's pickup truck. I spot him and Maddy sitting in the bed of it, talking to a group of kids from the baseball team. All but two of the boys drift off as the screen flashes a five-minute warning and a reminder of the radio station to tune to for sound.

"Hop up—there's plenty of room," Maddy says, shuffling blankets around as Abbi and Cam get settled and Luke's friends climb in. Maddy helps me up into the bed of the truck, and Luke shuffles sideways like he's going to sit next to me. Luckily Maddy plops down in the space, and he takes a seat next to her instead.

"There are more blankets and stuff in the truck, if you need them," Luke offers.

"I'm good," I say.

"Sera's my blanket," Maddy says, stretching her arms around my shoulders and squeezing.

I laugh, relieved that there's space between Luke and me. I get a text from Jackson just as the movie starts.

Jackson

Running late, but I'll be there soon!

I ignore the nerves in my stomach, text him where our spot is, and tuck my phone away.

I hadn't looked up what was playing, so when the small blue image of dolphins appears, and a British voice-over crackles out of the car speakers, I gasp a little too loud and look over at Luke.

He's looking at me too, delighted as he mouths along with the movie.

So long, and thanks for all the fish.

They're playing *our* movie. Abbi looks a little suspicious as we both dance to the intro song and sing all the words, but it's harmless. Just two friends vibing.

Ten minutes in, I desperately need a snack.

"I'm going to get snacks," I say quietly as I slide to the end of the bed and hop off. "Anyone want anything?"

"I'll come," Luke says, jumping over the side and landing next to me.

"I'll take some popcorn," Maddy says, eyes glued to the screen as Ford and Arthur argue.

"Gummy bears, please," Abbi adds, giving Luke a side glance and raising her eyebrows at me. Cam squeezes her knee, and she says, "And Junior Mints," before pulling him in for a kiss. I smirk at her when she finally pulls away and mouth *Strike two* while she sticks her tongue out at me. Then I turn and skip off, grinning.

"What are you so pleased about?" Luke asks as we move quietly toward the food trucks and the fundraiser tent.

"Oh, nothing, sister stuff," I say. We make it past the last cars to the dock.

"Ah, got it. My little brothers are like that. They have, like, a secret code between the two of them."

"Not with you?"

He shrugs. "I'm too old, I think, and with my dad gone . . . I've definitely taken on some semi-parenting stuff that means we're not always on the same side."

"I'm sorry. That sucks." He shrugs again, one strong shoulder rising and falling.

"I'm sorry too. For what I said about your art. I don't think it's kid stuff, really. I just, well, I can't really play around with hobbies anymore. My mom really needs to be able to rely on me, and art doesn't help pay the bills or for Adam's lacrosse equipment and Oliver's skateboards—which I swear he keeps wrecking on purpose." He shakes his head and laughs. "You should see his kneepads. That kid is fearless."

"It sounds hard," I say, feeling guilty again for not having known how tough the divorce has been on him. "And unfair." I work out carefully how to say what I'm feeling. "They're your brothers, not your kids."

"I don't mind helping," he says firmly. "I want to be there for them and my mom."

We come up on the main tent, and Luke pops in to say hi to the organizers, but it quickly becomes clear that he's one of them too. While I wait for him to help someone with an issue with the second movie, I stare at the poster taped up beside the tent. It has an old-school 1940s advertising vibe, with a classic car at a drive-in, an illustration of the footbridge on the screen. The lines are clean, the font sharp. I can't believe I missed this. It's Luke's.

He reemerges from the tent. "Sorry, being the youngest volunteer means answering a lot of questions about tech. You ready for snacks?"

"Yeah. No. Wait. I think I missed it before because of all the color," I tease, pointing to the poster, "but this is yours, isn't it?"

Luke tries to brush it off.

"Yeah, it was cheaper than hiring a real designer."

"Luke," I say, "you *are* a real designer. This is awesome."

"Thanks. Should we grab the snacks?" He changes the subject quickly, pointing to the line by concessions.

"Yeah." I fall into step next to him, not sure why he's being so weird about the poster. Behind us, on-screen, Earth implodes.

I catch Luke watching me watch the movie, and something clicks in my brain.

"Wait . . . did you pick the movie?" I ask, looking at him.

"Uh . . ." Luke scratches the back of his neck. "Yeah." He starts to play with the frayed edges of his T-shirt. "When I knew you'd be here, I switched it. It's your favorite," he says.

I reach out and squeeze his hand in thanks. Even though he has no idea what's been going on with my health, it feels like he still knows how much this summer means to me. Luke grips my hand, his calloused palm familiar and warm. He looks down where we're linked, then up at me. The movie is the only thing casting any light, so we're standing in shadow. In the dark, his eyes look like a deep, cozy part of the ocean as they hold me there, pinned. My heart races and my fingers go cold. I should let go. Why am I not letting go? It's like the pieces of my heart sitting in his chest are magnets tugging me in. I feel like I did when we were sixteen, intense and desperate. I'm heartbroken all over again remembering that I wanted to be with him more than anything, and he . . . didn't. I don't want him to see what I'm feeling, to pity me.

My eyes flick to his mouth, which is quirked open like he's about to say something, but before he can, a girl comes out of nowhere and throws her arms around Luke's neck. He drops my hand like it's on fire.

"Izzy!" he says, turning to hug the girl back. "When did you get home?"

My stomach turns. Izzy's a local, a grade above us, and though she didn't go to Blue Honeybee, she was always around. Very into music and films and, the last summer I was here, Luke. I bite my lip, suddenly anxious and uncomfortable. I would turn and walk away, but that would just invite questions I don't want to answer.

"Today!" she says, brushing her pink hair out of her eyes. "I wanted to surprise you." She tousles the top of his head with a manicured hand, even though she's barely able to reach. "You've let your hair get long. But you're wearing the shirt I sent." She smirks, tugging on the hem of the T-shirt featuring an anime character I hadn't known Luke even liked.

Luke laughs and gestures at Izzy's hair. "I like the pink."

"Better than the blue from last summer, right?"

"Will it bleed off any less?" Luke teases.

She lightly shoves him. "I ruined *one* hoodie."

"My white vintage Pats hoodie," he reminds her, though he doesn't actually seem mad.

They're flirting, I realize like an idiot. Something is clearly going on here that I've missed. More than just what I know from two years ago. When Maddy said Luke didn't do serious, maybe she left Izzy out because she didn't want to hurt me.

"Sorry," Izzy says, turning away from Luke to face me. "We're being rude."

"Oh, this is my old friend Sera. We're neighbors. You've probably met," Luke says.

"The heart girl!" It's apparently now my turn for a hug. "Of course. Glad to see you're back this summer."

I clear my throat and find my footing. "Me too," I say. "Should be a fun summer." I force a smile.

"There's nothing quite like the summer before college. You'll see." She slides her arm around Luke's waist, and I feel a lump growing in my throat. "But there's also nothing quite like coming home either. Can you believe I actually missed Northport?"

"When you had all of Cleveland at your feet?" Luke jokes.

"Did you know it's *landlocked*?" Izzy shivers. "Not an ocean for a thousand miles. I felt more myself as soon as I could see the Atlantic."

I nod like I know what she's talking about, but I don't have anything to add. There's a lake in Ohio, right? A Great Lake? Isn't that enough water for her? I pinch my lips together in what I hope is a sympathetic grin.

"That's why I can't imagine leaving," Luke says, and it's my turn to look at him funny. When we were little, all our dreams involved going to see the far corners of the world, getting lucky enough to fly into space for real.

"It's nice to know you'll be here." Izzy plants a kiss on Luke's cheek.

The ground beneath me tilts like the earth is trying to fling me off. I take a deep breath and stare intently at the head of the guy in front of us. But my eyes keep trailing back to where Luke and Izzy are glued to each other.

Thankfully the line moves forward quickly as a huge group of younger teens move away with their snacks, and I wrench my gaze away from Luke's hand on Izzy's hip, embarrassed. I order all the food and pay, remembering to ask Izzy if she wants anything, and Luke takes two of the trays while I grab the last one. I'm quiet on the way back to the truck, letting Izzy fill the air around us with updates meant for Luke and Luke only. The moment from before sits heavy in my chest, so many things unsaid but understood. *We're just friends. We're just friends.* I repeat it to myself.

As we make it back to Luke's truck, I'm delighted to see Jackson there. He's chatting with Luke's friends about the Red Sox, but he jumps up to help with the tray of food and drinks.

"Thanks," I say as we hand everything off. "Glad you could make it."

"I love the drive-in," he says with a grin. "Couldn't miss it." He climbs back into the bed of the pickup truck, then turns and takes my hand, helping me up.

Abbi wiggles her eyebrows at me and helps make space for the two of us to sit on the end next to her and Cam. Jackson's arm ends up resting on my leg. He smells like some sort of spicy cologne, and it's nice to have the warmth of him next to me as the night continues to cool off. He's seen the movie before too, so he doesn't mind when I end up saying some of the lines quietly to myself before the characters do.

I glance behind me quickly and see Izzy curled up to Luke's side. She's watching the screen, rapt, so I guess she gets points for not hating it. Luke looks at me, then at Jackson. I see a flash of something unreadable in his eyes. I turn away, leaning more into Jackson, and though heat tingles across my neck like Luke is staring, I don't look back.

CHAPTER EIGHT

Sera

On Friday I go straight to Maddy's parents' diner after camp is over. The place is packed, so I take a spinning seat at the far end of the counter and wave to Maddy to let her know I'm there.

"No rush," I say, pulling out my notebook to work on my ideas for the fellowship application. I have to submit three cohesive pieces and write an essay. I've been toying with finally doing some self-portraits and writing about my heart, since it is the thing I know best. I send Iris a text to ask how Paris is, and she sends back a few photos of the view out her window. There's a cobbled courtyard covered in potted plants and a teal Vespa leaning against a vine-covered wall. She asks how the first week of camp was and if I've decided on a theme for my application yet. I send a thumbs-up on both and tell her I'm working on it today. It's not ready for her critique yet.

Maddy comes over with a milkshake and a plate covered with an upside-down takeout container and leans on the counter, sighing dramatically. She looks exhausted, and I feel a twinge of guilt for how hard she's always working. Her glasses are smudged, her hair frizzed. She's been here all day, and I know she's dying to leave. There's a group of younger teens in the corner booth who are counting out their change before they order, reminding me of us, of simpler times. Five years feels like such a long time ago. I hope no matter where I am in the next five years, I'm still coming down to Northport for at least part of the summer. And I hope that Maddy has her own bakery business and isn't tied to the diner.

"When are you off?" I ask, stirring the shake and taking a spoonful of the whipped cream off the top.

"We still close at eight even though it's Friday on the Cape in the *summer*. Usually I think it's crazy that my parents don't want the extra hour or two of dinner service, but today, thank god. It's been chaos."

"The weather." I nod knowingly, looking outside at the sideways rain that's been coming down all day. "The kids at camp were all worked up too."

"You have the weekend off, though, yeah?"

I nod and take a sip of the peanut butter–chocolate milkshake. "Wow, that's amazing."

"Right? My own special recipe. A few hundred more of these will pay for culinary school. I think." She shrugs. Something crashes in the kitchen and the line cook, Maddy's cousin Kris, shouts out that she's fine. Maddy sighs. "Maybe in five years."

"And what's this?" I point my spoon at the covered plate, and Maddy straightens up, her eyes twinkling.

"Cookies. You're gonna love them. They're kind of like the

sequilhos my mom makes, but I added shredded coconut and vanilla." She slides the plate closer, and I pick up a cookie.

I take a bite, and Maddy's right. I do love them. They rival the baked goods at Lorell's, and I tell her as much.

"Seriously, Mads, this might be the best thing you've ever made."

"You always say that," Maddy says, taking a cookie for herself. She points to my notebook. "What are you working on?"

I tell her about the fellowship and the application process, the house I'd get to stay in in Paris next summer. Her eyes grow wide behind her glasses.

"That sounds so cool. What if . . ." Maddy starts, and I sit up taller. Maddy's *what-ifs* are usually followed by spectacular ideas. "What if I came with you?"

"Yes! I mean, can you?" I look around the diner again, knowing Maddy's parents rely on her.

"If I give my family a heads-up, I think so. I've already been talking to them about this Parisian bakery course."

"Oh my god. Yes. It would be amazing to go to Paris together. We'd eat all the best pastries."

"Maybe we can go backpacking too. Do a real European gap year," Maddy adds.

"Yes," I say. "It's decided. We're doing it."

Maddy laughs. "We better start saving up."

Two meals pop up in the service window and Maddy spins off to deliver them. As she does, the bell above the front door chimes, and a girl our age with brown skin and sleek black hair comes in. She has big headphones on and is clutching a sticker-covered laptop to her chest. I smile a little to myself as she catches Maddy's eye—she's totally Maddy's type. Maddy tells her to sit anywhere, then goes and takes the tweens' orders and greets a family of six that has just piled in. She comes back around the counter, picking up fries from the window and sliding them toward me.

"Who's that?" I ask, tilting my head toward the corner booth where the new girl is getting settled.

Maddy shrugs, but there's a mischievous smile playing at the corner of her mouth. "Don't know. Summer person, probably." I raise my eyebrows, but Maddy doesn't take the bait.

"Do you want a burger too?"

My mouth waters. Of course I want a burger, but there's already more salt on the fries than I'm supposed to have in a month. I pop one in my mouth while it's still hot and moan in appreciation.

Maddy quirks an eyebrow at me. "You never had a fry before?"

"It's been a while since I've had one this superb." Heart-healthy food is fine until it's all you get, even when you're on your period and craving Cheetos. Then it's torture.

"Ah, your heart? Thought you were good?"

"I am. Just supposed to watch my salt, but I've been so good all week," I say as I eat another fry. "Better make it a turkey burger because I'm going to eat too many of these fries."

Maddy snags a couple fries off the plate and nods.

"So, where are we going on our Eurotrip?" I ask.

"Hmm . . . Amsterdam, maybe Oslo? Berlin?"

I write *Berlin, Amsterdam, and Oslo* really big at the bottom of my page.

"Yes! I'll start googling hostels."

Maddy shoots me a grin and goes to run more food orders. She lingers a little longer than needed as she pours coffee for the girl in the corner, but I can't catch what they're saying.

I'm jotting down other ideas for my application when my phone lights up next to my milkshake. It's Jackson, asking if I want to go to dinner soon. After the drive-in, he walked me home, since Abbi went to Cam's, and I found out his mother is an artist and has taken him all over the world to see some of the greatest museums. I'm dying to hear more. I smile and send a yes. Maddy resumes her position across from me at the counter.

"Was that Luke? What's going on with you two?" she asks, looking excited.

I swallow, my mouth cottony. "There's nothing going on. That was Jackson."

She looks at me, quiet, waiting. I hold out. Maddy sighs.

"Something happened at the drive-in, before Jackson got there. Was it just that Izzy's back? Because they're not serious. They were on and off all summer last year."

"Seemed serious." I try to keep my voice light. "And I don't care, really. Luke can date whoever. We're just friends. Did you get her name?" I glance at the girl in the corner booth, who is opening her laptop and emptying sugars into her coffee.

"Sienna." Maddy blows her bangs out of her eyes. "Stop deflecting. So, you two talked? Like, for real, about . . . everything that happened? And he knows about your heart?"

"You hypocrite." I shake my head. "And well, no, not in detail"—I shrug—"but we agreed to be friends again. I'll tell him about my heart soon. I swear. But I'm fine and it's not really important now." I don't mention the moment in the dark at the drive-in.

Maddy smirks. "You two aren't meant to be just friends."

"No one is meant for anything, Mads. We both made choices, and his was clear."

Jackson sends me a thumbs-up, and I show Maddy my phone. "Plus Jackson is new, and he's nice. And he's *hot*." I reach for another fry and Maddy takes it right out of my hand.

"Hey!"

"Sure, so hook up with Jackson, whatever. But you're still avoiding them, aren't you?" she says, pointing the fry at me.

"Avoiding what?"

"Your feelings for Luke."

"I don't have feelings for Luke."

"Liar!" Maddy's voice rises, and there's another crash from the kitchen. The family in the corner whips their heads her way, frowning. Sienna looks over too, concerned, and Maddy tucks her hair behind her ear. "Oops." Maddy laughs as Kris shouts that she's okay again, then leans closer and lowers her voice. "I didn't push last year 'cause, well, you know, but come on, you'd be so great together. He literally has two pieces of your heart. Tell me a more storybook romance beginning than that."

My heart flutters in reply, and I sigh. "I really don't want to talk about it, Maddy."

"Maybe you need to," Maddy says, gently cutting through my bullshit.

"Maybe," I admit, "but I just want to move forward, not back."

"But what if you left something good behind?" Maddy asks.

Thankfully more food comes up in the service window and she leaves me with my thoughts.

She's not wrong. Sometimes it does feel like two summers ago Luke and I missed out on something great. By July I was sure Luke and I were going to be getting together, but it just kept not happening. At the end of August, the camp hosts a dance at the high school, and I was positive Luke was going to ask me as his date. There'd been so many moments all summer where it felt like something was about to happen that kept getting interrupted by our friends or siblings or even my own nerves. Then, a week before the dance, he stopped me on our bike ride home, pulling us off into the grass at the corner of Beach Rose Lane.

"What's up?" I asked. "You're going to be late." He was due at the shop to help his dad with some delivery orders.

"It's fine." He pushed his hair out of his eyes and smiled his mischievous smile that crinkled his eyes and set off butterflies from my chest to my toes. "Meet me at our beach tomorrow night. Ten? After your tournament."

"Okay," I said. My heart raced. I had a feeling this was it; he was going to ask me to the dance, tell me he liked me as more than friends. "Why?" I half whispered.

"I'll tell you tomorrow, Watkins," he said, his eyes playful.

Because my tournament would take all day, I'd already picked out the skirt and tank top I wanted to wear when I saw him. I set those out next to my shoes so I'd be ready to go as soon as I was home. My whole team had been working hard to make it to regionals, but that morning I was just as excited for the day to be over so I could finally find out if Luke was feeling the way I was.

I was tired in the first few games, and slow, but we were winning, so it was fine. I had a headache by the time our last game started, and we were down by five with very little time left. The other team sent a serve flying over the net. I lunged for it even though it was in my teammate's zone and collided with her. She was pissed for two seconds, until she realized something was really wrong and shouted for our coach. I was way too dizzy to get up. The sand beneath us was pulling me down, the sky twisting up, my headache radiating down my neck. Then I passed out.

I came to in the ambulance. I was going through my third echocardiogram with the stone-faced tech at exactly the time Luke had told me to meet him. In that minute, my whole heart felt heavy and sick. Something was wrong with me, and though it would be a week before I met with Dr. Lee and got the confirmation of how bad it was, I couldn't fathom telling him one of our worst fears was coming to pass. I always thought this would be something we'd weather together, but I felt so alone, and I wanted Luke, my *friend*, not the flirty boy who might break my heart. So I texted him that I couldn't do this. I didn't want him to look at me differently. Like my whole family had been looking at me that whole night.

Back at home, my parents started packing up to leave the Cape a couple days early. I wanted to mope by myself, but Abbi wouldn't leave me alone.

"What's wrong, Sera?" she whispered, climbing into my bed

long after we were supposed to be asleep. "Other than the obvious," she added as I wiped my eyes. "Spill."

"I was supposed to meet Luke tonight." I gulped down tears and curled into a ball. "I *like* him," I whispered to my knees, "and I think he was going to tell me he likes me too, but what does it matter now? I'm going to die, and there's no time."

Abbi, blunt as usual, told me I was being stupid, that we didn't know anything yet, and if anyone would get it, it would be Luke. She said I shouldn't give up on something before I'd really tried. So, under strict orders to be no longer than an hour, she covered for me while I snuck out. It was past midnight, but I tried the Beach at the End of the Universe first. When Luke wasn't there and didn't reply to my texts, I asked Maddy where everyone was, and she sent me the address of a house party in Dennis.

When I got there, the house was packed, different music playing on each floor, kegs in the tiny kitchen, beer pong on the porch. The space around the backyard firepit teemed with people, but I spotted Luke right away, the back of his hair standing up to the left like it always did. I had this brief moment of pure joyful anticipation, like everything would be all right after all. That's probably why I didn't see Izzy at first. But I couldn't *not* see her as soon as Luke leaned down to kiss her. I froze. Suddenly I was second-guessing everything—every small look and touch that had happened since the start of the summer. None of it had meant anything. Fighting tears, I rushed back through the house and out the front door before Luke saw me.

My family and I left the Cape two days later. I thought about trying to talk to him. To ask him if he'd ever really liked me at all. But I just couldn't. I needed to—I still need to—protect my heart.

Maddy interrupts my thoughts with my turkey burger, and I thank her before she's off to help two new tables.

I stay until close, committing to the idea of three self-portraits and drafting a few paragraphs for my essay. I also start a shared doc for Maddy and me to make plans for next summer in Europe. I watch the girl in the corner scrawl something on her receipt before she pulls up her hood and heads out into the rain. When Maddy locks the door behind her, I leave my stool to help her wipe down the tables and flip the chairs onto them. She lines the ketchups up on the counter and has me marry all the low bottles while she mops, blasting the new Chappell Roan as loud as the old speakers can handle. Once everything is tidy and the kitchen staff is gone, she turns the lights off and I go wait on the front step for her to set the alarm. The rain has finally passed, but the air is still wet, the street soggy, like all of Northport is sitting inside a huge cloud.

Maddy wipes her bangs out of her face and sighs.

"I'm sorry," she says, fiddling with her keys. "For pushing you about Luke. I just really love you both, and I like a good story, and you two could make a really good one."

"Not all good stories make good realities," I say.

She nods. "Like his parents."

"Yeah. What went down there?"

She shakes her head. "I don't really know. I think Mr. Tisdale cheated, but all I know for sure is he left, and Luke was . . . furious, but really sad too. You should ask him about it. He was always more open with you."

"I don't think he wants to tell me," I admit.

"A lot has changed, huh?" Maddy says, then throws an arm around my shoulder and squeezes me to her side as we walk around the back to her car. "I'm glad you haven't."

"Never."

"Okay. No yelling at me. But if this summer, heck, if the next few years are supposed to be about going for what you want while you can . . . are you sure you don't want to give things a shot with Luke? I think you're just being a chicken," Maddy says as she unlocks her old Toyota sedan and we climb inside.

"I'm not being a chicken. I'm being practical." I cringe as I remember Luke saying the same thing about his family situation and how badly I wanted to argue with him. But this isn't the same. I don't want to languish. I want to be all in. "And I want a new beginning. Anything could happen with Jackson, but at least it'll be different."

"Okay. Okay. Fine. I hear you. I'll drop it. Enough moping about the past. Go have your romance with Jackson, and I'll start looking at the map I know you're dying for me to put notes on."

"Really?" Maddy nods, and I do a little dance in the passenger seat. "Okay, now spill. What did Sienna write on her receipt?"

Maddy pauses, then reaches into her pocket and pulls the receipt out. I snatch it.

"Her number?!"

"Her number." Maddy grins, and I poke her on the shoulder,

demanding she text her, until she does. "There," she says, throwing the car into reverse, "now we'll both have hot summer people blowing up our phones."

*

At home I find Mom on the back porch reading and sipping wine. Dad's in the living room watching the Sox game, and Abbi's in the kitchen making sundaes with Cam. The house is quiet but not silent. Lived-in and still at the same time, like a snapshot. After all the rain today, the air smells fresh and clean. I used to love quiet nights on the Cape, but there's something missing from this one. Maddy's questions have me thinking about Luke. On rainy days when we were little, he'd come over and we'd camp out in my stairwell, pretending we were hiding from dragons or stuck on an infinite staircase. Two summers ago, we spent a lot of those rainy days watching old movies, the space on the couch between us shrinking, me waiting for it to disappear. I try thinking about him as just a friend, but my mind can't untangle our friendship from all those deeper, heated feelings of want and hurt.

I slide onto the love seat next to Mom. "What are you reading?" I ask. She pulls me into her like I'm still five and tells me about her book—something historical about siblings getting through a war.

"It sounds sad," I say, reaching for her wineglass and taking a small sip after she nods permission at me. The liquid is cold and sharp, and tastes like lemon juice mixed with grapes. "Bleh," I groan, handing it back to her.

She chuckles. "It grows on you," she says, taking a big sip and putting the glass back on a coaster I made at camp when I was eight. "You'll have to learn if you're going to Paris. And the book is sad, but it's nice to feel sad sometimes."

"Did your therapist tell you to tell me that?"

"No," she says, threading her fingers through my hair, "just an observation."

She doesn't really need to say more. We both know what she's thinking. I snuggle in a little more and let her baby me for a few minutes. She smells like clean laundry and hand lotion. The steady scratch of her nails against my scalp makes me sleepy.

"Kids are exhausting," I mutter, closing my eyes. She laughs silently, her stomach bouncing my head a little.

"Oh, speaking of kids, we're having Paula and the boys over for a barbecue tomorrow."

I pull the blanket off the side of the love seat and draw it over myself. I can't tell them to cancel. Paula is Mom's friend and they're our literal neighbors. It would be weird if I objected to a casual barbecue.

"Okay."

"I know something's changed. That you and Luke aren't as close. Was it your health? I know you asked us not to tell them details, and we've respected that, so is it something else? You know you can tell me."

"Something else. He still doesn't know about the heart stuff, and I don't want him to. Yet."

"Okay, honey, but I'm sure he'll be understanding. You share the same history."

"Maybe. Can we just not bring it up?"

"Of course."

We fall quiet for a while as the yard darkens from purple to navy to black. Mom goes back to her book, the pages slicing through the quiet alongside the spring peeper frogs hiding back in the woods. When I fall into a light doze, Mom shakes me gently. "Get to bed," she says.

I head inside, passing through the living room to say good night to my dad.

As I trek up the stairs, I feel the full weight of the busy week settling into my bones. I pause and take in the photos of Luke and me halfway up. We're at camp, showing off our wimpy muscles in our swimsuits. We painted our scars bright red to show the kids teasing us we didn't care what they said. Our scars were special; they meant we'd survived. I sigh. I want an easy path back to those kids, or at least to what's between them. A fierce kind of protective love.

After I shower, I sit on the footstool in front of my vanity and brush out my hair, putting in the fancy leave-in conditioner Abbi got me when I got sick two years ago. There's barely any left. The me in the mirror looks healthy enough. My skin is a little tanned from the days in the sun. As I go through my skin-care routine, I try to picture her older, at twenty, before our new heart arrives, then thirty, forty-five. I push fast-forward on her face, where I imagine I'd wrinkle and sag, and when I squint, I can see her—me but old, ancient, at least a hundred. She's beautiful. Her gray hair wild, her thick glasses held on with a beaded chain made by some grandkid.

What would she say about how to live *now*?

CHAPTER NINE

Luke

I try to get out of the barbecue at the Watkinses' by telling Mom I've been called in to cover at the marina, but she isn't buying it.

"I called Georgie ahead of time and double-checked they hadn't put you on the schedule," she says as she wrestles Adam into a button-up. I don't know why she's torturing them with nice shirts. It's just the neighbors. I'm pretty sure Mrs. Watkins was there when Oliver was born. I remember her showing me how to hold him.

"I know you and Sera had a little falling-out, but you're eighteen, honey. Learn to patch things up."

My phone buzzes in my pocket for the fifth time in the last ten minutes. Izzy wants to hang out, and I've been avoiding her. It's not that I'm not happy to see her, but with Sera back it's just . . . confusing.

"I'd like you to come," Mom says as she directs Adam toward

the front door and pries a Nerf gun out of Oliver's hands. "Please. They're like family."

We let the unsaid thing sit between us. That with Dad out of the house we've been trying to rebuild what *family* means, to varying degrees of success. I nod and stop Oliver from reaching for his Nerf gun again.

"Heyyy," he says, pouting.

"There's stuff to do over there," I promise him. "Let's go."

I text Izzy that I have a family thing but that we can hang soon.

Like the shirts have added some weird formal tension to the day, Mom also has us go around to the front door and knock. I take a couple deep breaths, shake out my hands, and prepare myself to look at Sera like I look at any of my other friends. I wish I were more ready, though, because she's the one who opens the door. She's wearing a Mass MoCA T-shirt and denim shorts, and she looks beautiful. My heart lurches in my chest. I notice she seems nervous to see us. Her smile is a little forced.

"You knocked!" she says, surprised, and I give Mom my best *I told you so* look. "Come in. Welcome. You remember the way through to the backyard, right? The house hasn't changed, that's for sure. Same creaky floor, and watch your step between the living room and the kitchen. But you know that. Duh!" Sera clamps her lips together like she's forcing herself to stop talking.

Mom and I step inside, and Adam and Oliver dart past Sera, heading straight through the house to the backyard. I cringe, hoping they don't knock something over. Abbi swoops in, dodging the boys, and gives Mom and me quick hugs.

"So good to see you!" she says, beaming. She takes the eggplant Parmesan Mom has and starts asking her about her garden. Mom follows her and then Mr. Watkins appears. He's taller than even me, and looks most like Abbi, with dark red hair that's started to gray since I last saw him. He pats me on the shoulder and pulls me to the living room, where the sports news is going over the Sox game from last night.

"Did you catch the game?" he asks, hitting pause on the remote and scrolling back. "Did you see this play? What a mess."

I laugh, taking in the living room, which looks the same. I spot the photos of Sera and me still lining the wall next to the staircase. "Yeah, they really almost lost it all in the eighth." I swallow, surprised the photos are still there when Sera did such a spectacular job cutting me off. I wonder what her family knows about why she ghosted me.

Mr. Watkins launches into a statistics rant, and I remember he's a math professor. I'm trying to keep up, but I catch Sera out of the corner of my eye. She mouths *Good luck* as she points at her dad. Then she slips away down the hall toward the kitchen.

I listen back in to Mr. Watkins's statistics spiel and offer my own two cents, saying that if they hadn't intentionally walked the player before, we probably wouldn't have needed the extra inning to close. He nods.

"Smart observation. So, tell me about this state championship game we missed."

At least that's an easy ask. I fill him in as we head through the house to the open sliding glass doors that lead from the kitchen to the backyard. Talking about baseball is easy. When you break the rules of what's expected, it's fun, thrilling even, and makes for a good story. A game was a game, no lasting ramifications.

Outside, Mom and Mrs. Watkins are fussing with the grill. Adam and Oliver are doing circles in the yard and playing on the old playset while Mom explains that their parkour instructor made her promise to stop them from doing tricks outside class. I give Oliver a look when he catches me watching him swinging a little too high on the swing. He makes a face at me, then hops off. Once both his feet are on the ground, I head for the cooler at the end of the picnic table, where Sera is sitting on the edge. She's watching my brothers with a smile on her face, and I wonder what she's thinking about. I catch myself wanting to ask but I don't know if we're there yet. At our beach it felt like things could go back to normal, but since the drive-in, Sera's been hard to pin down again. She's busy teaching, and I'm busy with my jobs and Izzy. Sera also might be seeing that Jackson guy. I don't know. Maybe this is just what happens when you grow up and take on more responsibility—less time for friends, particularly ones who have let you down.

"Even baseball scares me," Mom is saying, "after Luke's knee injury."

Sera turns and glances at my leg as I lean down to get a soda. I accidentally brush my arm against her calf as I stand up, and she flinches back, catching herself before falling off the table. The awkwardness from the drive-in rushes back, the way her face closed up when I forgot to let go of her hand.

"You okay?" I ask as she rights herself. She nods. That's

when I notice she's still wearing the *EBE* bracelet I made her when we were ten. My heart clenches. *What does that mean?* I wonder, but then I remember the way she was cuddling up to Jackson at the drive-in.

I must be hovering too close, because she jumps down and scoots around me as Abbi puts on some music. As she brushes by, I smell citrus shampoo and vanilla perfume and my mind starts to act like I'm sixteen again and can't take a hint. I swallow and shake my head, opening the soda as Sera takes the phone from her sister and starts adding songs to the queue. Abbi whispers something at her, and she brushes it off, glancing at me quickly, then away again.

Oliver comes sprinting back to the patio, pausing at the cooler to take two sodas before I can tell him not to. I settle in at the table and keep an eye on them. In less than ten minutes they're turning cartwheels in the grass and Oliver has lost a shoe and Adam his collared shirt, which he has affixed to the top of the tree house as a pirate flag. I spot Sera out of the corner of my eye heading back into the house.

Mrs. Watkins keeps saying it's fine, but I can tell all the chaos is making Mom upset. I'm about to tell them to calm down or we're not getting ice cream tomorrow when Sera comes back out and gets their attention with a couple of huge sketch pads.

"Do you guys want to make some pirates?"

The boys stop what they're doing and rush over, asking a hundred questions. Sera explains her plan: to make some large drawings they can tape up on the back fence or the bushes to act as targets. Oliver is immediately into it, making Adam lie down so he can trace him.

"I'll make an enemy boat," Sera says, settling onto the grass. As she tears a piece of paper away for Adam to draw on, and helps Oliver open a brown Magic Marker, I'm pulled back into a memory from two years ago.

We were working on the camp float for the Fourth of July parade in Barnstable. Sera had only been back for a couple weeks, and everything felt different. Had she always looked at me so intensely when she talked? Had her eyes always been a rich, dark brown at the center? Had she done something new to her hair, which kept catching the sun? We were alone on one side of the float, painting the papier-mâché copy of the Blue Honeybee. All of a sudden I felt nervous to be one-on-one with her, like I didn't know how to talk to her.

"So, um, what happened with that guy you were dating?" I asked as I reached past her to re-dip my brush in the paint. I knew she'd just broken up with Ethan, a boy from her school, about a month ago, but she hadn't told me why.

"Oh"—she paused, readjusting the bee's antennae—"I don't know. I mean, he was nice. He got me that cool book of hyper-realistic paintings of science fiction worlds. The one I showed you."

"But?" I asked, trying not to sound too interested.

"I guess . . . it just didn't feel special." She shrugged, pushed her hair out of her face, and got a smear of paint on her cheek. I smiled.

"I get that," I said.

"Yeah?" Her eyes met mine and stayed there. I couldn't stop looking at her. It was the first time I wondered if she'd ever want *me* to be her boyfriend. Butterflies exploded in my stomach at the thought, but my nerves got the better of me and I glanced away. Before I could say anything, Ryan O'Rourke, the senior in charge, had come back around to help us, and the moment was over.

Still, that day, every little move and look felt like it meant something. When Sera handed me the paint bucket and our hands touched, they lingered—didn't they? When she came over to give me advice and leaned against my shoulder to point out what she thought I should change, her breath so close to my ear—that was flirty, wasn't it? When I finally told her about the paint on her face and went to wipe it off and she blushed—was she feeling that tug in her gut too?

I swallow down a sigh and go to help her with my brothers. Sera's feet are bare, the bottoms a little green. I sit next to her.

"Want some help?"

"Sure." Sera moves over so there's space for me to sit and work on the other half of the page. She hands me some markers, and when I grab them, goose bumps rise on my arm at her touch. But Sera just turns back to the drawing, reminding me I was a fool for thinking I could turn our friendship into something more. The quick, painful memory of the night she stood me up comes back to me. My anxiety when she was late, turning into tearful disbelief, then anger, when she told me she couldn't do this. I want to know why, but more than that, I want to be friends again.

We sketch quietly for a few minutes; the boys have finally calmed down. Through the trees, the sun falls in broken yellow splotches across the yard, warming our cheeks and shoulders. My phone buzzes again, and I scramble to shut it off, like I've been caught. I wish I could just get wrapped up in Izzy like last summer. Maybe I should. She's fun, and it's comfortable knowing that it's not going to get serious because there's a clear end date. A few minutes later, it's Sera's phone that lights up with a text message. She looks at it and smiles, typing back a quick response. I wonder if it's Jackson, but I can't ask that without sounding jealous.

"You're good at this," I say as she gives Adam the okay to run his *Pirates Only* sign up the tree house.

"Yeah? Thanks. I'm loving teaching."

"That's great," I say, picking up a brown marker and scribbling on the edge of Adam's other abandoned drawing. "I miss camp." Getting lost in my art was always something I looked forward to, and making posters for town events scratches some of that itch. But art will always be there, waiting for me to have time again.

"You should come by sometime, then," Sera offers, smiling at me for real as she watches me sketch.

"That would be fun."

"Just don't let them see you're a better artist than I am," she says, still looking at my stupid drawing. "Or my expertise will be questioned."

"Yeah, right. As previously mentioned, I'm a hobbyist—you're the expert."

"*And* you gotta keep it zipped about the old days. If they find out it was *our* idea to start the annual last-day-of-camp paint fight against the theater kids, I'll have no authority at all," Sera says.

I laugh. "Fine. Deal."

"Glad that's settled," she says.

"So," I say, adding a cannon to the front of the boat. "Tell me about this gap year thing."

CHAPTER TEN

Sera

On Monday, inspired by Oliver and Adam's pirates, which are still all over our backyard, I have the kids spend the morning coming up with ideas for self-portraits. I have them write down a list of all the things about themselves they can think of. We do physical stuff but emotional and character stuff too. Things I'm thinking about for my fellowship application. I try to stay focused, but once or twice, I find myself glancing at the door, hoping Luke takes me up on my offer. But the morning goes by and there's no sign of him.

After lunch, we're scheduled to walk down to the beach. Jayda, the lifeguard, is an old friend of Abbi's. She shouts hi to me as I herd the kids across the hot sand toward her. For anyone who doesn't want to swim, we've got salt-worn easels hidden under the lifeguard stand, and I'm lugging the bag of art supplies along with Frisbees and other beach games. It's only an hour, but I'm definitely tired by the end of it.

Once we trek back to the studio, I have the kids set up their stations with the materials they want to use to fill in their outlines.

"Remember, you don't have to finish today. This is going to be our open project this week, so you can add to it between now and Friday and we'll do presentations then." I settle back on my stool and wait for hands to shoot up into the air when they have questions, then move carefully among them one at a time. I sit next to them on the ground, listening to their ideas pour out of their little heads. There's so much energy in each kid, it's like they radiate imagination.

Suddenly there's a knock on the door, and I turn hopefully. But it's just one of the parents, here for pickup a little early. I ask everyone to start cleaning up, helping the kids hang or lay their pieces out to dry until they come back Wednesday. My phone buzzes in my pocket, and I check it as the kids start clearing their spaces.

Jackson

Any chance you're free for dinner tonight?

Maybe it's good if Luke doesn't show up today. I don't need the confusion. I like Jackson, and I haven't liked anyone besides Luke in so long.

Sera

Sure! What time?

Jackson

7pm at my house? I'll send the address.

I gulp. Dinner at his *house? Fresh start. Fresh. Start,* I remind myself.

Sera

Sounds great! See you then.

As we're wrapping up, one of the students who I used to babysit comes up to me holding a piece of paper.

"Miss Sera?"

I still can't help but smile at being called *Miss*. "What's up, Rose?"

She hands me the paper. "Do you want to come to my softball game this Thursday?" The flyer tells me it's the July 1 season opener over at the middle school fields. Rose is staring at her paint-splattered shoes waiting for an answer. I have a vivid memory of the year I first had Miss Iris, and how anxious I was to win her attention and approval. I kneel down and take the flyer.

"I'd love to, Rose. Thanks for inviting me."

She lights up, one tiny megawatt grin, and skips off to her dad waiting at the door.

I look around to make sure everyone is gone and then decide I'm not ready to go home. I take my stuff to the open studio, where I've been working on some landscapes instead of my fellowship pieces. I drop my bag in the corner I've claimed as mine and set everything up. I unfold the printed application I've been carrying around and set it next to a blank page. Even though I decided on self-portraits, I'm struggling a little with my theme. The essay needs to answer a few questions about the project you want to work on if accepted, and the first one is: *Why is this work important to you? What is it telling the world about who you are?*

I sigh and flip through my sketchbook to a self-portrait I did last year when things were awful. I'd never done one before, and I'm proud of it, but it was tough to draw. I could feel every unsaid thing I wanted to scream at the universe leaking out of my pencil onto the page. It's not pretty or soothing, like my landscapes are. Doing more of these means thinking about the fact that even though the surgery and my new medication have extended my time before my next transplant, that's still waiting for me, blocking me from seeing too far down the road ahead. I trace the edge of my face on the page, so glad not to be that sick girl anymore, but still worried I'll be her again too soon. I wish I could draw her a better future. I jot that down. I chew on my pencil, thinking about the pieces I could create. Maybe I'll do one from when I was little and proud of being a survivor instead of tired of it. The theme could be about embracing all parts of my condition: the good, the bad, the possible. The idea is still a little half-baked, but I think I can make it work.

Like she knows I'm struggling, Iris texts me right then. A picture of her view somewhere in the French countryside.

Miss Iris

It's not the beach but it's beautiful! Hope the kids are being nice to you. Let me know if you have any issues!

I text back a picture of my setup and tell her the kids are being angels even though I did find a rogue handprint on my back today.

Miss Iris

a blank page contains the universe!

I take a deep breath. She's right. I start writing out the ideas for three main pieces. Me at eight, me now, and me in ten years. Three decades, three attitudes toward my heart. But all three underwater, under the pressure of time. I sketch the me now first and write a list of descriptors on the right side of the page. I want to paint myself looking forward. My gaze should be almost over the head of the viewer. I can hear the ocean out the door, echoing across the dunes. I breathe in time with the ebb of the tide, let go of my worries and just sketch, disappearing into the fine lines building up under my pencil.

I've lost track of time, a good sign of the work going somewhere promising, when I hear the barn door creak open. I put my pencil down, lean away from my sketch pad, and turn my sore neck. Luke is walking toward me. *He came,* I think as my face breaks into a smile.

"Okay if I set up here?" He points at the station next to me, and I nod, still a bit surprised even though I'd been hoping he'd come. I'm delighted to see he has his old art caddy with him, TARDIS stickers intact, along with a canvas tote. He opens the bag and pulls out a canvas painting.

"There's no black in that." I laugh, taking in the details of the choppy ocean scene. He's used dark shades of many colors, but no actual black. He tries to hide a smile from me.

"That was the assignment." He shrugs, opening the caddy and digging around until he's pulled out a dozen or so rocks, all smooth black specimens that he starts lining up at the base. "Multimedia. But outside our usual medium, so no digital and no black for me." He glances at my sketch pad, then at me in a way that makes me wonder if the kids got paint on my face too. "I actually was thinking about that one project you did years ago, when you glued rocks and shells into a painting. I thought it might bring dimension to have some at the foreground. And I'm not really happy with the top left corner." He bites at his lip and steps back, and I tell myself not to ogle. *You don't ogle at friends.*

"It's really good, Luke," I say, picking my pencil back up.

He shrugs again in reply, already sunk into his own focus. I drift back to my own work, and soon it's like old times. We work side by side, and sometimes we turn and look at what the other is doing, offer a little comment. Luke points out that my nose looks a little flat, and I thank him and suggest he stop thinking the rocky base of his piece needs to be perfect. I tell him that the shoreline looking off-balance will feel more natural.

After another hour, my legs can't stand being still anymore, so I start to clean up, storing my easel and putting my sketchbook in my bag. Luke leans his work up on the drying rack and then asks how I'm getting home.

"Riding." I nod toward the parking lot, where I left my bike this morning.

He follows behind me out of the barn and up to the path. "What's the piece you're working on for?" he asks.

"A fellowship. The same one Miss Iris is at, for next summer." I feel a rush of excitement at the thought of Paris. "The chance of me getting in is slim," I admit, "but if I do get accepted, Maddy is going to meet me there. We want to do a backpacking trip afterward."

"Maddy's been dying to go to Paris." He laughs. "That sounds great. Your parents don't want you to go to school?"

"Oh, they definitely want me to go to school, but . . ." This is exactly where I should tell him what happened with my heart two years ago, where I could lean on our history, our shared understanding of how the universe doesn't really owe us anything, especially not time. This is where I should tell him how scared I was and how I don't want to be scared anymore. But then he'd ask more questions, and I'm not sure I can answer those yet. "I've asked them to give me some time to decide what I want to do. As you've mentioned, art school isn't super practical . . ."

"But you *could* go," Luke says, a little sharp.

"I guess, but—why?" I look over at him as we pass the storage shed.

"Why?" He sounds frustrated, and I feel a little defensive.

"Yeah, like, at least with the fellowship I can focus on one thing I know I love to do. I wouldn't have to decide what I want study for a whole four years and then what I want to do with the rest of my life." I swallow down my anxiety. "And the commitment is short, so if it, like, doesn't work out, and the work isn't good or something, then I didn't waste too much of anyone's time."

"Your art definitely isn't a waste of anyone's time, Sera."

"Neither is yours, Luke."

We fall quiet. The beginning of an argument sits between us, and neither of us wants to take it any further. Luke clears his throat and changes the subject.

"Remember the sleepover before seventh grade? When we stayed overnight?" Luke asks as we approach the theater building. The theater kids glance over at us through the open doorway and turn their music up louder.

I smile at the memory. We were thirteen and terrible.

"I still don't think it was a bad idea to sleep on the beach," I say.

"If only we had accounted for the tide." Luke shakes his head. "Though in our defense, it doesn't change as dramatically at the Beach at the End of the Universe, so we weren't used to that."

"Yeah, so at like four a.m., no moon, I woke up to you screaming that the kraken had you." I can't stop the bubble of laughter that escapes me.

"I was closer to the water than you! That's one hundred percent what it felt like. Cold, slimy tentacles wrapping around one side of me." He's laughing now too, his green eyes shining.

"I think they canceled sleepovers after that."

"Really? That sucks."

"Well, we did wake up the whole camp and scared the pants off the littles. I don't think they went swimming for weeks."

Luke's laugh settles, fades. "Good times," he says, still smiling at me. The way he's looking at me warms me up, like I'd been cold and not known it. Then he reaches for me, pulling me off the path, and my heart lurches at the contact. "Incoming," he warns as a string of kids runs past us shouting "Sorry" and dodging water balloons. Of course—he's just being kind. He's not touching me for any other reason. He lets me go, and the back of his hand brushes mine as we step back onto the path. I breathe a little easier once we're moving and there's more space between us again.

At the bike racks, I free my bike and slip my helmet off the handlebar.

"Thanks for coming," I say. "It was nice not to be working alone."

He nods, shoving his hands in his pockets. "Thanks for the invite."

It's a little awkward between us again. I want to say more, so much, but it doesn't feel like the right time. I'm not sure it ever will.

"Do you want to go grab an early dinner at the diner? Maddy's been mad I haven't come by to try her newest pie."

"Oh." I'm surprised, and a part of me wants to say yes, to slip back into a familiar routine with him, but I can't, of course. "I have something tonight."

"A date?" he jokes.

"Yes, actually. Haven't you heard of those?" I joke back. I think I see his smile fade briefly, but in a flash, it's back again.

"Cool. Have fun, Watkins," he says.

Abbi lets me borrow her car for the evening so I can drive myself out to Harwich Port. It's only thirty minutes away, but I'm late because I couldn't figure out what to wear. When I pull into Jackson's driveway, I'm glad I landed on a sundress and sandals and not the T-shirt and shorts that were in the running. The house is all white and massive with two columns framing the entryway and a balcony jutting out from the second floor.

As I make my way up the front steps, I quickly check my phone camera to make sure I look okay. I fix my hair a little and then press the doorbell. The sound echoes deep into the house. A woman in a maid's uniform answers and welcomes me in. I try not to gape as I follow her down the long hallway to the right of the grand staircase. We pass a library, a room with a pool table, and a large sunken living room. I shiver in the AC, which Dad still won't let us turn on yet at home. In the kitchen, Jackson is sitting at a long white marble island talking with a woman in a white chef's jacket. The maid ducks out of the room, and I can only hope my eyes aren't completely bugging out of my head.

"Hey, Sera," Jackson says, his face breaking into a grin. He gets up out of his seat and gives me a quick hug. My cheek presses into his chest—he's a full head taller than me. "You're right on time. Do you like ravioli?"

I laugh, nervous. "Who doesn't?"

"Great. My parents are going out, so it'll just be us." His smile widens, his eyes lighting up. His golden hair is swept off his face, like he just got a haircut.

"Cool." I turn to the chef and say hi. She just gives me a wave and returns to breaking down the lobster she has on the counter.

Jackson leads me out of the kitchen to a huge white stone patio, where there's a set of cozy-looking couches around a firepit and a tray with lemonade and iced tea.

I take in the backyard. The perfectly manicured emerald grass stretches toward the drop to the ocean. The water is choppier ocean-side, the waves a little louder than in Northport.

"It's so pretty back here," I say, awed. The sun is only just starting to set, and the few clouds over the ocean are slightly pink. Jackson brings me a glass of lemonade and gestures to the wooden walkway that leads to the shore.

"We can go walk on our beach for a little, if you want?"

"Sure." We walk their stretch of private beach, and I ask Jackson about his summer plans. He launches excitedly into a spiel about sailing, and something called a regatta. I nod along like I know what he's talking about, but it's all a bit hard to follow. I like that he's excited, though, and I make a mental note to look it up when I get home. When the sky starts to get dark, we turn back. We eat in the kitchen, at two place settings on the corner of the island. I try to relax, but the lobster ravioli is so good I can't quite keep my cool.

"My friend Maddy would *love* these," I say, finishing off another two that Jackson just added to my plate from the pan on the stove.

"Take some back for her," he says. "I'll make you a to-go box."

"If I don't finish them first!" I laugh, and he looks pleased as he sits down next to me again and pulls his chair a little closer.

"Have you been to Italy?" he asks.

"No," I sigh, trailing my fork through the sauce and letting my knee bounce off his. "Someday, maybe. Have you?"

"A couple times. You'd love it. The summer is hot, way more humid than here, but there's so much to do."

"And eat," I say, taking a final bite of the pasta on my plate.

When we're done, we take bowls of ice cream out back. Jackson starts the firepit, and I ask him about where else he's traveled. When I tell him about the Paris fellowship, he asks to see some of my paintings. My chest tightens for a moment, but I brush it off and show him the start of my self-portraits for the application. I tell him about how I hope to finally get to travel through Europe next summer with Maddy.

"Wow." He leans closer, putting a hand on my knee. "These are great, Sera."

"They're just sketches," I say.

"They're *good* sketches," he whispers back, looking me in the eye and brushing a loose piece of hair behind my ear. "They look just like you. You'll get in." I shiver at his touch and scooch closer.

"You think so?"

He grins again. "I know so."

I reach out and trace his bottom lip, smiling as his blue eyes glow in the firelight.

"Can I . . ." Jackson starts to ask, looking at my lips.

I nod once.

He takes my face gently in his hands. The kiss is sweet. But when he pulls away, I feel like I'm still waiting for something. The kiss feels like a question I don't know the answer to.

I'm still thinking about Jackson's lips when I flop onto my bed at home. Next door, the house is dark and quiet, but out my window I can see Luke's room is lit up. His curtain is drawn closed except for one corner, where I realize he's put up his old tin can phone line. It's not connected to mine anymore, and hasn't been since before we were ten, but the sign is unmistakable. He's up to chat if I want to. My throat tightens, and all at once I feel a deep, aching sadness for what could have been.

CHAPTER ELEVEN

Sera

On Thursday, Mom and Abbi drop me off at the middle school softball fields before they go to get mani-pedis. We had to stop by the pharmacy first, because the extra labs Dr. Lee requested last week finally came back and she wanted to adjust my meds a little. Even though the dose is only a tiny bit higher, my family's being a little clingy, as they're prone to do whenever we're reminded of how bad last year was. What they don't know is that I called the salon and paid ahead, now that I'm making my own money. I can't wait for them to come back all annoyed that I'm taking care of them instead of the other way around.

Maddy pulls up at the same time, running late with her little sister, who shouts an angry "I told you so!" before sprinting toward the fields.

"Hey!" Maddy gets out of her car and walks over to pull me into a hug. "Hi, Mrs. Watkins. Hi, Abbi," Maddy says.

"Hi, honey," Mom says. "How are your parents? No more issues with the landlord?"

"They're good and no issues. He's been delightfully absent since you spoke with him." Maddy switches her regular glasses out for sunglasses that are just as big but still cool with their bright orange frames. "Are you staying?"

Abbi shakes her head. "No, we're just dropping off Sera," she says, and I can hear the post-pharmacy-visit anxiety in her voice.

"Great!" Maddy says, looping her arm into mine. "I'll watch our girl. You two have a great afternoon." She pulls me around without waiting for them to say goodbye. I'm so grateful I promise her as much candy from concessions as she can possibly eat.

"On your part-time art teacher salary? For me? Wow, I'm spoiled."

"Please, it's the least I can do. Those two have been hovering all morning."

"Why?" Maddy asks, her eyebrows knitting together. The medicine thing is actually good news. This is the dose Dr. Lee wanted me on; we just had to work up to it.

I shrug. "They like to fuss. Okay, so I need to find the . . ." I pull out Rose's flyer and point to the circled team name. "Sandpipers."

"That's Marissa's team! Perfect. I think they're on the back field." We walk past the concessions stand, where we say hello to the Stones, who own Lorell's. I buy myself some sour worms and a Snickers for Maddy while trying to convince her to bring Mrs. Stone a batch of her newest cookies.

"Cardamom cookies with yogurt chips," I tell her. Mrs. Stone's eyes light up, but Maddy insists they're not ready.

"When they are, you bring them by. Okay?"

"Promise."

We fill up our waters and stuff the candy into the cooler of orange slices Maddy has with her so it won't melt. Then we locate the Sandpipers by spotting Marissa's long brown ponytail on the field closest to us. She's stretching with Rose, who stops and shouts when she sees me.

"Hi, Miss Sera!"

I wave to her as Maddy and I find an open space a couple rows up in the bleachers. But I almost trip when the coach stands up from the end of the bench and looks around for who Rose is so excited to see. Maddy has to lower my frozen arm down and tug me into my seat. It's Luke. Of course it's Luke. He gives me a confused smile and calls the girls into a huddle.

"Ugh, he's going to think I'm stalking him. We hung out a little Monday, but it was awkward. He asked if I wanted to grab dinner, but I had those plans with Jackson."

"Oooh, *plans*. Is that what they call it now?" Maddy stifles a giggle.

I feel my cheeks heat up. "Anyway, Luke and I are trying to be friends, but it's just been . . . weird."

"Just act natural," Maddy says. "We're here to watch my sister play, that's all."

"Right, right," I reply, crossing my legs and straightening my posture.

Maddy looks over at me and smirks. "That's not acting natural."

"Whatever," I say, slouching again and pulling my ponytail over my shoulder.

Luke looks over at us again quickly, and then back to the team as he has them put their hands in for a cheer. I feel my cheeks heating up. He's wearing his baseball uniform, and I now vaguely remember that the flyer said the high school team would be playing an exhibition game afterward against the local firefighters and first responders. I don't know how I wasn't prepared to see him.

I chance a look at him again. Luke is handsome already, but in his uniform he's downright hot. There's no ignoring it or pretending he's still the nerdy boy from next door who happens to have pieces of my heart in his chest. The whole outfit is formfitting and shows exactly how much he's grown in the last couple years. His biceps strain against the edge of the short-sleeved jersey with his last name in maroon across the top. Then I notice the number on his jersey.

He's number forty-two.

The answer to the ultimate question of life, the universe, and everything, from The Hitchhiker's Guide to the Galaxy.

And there's a small light purple towel hanging from one of his back pockets.

"Are you looking at his ass?" Maddy asks. "Because I kind of get it." She leans forward like she's trying to get a closer look.

"No!" I whisper-yell.

"Hey, we can all appreciate a nice butt."

Finally the Sandpipers take the field for the start of the game. Noticing Luke in this way is overwhelming, and I feel a little guilty because even though I've hung out with Jackson a few times, I don't get lost in my head thinking about *his* calves. Maybe I need to try a little harder there. I pull my phone out and ask if he wants to come to the exhibition game later. When I look back up at the field, I tell myself that Luke's just another hot guy—there are plenty of those. I went to prom with one two months ago, I'm going on dates with another, and Paris will be full of them for sure.

The Sandpipers are playing against the Minnows, an equally adorable group of kids. We cheer Rose, Marissa, and the whole team on as they keep the score at zero–zero until the third inning, when Marissa whacks a ball so far even she's shocked. Luke shouts at her to run and she sprints off, making it all the way to third before the other team brings the ball back in.

Rose is up next, and I cheer with the rest of the crowd as she focuses in. There's a buzz in the crowd even though this is kids' softball, and my heart warms to be back in Northport again, among people who care about the little moments of life. Who slow down to go to kids' sports games and throw fundraisers for footbridges that are actually fun and bring everyone together. Rose sends the ball flying over the first baseman's head, bringing Marissa's feet slapping over home plate. Rose does a little dance at second base, and I whoop as loud as I can for her. The next girl is struck out, and the inning ends.

Maddy stands up and stretches, grabbing the cooler. "I'm going to see if they want these before the next inning starts. It's hot. You wanna come?" She tips her head in Luke's direction, and I'm about to say yes when I notice Izzy bounding onto the field. Luke slings an arm over her shoulder as she pulls a water bottle out of her bag and hands it to him. He chugs it down and thanks her by bopping her on the nose with the empty bottle. They fit so well together. She's wearing sunglasses, but they can't hide the way she lights up as she talks to him. Some of the girls come over, shy but excited to say hi to her too. They all clearly know her. She must come to these things a lot when she's not at school. Serious or not, she's important to Luke. My heart clenches, and I remind myself that I'm not *from* here. Being a local is a big deal in Northport. In that way, Izzy and Luke are perfect for each other.

When the game is over, we grab more snacks and follow the considerable crowd over to the exhibition game. Marissa is giddy from the win, and I'm surprised the usually sports-averse Maddy is invested too.

"You can see the Northport boys at their best. God knows when Luke and the other seniors are gone they won't have the same winning streak."

Marissa argues that that's not fair, it's a team sport and he's just one person.

We squeeze into the packed stands around the main field, and I text Jackson our location so he can find us in the crowd. We end up behind Izzy and some of Maddy's and Luke's other friends. Luke's mom and his brothers are here too, down in the front, and Adam stands on the bench wiggling his arms at me. Paula turns her head and waves. Luke appears next to them, and Adam wraps his arms around Luke's waist, looking up at his brother like he invented the sun. Luke laughs, then looks up. His eyes land right on me, and my breath catches in my throat. But then Jackson slides into the row with us and puts his arm around me. I lean into him as Maddy runs through the rest of the roster and the high school team takes the field.

I recognize most of the guys on Luke's team, and they've all grown similarly, though none of them seem as charismatic as Luke. He stops to talk to at least five or six more people as he heads back to the field. Jackson asks if I'm rooting for one side or the other.

"Hmm," I say, thinking. "I'm going with the boys."

"My money's on the old folks," he says.

I laugh. "Suit yourself."

The fire chief is up to bat first, and she makes a big show of trying to get the ump to walk her, eventually getting her way, to the delight of the crowd.

"So it's not a real game?" I say to Maddy, reaching into the cooler for some of the candy.

She shrugs. "I don't really pay attention." She taps Izzy on the shoulder and asks the same question.

"I think it'll pick up," Izzy says, pointing to the lineup of first responders, who, unlike the chief, look fresh-faced and young, ready to play. "Don't worry, we'll get to see Luke at his best. He's not one for going halfway."

"Oh, I was just curious," I say. It comes out all in a rush, and I quickly turn and offer Jackson some sour worms.

She's right, though. The next two batters get on base, and the crowd quiets as the pitcher throws the ball to one of the EMTs. The first two pitches are strikes, but he connects on the third pitch. The ball goes whipping toward the third baseman and Luke, who plays shortstop. It looks like there's no way either of them will get there in time—until Luke does. He dives, catching the ball with an outstretched hand. I cringe as he lands hard on his right side, but he's up in an instant, the ball flying toward home to catch the runner out too. The crowd goes nuts. Izzy's jumping up and down, hollering with the rest of them, while Maddy claps and Marissa shouts, "Go, Coach Luke!"

"Okay, maybe you chose the right team," Jackson says with a laugh.

Luke dusts off his uniform and tips his hat to the crowd. The fact that he has this wider life now, friends who used to be bullies now teammates, girls who'd never looked at him twice fawning over him, townies who proudly say "That's our boy" like they raised him instead of giving him a hard time for preferring art camp over fishing at the docks. I feel like I'm stuck in a cheery Hallmark movie, just one of those extras lingering on the fringe.

During the third inning I tell Maddy I'm feeling tired, and I ask Jackson to take me home. We slip away, and I wait in the parking lot for Jackson to pull his BMW around. My back is to the field, but I can still hear the announcer's voice echoing over a wave of cheers.

"And that's a home run from our own Luke Tisdale, number forty-two, Northport's finest, showing us how it's done!" I'm proud of him, I realize, beneath the loss, knowing he's no longer just *my* Luke. He's found a place here, made it his, and maybe me not fitting in it anymore is just the way it's meant to be.

CHAPTER TWELVE

Sera

One of the best features of Northport is its Fourth of July celebration. While the town doesn't have its own parade, it has the best carnival and fireworks by far. Jackson invited me to spend the weekend with his friends on Nantucket, but I wanted to spend the holiday here. My whole family went down to the carnival on Harborside with Paula, Oliver, and Adam. Maddy placed second in the pie contest—right behind Mrs. Stone, of course. Luke was volunteering again, but he'd appear every couple of hours for hot dogs or fried dough, to challenge me to games, and to take his brothers on the rickety rides. It was almost like old times. Poor Dad has a migraine by the time we're home to pack our picnic dinner and begs off for the rest of the night.

"The fireworks can go off without me," he says as he pulls an iced eye mask from the fridge. "If that's okay?" He turns toward the hug I wrap him in and holds me tight for a minute while Mom and Abbi fuss around and get him meds and a glass of water. It's too bad he's not feeling well, but it's nice to be the one taking care of someone else.

"Pizza?" Abbi asks, once Dad's gone to bed, standing in front of the nearly empty fridge. "It'll travel well."

"Fine with me," I say, sliding into a chair at the kitchen table and lifting my prizes out of my bag. A tiny stuffed whale, a new set of playing cards featuring different types of sailboats that I slip into the napkin holder, and bright pink jelly shoes I'll give to Maddy because they're a little small. "Can we not do one of those heart-healthy ones, though? I'd die for some real pepperoni."

Abbi shrugs and looks at Mom, who is too tired to argue. My last check-in with Dr. Lee went great. She's happy with how things are looking with the adjusted medication.

I prepare a bagged salad in a Tupperware bowl with a lid as Abbi heats up the oven. Mom admits there are Oreos hidden in the pantry, and I grab those too, shoving them into the picnic bag along with our travel utensils, waters, seltzers, and a couple of Mom's mini wines. While the pizza heats up, Abbi and I change, running through several different outfit options to accommodate cuteness as well as potential cold from the wind or humidity. I settle on simple jeans and a white tank top that dips a little lower than Mom approves of and tie an old navy-blue hoodie around my waist. I dab glitter on my eyelids and throw on some star-shaped earrings before putting like eight mosquito-repelling stickers along the hem of my jeans.

I grab the food, Abbi gets the beach chairs and a blanket, and we pile into the car. When we get to Northport Beach, it's already more than half-full, but Mom's been texting Paula, and she saved us a spot. She's gone all out for their picnic, and Oliver and Adam are sitting quietly, devouring deviled eggs, pigs in a blanket, and her famous brownies.

"Hi, Sera," Adam says as I sit down. "Do you want a brownie?"

"What kind of question is that?" I ask, and when he looks at me confused, I laugh. "Of course I do. I'd never say no to one of your mom's brownies."

"Well, duh." He laughs and cuts me a piece, placing it on a blue napkin before passing it over carefully. I take it with as much seriousness as I can manage.

"Thank you, sir."

"You're welcome . . . ma'am." He bows back at me, tipping an invisible hat. I laugh and reach out to muss up his hair. He suddenly looks so much like Luke when we were little that I'm hit with a hard feeling of nostalgia.

Soon the beach is full, as if the whole town is here, even though sunset still hasn't fully darkened the sky. I'm trying not to get antsy, but it's bothering me that Luke isn't here with his family.

"Paula," I ask, "is Luke here?"

"Oh, somewhere." She gestures at the crowd. "His friends came and stole him a little while ago, once he was done helping set up. You should go find them."

I do need to find Maddy, I justify to myself as I stand up. She promised to bring a batch of her newest cookies as a test run for the ones she's making for the annual blood drive next weekend. "That okay, Mom?" I ask.

"Sure, honey, just bring your phone so you can find your way back when it gets dark." I wave my phone at her and head off toward a group of kids I recognize from the bonfire, keeping an eye out for Maddy's brunette bob or Luke's towering frame. *I'm glad I'm here,* I think as I weave around families on the beach. Doing something new with Jackson's friends might have been fun, but I missed this tradition.

I hear my name and turn. "Sera!" It's Izzy, just a few feet away, sitting on a blanket next to Luke.

"Hey," I say. "Happy Fourth."

"Wanna sit?" Izzy says, motioning to the spot next to her and moving a small cooler over to make space. She opens it to pull out a couple beers. I look at her cozied up to Luke and shake my head. Luke opens his mouth to say something, but I cut him off.

"I have to find Maddy, but thanks," I say. I turn to go, trying to swallow down the sudden lump in my throat.

Seeing them has opened a crack in the wall around my memories from two summers ago, and that Fourth of July comes racing into the front of my mind.

That summer, Luke and I had plans to go watch the fireworks from our beach. I packed snacks and blankets and met him on his back step.

"Hey," he said, smirking, as he opened the door. "Look what I scored." He held up two packs of sparklers and a couple beers.

My heart sank a little. I didn't want to drink. We weren't supposed to. I knew his doctors told him almost the same things as mine told me, even though he didn't need to be on immunosuppressants like I did. But I felt weird saying that when he was excited, and I didn't have to have one. Plus he did seem a little cheerier than he'd been for the last few days. Something had been bothering him that he wouldn't share with me no matter how much I bugged him about it.

"Oh," I managed, "okay. Ready to go?"

At the beach we set everything up on the rock, and Luke drank one of the beers while I nibbled on snacks.

"What's going on with you?" I finally asked, when he'd finished the can and crushed it under his heel. He ducked his head away from me and shrugged.

"Nothing."

"*Nothing* doesn't make you drink beer when you've never had it before," I said, a little angrier than I meant it to come out.

"I've had beer before, Sera," he said, bristling. I wanted to demand when and with who, but I felt silly and childish. Instead, I scooched closer to him. The sky was dark and clear, the moon low, stars out galore.

"Show me the constellations?" I asked.

To my relief, he leaned into me, a warm pressure that my body focused in on. The backs of our hands were touching. Luke looked down and intertwined his fingers with mine. Our eyes met. He squeezed my hand tight, and I could feel our heartbeats pounding away together in my palm. I leaned a little closer. His breath smelled sour and bready, and it cut straight through the thought I'd had, that maybe I could kiss him. I wrinkled my nose at him and turned away, grateful I hadn't done anything stupid.

"The constellations are up there," I joked, letting go of his hand and pointing to the sky above us. But Luke didn't look away.

"I don't want to look at the constellations, Sera," he said, taking my hand back. My heart started to race, each beat climbing up into my throat.

"What else are we supposed to do while we wait for the fireworks?" I asked, wondering if he was thinking the same thing I'd been thinking before. That it was romantic, out here on our space rock, no one else for miles.

Luke shrugged, then reached for the second beer, breaking the spell. I shifted away from him just as the first fireworks started a mile offshore, vibrating the air around us. I felt lightheaded suddenly, and a little dizzy. I dropped my head onto my knees and closed my eyes for a second.

"Hey, you okay?" Luke asked, looking at me through tired eyes.

"Yeah, fine. I just . . ." My head was still spinning, and I wouldn't know it for more than a month, but my heart was struggling right there without my knowing. "I don't like the smell of the beer," I said.

Luke leaned away from me. We sat in silence as the fireworks went off. After the finale, my ears were ringing. The shimmer and crackle of the last explosion was raining down on the water, but the silence was still there between us. And it only grew.

Now, as I try to find Maddy in the crowd, I'm having trouble with my emotions. I can't stop picking them apart. I look down at my outfit. Was I trying to get Luke's attention tonight, with my scar peeking out and the cute red bra under my white tank? Maybe. Ugh. I don't know.

"There you are!" Maddy finds me and pulls me out of my head and over to her beach blanket. I'm a little surprised when Luke and Izzy join us, since they seemed so happy just the two of them, but Maddy makes space for them right next to us, even though I wish she wouldn't.

"Hey," Luke says, stuffing his hands into his jean pockets. He's relaxed, happy, and I wonder how much he's had to drink.

"Hi," I mutter, moving my eyes from him to Izzy, who is carrying a giant stuffed octopus I mistook as a pillow when I saw them before. She's wearing it draped over her shoulder like it's part of her outfit.

"Nice sea creature," Maddy says, squishing one of the orange tentacles.

"Luke won it for me," Izzy says, gushing, as Maddy helps reposition it a little.

I tell the jealousy in my stomach to chill out even though I want to scream.

"I'm going to grab a Popsicle," I say, turning and leaving before offering to get anyone anything.

I throw my brushed-until-silky hair up into a messy bun as I walk and pull my sweatshirt on even though it's not that cool yet. I want to erase all the evidence of my efforts to try and look nice. I wish I'd worn pj's and maybe a paper bag over my head. The Popsicle line is long, but I need the time to cool off, so I step to the back and start scrolling through my photos. I'm looking for a photo I took of Maddy at the diner weeks ago when I land on a picture I took of Luke's drawing the night of the barbecue. I pause and zoom in, admiring how he made so much movement happen with so few lines. I text it to Iris, asking her what she thinks.

"Hey." Luke surprises me from behind and I almost drop my phone.

"Whoa." I turn, annoyed. "Hi, again. Are you following me?" It comes out harsher than I mean it to.

"No, I just can't resist a Firecracker pop," he says. He smiles, and I give him a tight-lipped one back, then continue looking at my phone. Summer, summer, graduation, prom, Iris's show in Boston—my year flickering across my screen while Luke stands there.

"Are you mad at me or something?" he asks.

"Nope," I try, but even I can hear the bitterness in my voice. I slip my phone into my back pocket.

"Yes, you are, Sera. I can tell. Why?"

He's really trying to be nice, which is why I'm so pissed at myself when all I can say is "Are you dating Izzy?"

"No." He looks legitimately confused. "Izzy and I aren't dating. We're just friends. Like *we* are. Or we're supposed to be. Do you *not* want to be friends?" He takes a step closer, and I flinch away.

"You two are friends with, like, benefits, though, right?"

He sighs and steps back again. "Why do you care? Aren't you doing the same with that rich kid? Jackson?"

"No." I waver. "But it's casual. He knows that."

"Right. Well, same with me and Izzy."

"You clearly like her a lot," I accuse him. "What's up with claiming it's not serious?"

"It's not like that," Luke says, shoving his hands in his pockets.

"Cool. Well, you fooled me. Ever consider you might be fooling her too?"

Luke stares at me, and I want to shove him like we're ten and he's just broken my Lego Millenium Falcon into its individual pieces.

"Look, I just want our friendship back." His voice is calm, low. I want to tuck myself up inside it. "I thought you wanted that too."

I look down at my shoes. If I could've just followed through with what I said by acting like his friend instead of a jealous kid, we wouldn't be here.

"I do want that." I sigh. "Can we just forget this?" I ask, meeting his eyes.

"Forget what?" Luke says with a smirk.

I feel the tension dissipate a little and point to the moving line. "You want one, right?" Luke's eyes search my face. I feel like he can tell there's something I'm still not saying, and there is, but right now isn't the time.

"No. I'm fine, actually. I should get back. My mom is probably dealing with Oliver forgetting his Lactaid right about now. Catch up later?"

"Sure." When he doesn't leave right away, giving me a look that pricks at my heart, I add on a "That would be great." And that seems to work. He leans in like he's going to hug me, then stops and awkwardly pats me on the shoulder like I'm one of his teammates before he disappears into the crowd.

The first firework goes off, alerting everyone that the show will start in five minutes. I move to the back of the beach, as close to the dunes as I can get, my Popsicle melting into the sand between my feet. The sparks of that one solitary explosion fade away into the blue-black sky, and I feel like I'm the thing that's been shattered into a thousand pops of light, but I don't know what to do about it.

CHAPTER THIRTEEN

Sera

On Tuesday, I have the house to myself. Mom and Dad are out shopping for a new dishwasher, since ours announced its retirement last night. And Abbi is out at the beach with Cam. I set my easel up outside on the patio and try to make real progress on my first fellowship application piece. I've gone for a bigger size than I'm used to, and my order of 24-by-36-inch watercolor paper just came in yesterday. I start in a corner where there's nothing but ocean water, playing with oversaturating and blotting. I try out different colors for the layer underneath the blue until I'm happy with yellow. It creates an interesting glow effect. *Although* . . . I feel the idea creep up on me like the sun has struck me in the back. I could use a different color for each one. It would set their moods. Golden yellow for childhood, dark purple for now, and maybe light green for the future. I get as comfortable as I can on my stool and start in with one of my larger brushes.

I'm so lost in the process that I don't hear Maddy come in until she's right behind me.

"Earth to Sera!" she singsongs. I yelp and almost fall off my stool. "Oops. Sorry." She laughs as I turn and flick my brush at her.

"Maybe you should add becoming a spy to your potential job list."

"Nah." She recovers and pulls off her glasses, waving them in my face. "I'm too memorable."

"True." My heart finally slows down, and I start to collect my brushes to take in and clean. "What's up?"

"So, I took off work early, and I'm feeling like spending some of these tips." She puts her glasses back on and flashes a sticky-looking wad of small bills. "Wanna get a late lunch and go shopping?"

"Totally, let me change."

"No, no, no." Maddy grabs my elbow and leads me into the house. "You're perfect. Comfy and in easy-to-take-off clothes. All the better for trying things on." She gestures to her own outfit. She's wearing black leggings and a white T-shirt that has seen better days. Throw the apron she wears at the diner over it and I might ask her for a milkshake. I look down at my beach shorts and faded striped T-shirt.

"Okay, if you're sure this isn't a crime to wear in public," I say.

"I'm sure!"

I put my brushes in the sink, then slip on some flip-flops and grab my bag by the door. We wave at Paula, who is on her way out too, herding Oliver and Adam into the back of her little blue car. There's no sign of Luke or his truck. He must be at Nyeman's or working a shift at the marina.

As we walk through my neighborhood, Maddy points to the new aboveground pool the neighbors put up on the corner.

"I know Northport Beach is close, but I'd *love* a pool."

"I think I'd prefer an in-ground," I say as we pass by.

"Oh, like the fancy one at Ryan O'Rourke's house? Most epic graduation party I've ever been to," Maddy says.

I smile. It was epic. It also was one of those confusing days where things with Luke almost went somewhere.

I'd convinced my mom to buy me my junior prom dress early and met him there.

"You're blue, like the honeybee," Luke said, grinning when he found me by the dessert tables.

I did a spin for him in my silk dress, delighted. "Thanks. You look great!" I said, surprised by how grown-up he looked in his suit.

"It's my Christmas church suit," Luke complained, looking around the crowded yard like he was worried he didn't belong. Throngs of wealthy grown-ups sparkled in suits and gowns, holding champagne glasses. Platters of shrimp, grilled meat, and tiny lobster rolls seemed to replenish like magic. We were on the dance floor by the pool when Ryan came running through and jumped straight into the water. A slew of kids followed.

I raised my eyebrows at Luke.

"Oh no," he said.

"Oh yes," I replied. "Race ya!" I broke away from him and

cannonballed into the pool. He followed right behind me. We popped up out of the water, laughing. Luke's white shirt clung to his chest, and his lips were a little blue.

"Are you cold?" I asked, realizing I was shivering despite the warm night.

"A little," Luke said, floating closer. "You are too. I can tell."

"I'm great," I said, my chattering teeth giving me away.

Luke settled his hands on my arms, rubbing them, trying to warm me up. "You're freezing," he said, wrapping all the way around me until our noses were almost touching. Everything went still. The sloshing water seemed to settle around us, the music faded, and the chatter of the party guests was a distant hum. All I needed to do was lean in and kiss him, consequences be damned. I stepped a little closer, my skirt floating up around us like a cloud. That's when Ryan surfaced out of the water right next to us.

"Break it up, kiddos," he shouted. "My parents are pissed. Time to get out!"

Just another moment I misread, I tell myself as Maddy and I hit the corner of Main.

"I haven't bought new clothes in ages. It just seemed like a waste when everything was still so . . . uncertain," I say as we cross the street.

"Sure, I get that, but don't take this the wrong way: You're built for a style way cuter than Abbi's black-and-white hand-me-downs and your mom's oversized beach clothes. And now that you've got Paris to prepare for, you gotta refresh. Let me help redirect you?" Maddy begs.

"Deal," I say.

At the first few clothing boutiques we give each other shocked looks when we see the price tags. Still, it's fun to browse. We continue down Main to a big thrift shop. I collapse into an old fancy armchair inside, claiming I need a break, but Maddy isn't having it.

"You're totally fine. Get up. You're going to love this."

At the back of the shop is a wall of prints and paintings. A sign tells us that local artists donated the pieces and proceeds go to repairing the boardwalk. There's a huge oil painting of Northport Beach, a series of small paintings of boats in the harbor, and even some watercolor sunsets of Thirds Beach and the lighthouse. There's also a huge whale-shaped weather vane made of what looks like bone and driftwood that reminds me of Luke's grandpa's pieces.

"Okay, this is cool," I say. I lose track of time for a bit as I try to decide if I want this one painting of a humpback whale swimming up the canal. Maddy shouts my name from a few aisles down. I pull myself away from the painting and go find her.

"Where are you?" I ask, walking through the kitchen supply aisle and then a corner full of lamps.

"Over here!" I follow her voice to the clothing section, where she has a cart full of things to try on.

"See, it's not *new* or expensive, but some of this stuff is still so quality." She flicks through another handful of hangers in the dress section. "The rich people with summer houses like to dump practically their whole wardrobes every year and buy new stuff. Some of this still has tags on it."

I join her in looking for the most outrageous dresses we can find, before lugging our discoveries to the dressing rooms.

At the last second, Maddy drops a yellow dress on the top of my pile.

"You *must* try this. It's required."

I laugh. "Why?"

"Because it's a great date dress." Maddy's eyes shine, and she winks. "When are you seeing Jackson again?"

"Oh, um, I'm not sure . . . He's still in Nantucket," I say. He's been posting a lot, but I haven't heard from him much since he left. "But I'll try it. Do you need one, too, for any . . . dates?" I ask. "You still haven't told me what's going on with Sienna. I've seen her at the diner like three times now."

Maddy blushes. "Well, I wasn't sure it was anything . . ."

"But . . ." I egg her on.

"*But* . . . we've gone out a couple times and it's been fun. Her family just moved here and she's a rising sophomore at Berklee and into DJ-ing, and . . . me . . . apparently."

I squeal. "Maddy! That's great!"

Maddy blushes a little. "Early days, but I like her a lot."

I make a mental note to find something date-appropriate for her to try on too.

In the dressing room, we laugh about how short the curtains are as we try on giant colorful caftans and more blue-and-white-striped clothing than we can count. Then I finally pick up the soft yellow cotton sundress. It's covered in tiny white flowers. I drop it over my head and zip it up. It fits perfectly. I step in front of the big mirror outside the changing stalls and stare at myself. The dress falls slightly past my fingertips and flares out from a corset-like bodice. The sweetheart neckline ties with a bow at the center and covers all but the very top of my scar. The straps are these fun off-the-shoulder kind that aren't actually doing anything, but make my arms look strong. Maddy gasps when she comes out to see me.

"Sera, you have to get it."

I sigh. "It is really pretty." I do a quick spin and the skirt flares out and then settles again. I find the price tag, and it's only twenty bucks. "I'll get it," I say, then I pin Maddy with a glare. "But it's probably not for any dates. It's just a nice sundress, and I deserve nice things."

Maddy hmms as she turns me side to side. "In that case, you should wear it out, because I was lying before: Those shorts belong at the beach and the beach only."

"Monster." I gasp. "How am I supposed to trust you now?"

Maddy shrugs, then prances back into her changing stall and comes out in an orange-and-green caftan.

"Think this will be cool in Paris?"

"Maybe if you were eighty?" I say, draping my arms over her shoulders as she pulls on a green felt hat and looks at herself in the mirror. "And, like, loaded."

"Then it's perfect!"

I laugh and Maddy goes back in to try on the rest of her pile. I don't bother changing out of the dress, and I can't stop catching sight of myself in the mirror, imagining the perfect occasion to wear it.

When I get home, Luke is out front with his mom, hefting a huge bag of soil from his truck like it weighs nothing. His dark hair peeks out from underneath a backward baseball cap, and the side of his T-shirt has lifted up, showing a sliver of toned stomach. Holding my bag of new clothes, I walk over to say hi. That's what a friend would do, right?

"Hey," I say, lifting my hand to block the sun. "Need any help?" Though I'm not at all a gardener.

"Oh no, we're all set, Sera. Thanks, though. We'll be done soon." Paula smiles, wiping the back of her arm across her forehead. Luke drops the bag, and I can't miss how his gaze catches on my dress. A shiver zips up my spine. His cheeks redden before he turns abruptly and walks back to the truck for another bag of soil.

"Okay." I try to think of a reason to stay. In years past I'd just take him away when he was done with the chore. We'd go to the tree house or out to the beach and stay until sunset. Maybe bike to the candy store or to Frappie's for ice cream. He comes back and drops another bag farther down the garden bed.

"Actually I could use your help Thursday. If you're free?" he asks as he lifts up the bottom of his shirt to wipe his forehead. I stare at his elbow so I don't stare at his abs. "I'm taking Oliver and Adam out on the boat, and they've been asking nonstop if you can come too."

"Me? Really? Well . . ." I'm surprised he's asking me after the awkwardness at the fireworks. I try to think of a reason why I can't go, but realize I really want to. "Yeah, that sounds fun. I'm in."

"Cool," Luke says.

"Text me what time you wanna leave," I say, and walk past the rosebushes into my backyard.

Inside, my parents are bickering by the old dishwasher, which has been pulled out into the tiny kitchen, the new one sitting off to the side.

"We need to turn the water off first," Dad is saying.

"You didn't already?" Mom says, frustrated.

"No, you told me to wait!"

"When?"

"Before."

"Well, if it needs to be off, it needs to be off." She stands up. "I'll get it."

Dad gets up too, following her down the stairs, reminding her to be gentle. I shake my head and go up to Abbi's room to see if she's home. I need her help picking an outfit for the boat. I'd wear the dress, but it's not practical. I push into her room and find her sprawled on her bed. I toss my bag of clothes her way and slouch into the armchair by the door.

"Ooh, you went thrifting without me?"

"Maddy's idea," I say, feeling suddenly exhausted and like I need to catch my breath.

"Tired?" She looks worried.

I sit up, shaking it off. I check my watch for my heartbeat reading, but it's fine. "Yeah, we left before lunch."

Abbi whistles. "Long day," she says. She turns over my bag of clothes and gasps.

"Did I do good?" I ask, walking over to the bed and shuffling through the items I got. A handful of tops, a pair of shorts, two skirts, and a couple cardigans, plus the dress I'm still wearing.

"Can I borrow this?" she answers, holding up a black-and-white-checkered T-shirt I'd gotten for her. I can't help but feel a little proud.

"I got it for you," I say. "But I'll need to borrow it for Paris next year."

"Paris," she says, hesitant, looking at me head to toe. "Paris." The second time, she says it like she's casting a spell for my luck. I cross my fingers and sit on the bed next to her.

"Paris," I agree.

CHAPTER FOURTEEN

Sera

On Thursday, I meet Luke at the marina just before one, but as I walk down the dock toward his boat, Adam and Oliver are nowhere in sight. Luke is standing on the dock still, cell phone to his ear, an exasperated look on his face. As I get closer, I can hear him answering in terse one-word replies.

"Sure. Yeah. Okay. Did you tell Mom?"

He sees me and shrugs an apology as he pulls the phone away from his ear and mouths, *My dad.* I nod and let him finish, dropping my bag into the boat.

"I heard you," he snaps. "You tell Mom. That's not my job."

His brothers spent the last few days with their dad, and he was supposed to bring them back to Northport today, but it sounds like something's changed.

"Sorry," he says to me, sighing. "I gotta call my mom quick."

"It's okay," I say as I take careful steps down the slip and climb onto the boat, sitting on the edge. Luke calls Paula and tells her that he doesn't have the boys because his dad decided last-minute to get them tickets to a bouncy castle fair out near his place and keep them for another night.

"Yeah. I guess he's trying," Luke mutters. "Okay, see you later."

He hangs up and groans, rubbing the heels of his hands into his eyes.

"Do you want to reschedule?" I ask, not sure how to help. I'm used to my parents' bickering over little things, but it's always just between them. It's strange to see Luke mad at his dad, who he used to idolize.

"No, I still want to go out. Do you?" he asks, a hopeful look in his eyes.

"Yeah, it'll be nice. Like old times, right?"

His shoulders relax. "Yeah, great. We can head out to the sandbars off Sandy Neck. Go swimming?"

"Sounds great."

Luke joins me in his dad's old boat. It's a twenty-one-foot motorboat with a front bench and a couple seats at the back, and a tiny shade top over the captain's chair. Luke and I fight with the sunshade until it's up. I secure the cooler Luke brought in the back. I peek inside, finding snacks I know the boys would love, plus some sour candy he must have gotten for me. The gesture makes me smile.

Luke starts up the boat, and I unhook us from the dock. We push off, falling into a rhythm as I remember what to do. When Luke and I were little, we'd come out with his dad almost every weekend, taking our deckhand duties way too seriously and helping him catch fish for dinner, so everything comes back to me easily.

Per tradition, we wave at the old empty lighthouse that leans off the edge of a rocky outcrop. As we pick up speed, I pull out my sketchbook and sit up front. Facing Luke, I start sketching out his face, his hands on the wheel, the way the dark water behind him is cut through by the wake of the boat. I finish the sketch as he maneuvers us into a spot above the bright sandbar where we can drop the anchor.

Luke makes sure we're secure, then climbs up front to sit with me, carrying a couple seltzers.

"What are you drawing?" he asks, sitting against the front of the helm. I flip my sketchbook around and show him. He leans in and takes it from me, his face a carefully composed neutral expression.

"Wow, Sera, you've gotten even better. You did this in twenty minutes?" I smile, pleased, and take the sketchbook back.

"Thanks. Your face was hard to get with the shield in the way, though. Sit still."

He smirks at me. "I didn't agree to be your subject."

"Too bad," I say.

"You're going to capture my worst angles, aren't you?"

I snort. "Yeah right, like you have any." It just comes out. I feel my cheeks flush, but Luke just grins in response, his eyes crinkling, and leans back.

"Okay, do your worst, Watkins."

I flip to a fresh page and start blocking out the shape of his eyes and nose and lips. Luke fidgets. He pulls his phone out and asks what music I want. I shrug.

"What about one of the *Druid Detox* podcasts?" he asks. "I haven't listened to the new one."

"Me either."

Luke hits play and puts his phone in the shade beside him.

The podcast covers everything known or suspected about *The Soul Druid Chronicles*, and the new prequel is the subject of the day.

"I can't believe they don't like the connected backstories." Luke shakes his head as they hit a commercial break. I look up from my sketch to agree.

"Seriously. I thought it was brilliant. We always wondered, right?"

"Exactly. Like in book seven of the first series when—"

"Icari has the fever dream and wakes up—"

"And can't remember Thepha! *Thepha?!*"

"But he recognizes her *face.*"

"And we already know he's a reincarnation, so she had to be too—"

"But that she's the reincarnation of Aetha?!"

"Brilliant," Luke agrees. "How's my face?" He reaches out and takes the sketchbook from me.

"Rough," I say, even though I'm really happy with it already.

"Brilliant," Luke says again, a little softer, running his thumb across the swoop of his dark hair on the page. "You're going to get that fellowship for sure. I'll miss you all over again next summer." He hands the sketchbook back and stands up. Then he peels off his shirt and tosses it on the captain's chair.

"Haven't you been making anything new recently?" I ask as I start to slide off my shorts. I feel a little self-conscious in just my bathing suit. It's new—a bright red one-piece that Abbi said makes my butt look like a peach.

"Not really," Luke admits, swinging his legs around the side of the boat to dip his feet in the water. I climb over next to him and hope the water isn't too cold. "I've done a few posters for the town, and the events board paid for me to go to the International Poster Gallery in Boston last summer before it closed."

"It's closed?"

"Yeah, the guy retired or something. You can still see their stuff online."

"But it's not the same," I say, understanding the loss. "How was it?"

"Awesome." He laughs. "I went full nerd on the 1940s exhibit." He gives me a quick, unsure glance. "I almost stopped by to see if you wanted to go with me," he admits.

"Hmm," I say. I don't know how I would've handled that surprise visit. "Sounds like I missed out."

"You're right about that," he says, and stands up, wobbling a bit on the edge of the boat as it adjusts to his quick movement.

"Careful!" I shout, clinging to the edge so I don't fall in.

"Take cover!" Luke jumps and cannonballs into the water. The splash soaks my legs. I stand up and follow him. The water is a cool balm to the hot sun, and we play a half-hearted game of tag before I finally catch him. His shoulder is hot and firm under my grip.

"Race you back to the boat?" he challenges me, his eyes playful.

"First one gets the whole pack of sour worms to themselves," I warn him.

"Deal. Three, two, one." Luke takes off before he says go,

and I scramble away from the shallow sandbar after him. I win only because I come around on the side with the ladder. Luke grabs my ankle, and we're both heaving, laughing as we crawl toward the cooler.

"Fine, I'll share, I'll share," I say, to get him to let go. He releases me after a beat, the skin on my leg tingling where his fingers were.

We grab the candy and lay out our towels in the sun to finish listening to the podcast. I work on my sketch, and Luke tells me more about his plans for community college and his mom's business now that his dad is out of the picture.

"It just makes sense for me to stick around here and help out with the store," he says. It sounds like he's defending himself against an argument I haven't actually made yet.

"And that's what you want to do?" I ask, looking over at him. His eyes are closed and his brows knit together at the question. I want to reach over and smooth out the crease.

"It is," he says. He opens his eyes and looks at me. "For now." His lips turn up in a small smile, but his eyes don't look happy. Before I can say anything else, Luke hops up. "You hungry? Want to head back and grab pizza at Dockside?"

"Sure," I say.

Luke starts up the engine, and we head back toward Northport. He increases the speed, and I squeal as my hair whips around me.

"Slow down!" I shout through my laughter.

"Chicken!" he says, but he slows anyway.

At the dock, Luke expertly ties up the boat to the worn

wooden post. We walk side by side to Dockside's to-go window. The owner always donates free pizza to the blood drive, so I make sure to tip extra. Slices secured, I lead the way to the end of the dock, stepping over the rope holding an ancient *Residents Only* sign that's only there to scare off nonlocals. We find an empty slip and sit with our feet hanging over the water. Luke is quiet, watching the boats moving in and out of the harbor. I finish my first slice and put my plate down.

"That was really fun. Thanks for inviting me."

"Of course," he says, meeting my eyes. "I had fun too. Even if you are a wimp about going fast."

I scoff and slap his arm. "Sorry I don't have a death wish!"

Luke smiles. He looks down at his pizza, then back up at me. "But really," he says, "thanks for coming. Going out on the boat has been weird ever since . . ."

"Your dad . . ."

Luke nods but doesn't elaborate. I take the opportunity to ask what I should've asked years ago.

"Are you ready to tell me about what happened with your parents?"

He sighs, looks off to the left where another boat has just pulled in. I take a bite of my pizza and chew slowly, patiently.

"My dad cheated on my mom," Luke says finally, not meeting my eyes.

"Maddy said she thought that was it. But that's not all. Right?"

Luke shakes his head. "I'm the one that caught him." His voice is a strained whisper, both angry and sad.

"Luke, I'm—" I start.

"Don't be sorry," he says, shaking his head. "Thing is . . . I made it worse."

"No way. That can't be true. Nothing he did is *your* fault."

"I didn't tell my mom right away. I didn't know what to do."

"When did you catch him?"

Luke studies my face like he's not sure if he should share whatever he wants to say next.

"Two summers ago. Three days before you left."

My heart sinks. The day we were supposed to meet at our beach. The day my heart began to fail.

"He asked me to keep quiet because he wanted to tell her. But I only lasted a week, and when I told her she was devastated. They tried to work it out for a while, but she said she'd lost all trust in him. The divorce shit was the worst, all these stupid little fights over money and where we would live."

We're quiet for a beat as I rack my brain, thinking of what to say.

"Fuck" is all that comes out of my mouth.

Luke laughs. Sudden and loud.

"What?!" I ask, laughing along with him.

"Nothing, just, I don't think I've heard you swear like that before. But yeah . . . fuck."

The moment sits lightly between us, and Luke takes the opportunity to keep talking.

"I know I wasn't easy to deal with that summer, but they'd never fought before, and I really needed you."

"I know." I swallow and take a long, deep breath, the words on the tip of my tongue, but I don't want them to sound like an excuse.

We're quiet for a little longer. I watch the shadows dance on the water as a small group of minnows swims by, terns following in the purpling sky above.

"The first time I went out on the boat without my dad, Oliver fell over," Luke says, breaking the silence. "I wasn't paying attention, and he was too close to the edge when I made a sharp turn."

"Yikes. That must have been terrifying."

"Yeah. I freaked. If Izzy hadn't been there, it would've taken me way longer to get him. I completely blanked on how to turn back when it happened."

I try not to feel jealous at the mention of Izzy's name, but the feeling blooms in my stomach anyway. Luke is watching me carefully while I squirm. He doesn't miss much, I think.

"I'm glad she was there," I say.

He runs a hand through his windswept hair.

"Me too. Izzy . . . she's a good friend. She was there when my parents were fighting. She listened, but she also didn't let me get away with any bullshit," he says with a sad smile.

I think about Maddy accepting my diagnosis and not treating me any differently. My eyes well a little. "I know people like that. They're really great to have around."

"No kidding. I almost didn't sign up for baseball again senior year, and she tore me a new one." He laughs. "Said something about how I could grow up once I was done with high school."

"I'm liking her more and more," I say.

"I knew you would," he says, meeting my eyes.

"Okay," I say. I look out at the water, the harbor entry lights flashing on their buoys. I hear the tinny sound of '90s classic rock coming from one of the boats down the dock. "But she's not your best friend, right? Because that's my job," I say with a smirk.

"You were." He leans forward, pulling his knees up and resting his arms across them. "Why did you stop?"

"I didn't," I try slowly. "I just . . . I got scared," I admit. This is the closest I've come to talking about the night I bailed on him and then found him with Izzy. I meet his gaze and ask the next thing. "Why did you ask me to meet you at our beach?" I say quietly.

It's his turn to pause, consider his words. I watch him swallow, rub his palms against his eyes.

"I don't know," he says at last, looking away.

"I don't believe you," I push. I want him to say the full truth, and then I can finally off-load mine.

Luke scooches closer, his injured knee touching my thigh. His hand comes to rest with just his thumb over mine on the damp wood. I don't flinch away. My heart races, and every little edge of the hope I've tried to scratch out of my heart strains to fill itself in.

"I—" Luke starts, but then his phone buzzes in his pocket. He pulls it out. Izzy's face lights up the screen. "I need to go," he says, leaning away again.

"Really?" I ask, unable to keep the snark out of my voice.

"Yeah." He looks back up at me, apologetic. "We made plans."

"Fine." I stand up, balling my paper plate.

"Sera."

"It's fine," I say, managing to sound normal, but he hesitates.

"Really," I say. "I should get going anyway. Camp tomorrow. And Jackson's back from Nantucket tomorrow too. I'll see you at the blood drive this weekend."

Before he can say anything else, I leave, my footsteps echoing down the dock. I feel tears well in my eyes and wipe them away angrily. Friends? Yeah right. I can't stop feeling like it's supposed to be more, and that just keeps getting in the way. I need a reality check. I need to move the fuck on. I don't have any more time to waste.

CHAPTER FIFTEEN

Luke

July is our busiest month. The store is always slammed from the minute we open. At least the craziness keeps my mind off of the fact that Sera hasn't texted me back since we went out on the boat yesterday.

The regulars beeline for the back, ducking beneath the old Nyeman's sign to the area where they know Nana is hiding the best antiques. The newer people browse through all the boutique stuff up front—the Cape decor, table settings, and local artisanal foods. Mom pops in for a few minutes to get a book of samples for a client and leave the boys upstairs with Nana and Gramps while she's out. I barely pause all day. Between customers needing help and my mom's interior decorating clients stopping in with questions and requests, I'm swamped.

If every day was like this all year, maybe I could go to college for real, instead of just taking a couple classes at the community college. But summer is short, and the debt is long, and it's good that I barely have time to think of another way it could be.

Izzy comes in right at closing time and locks the door behind her, then flips the *Open* sign over. I thank her as I pop open the register and start counting out the drawer.

"Ready for date night?" she asks, leaning across the counter, smelling like peppermint ChapStick and sunscreen. I flinch a little at the word *date*, Sera's accusation from the Fourth still fresh in my mind. I don't think I need to check with Izzy that we're on the same page, but maybe I should.

"In a bit. How was the beach?"

"Crowded." She frowns. "The July Fourth crowds are still here. I wish there was like a Northport locals–only place, you know? So we didn't have to share." She plays with the pennies in the take-one-leave-one dish while I check the messages on the landline. There are a few voicemails for my mom, which is great. Summer rentals and new local buyers looking to decorate will hopefully carry us through the winter. A few people have asked for light handyman work, which I've got to schedule in, but since one of the cashiers quit, I've been too busy today to do that.

"Earth to Luke." Izzy waves a hand in my face, and I lose track of the fives I'm counting.

"Sorry, yeah, a beach for just us, sounds . . ." I think about the Beach at the End of the Universe, Sera lying back on the space rock in her bikini, the sun in her hair, her scream of laughter as she jumped into the icy water. I shake my head to clear her out of it. No matter what happens between us, I'm not sharing our beach with anyone else. "Cool, but probably unrealistic."

Izzy rolls her eyes, picks up the ones, and counts them for

me. "You ready now?" She hefts the tote bag she has over her shoulder. "I rented a bunch of those old sci-fi DVDs that you love from the library. I thought we could have a movie night, since my parents are still out on Martha's Vineyard."

"That sounds perfect, Iz." I smile. "Dinner first?" I ask, my stomach cramping. I shoved a bag of chocolate-covered almonds in my mouth around lunch and it didn't suffice. Plus Mom won't love that. They were ten-dollar almonds.

"Sure. Waterviews?" she suggests.

I waver. I love Maddy's family's place, and their prices are low, but Sera might be there.

"Maybe fish-and-chips instead?"

"Sure."

"Great. Give me five."

I slide all the cash into the deposit bag and head back to the office to lock it in the safe. I hate being in here, even though Mom's totally redone it. Every time it's like I'm going to walk in on my dad and that woman again.

Izzy and I leave out the back once all the lights are off. I lock up and head to my truck, opening the door for Izzy to get in. I move some of my random sketches off the seat into the back so she has somewhere to sit.

"Thank you." She leans up and kisses my cheek. The contact is brief, familiar, nice, but a little . . . empty. I can't help but notice it doesn't travel inward and sizzle in my chest the way even just being near Sera does.

Izzy's family lives inland, closer to the high school, in a newer development where half the houses' cedar siding is still fresh and yellow. We stop at the fried seafood stand and get our food to go. Izzy chats the whole time about how she's thinking about taking more film classes next year. I nod along, but I'm not fully here. I get like this a lot. This feeling like I'm living in a movie of my own life, a disconnect where my mind doesn't feel like it has any control over my body. I can't stop thinking about the rent that's due next week on the shop. I should've just asked Izzy to wait another fifteen minutes while I called and booked those consultations for Mom and the work for me. We need as much income this summer as we can get before the offseason hits and all the money leaves the Cape. Izzy notices I'm spacing and gently taps my arm.

"All there?"

I sigh and shake it off, turning to smile my thanks at her for pulling me out of it. "Yeah. I'm good. Just hungry."

Izzy's house is bright and open and unbelievably clean. It's like the homes Mom does decor for. Our house is nothing like this. She's an only child, so the entryway is populated by a table of photos of her from infancy until graduation last year. There are also family shots on the beach here on the Cape or on vacation. And a couple posed photos of just her parents. Sera's family has more money than us too, but I don't think about it as much with them. They're less intimidating than Izzy's parents are to me, but that's probably because I've known them longer. I don't know why I'm comparing them, though.

"Shoes off so my mom doesn't have a fit," Izzy reminds me. She kicks her sandals off on the tiled floor and drops her bag on the bench before heading toward the basement door. I slide off my sneakers and then go to the kitchen for plates and paper towels, knowing how careful we have to be to not make a mess.

Downstairs, Izzy's fiddling with an old gaming console under their huge wall-mounted TV. I put the food on the coffee table, along with the plates, and then collapse onto the massive L-shaped couch.

"I love this couch," I say, eyes closed. And for a moment, even though I'm wicked hungry, I swear I could fall asleep.

"I know you do," Izzy says, voice teasing and sexy and low. A small bubble of want creeps up in my stomach, and I relax. The thing with the kiss earlier was just a fluke. I'm not losing interest. If I did, I know where my mind would go, and it can't go there. "Okay. I got it working," Izzy says. "Which movie first? *Close Encounters, Blade, X-Men?* I also have all of *The X-Files.*"

"I vote *X-Men,*" I say, sitting back up and opening the food before the fries get soggy. *The X-Files* would take days.

"Nerd," Izzy says happily, popping the movie out of its plastic case and into the machine. We eat and watch in silence for a while. When we're done, Izzy gathers up all the trash and takes it upstairs. She comes back with a couple sodas and curls up next to me. Instinct has me wrapping my arm around her. I wonder who she cuddles with at school because I've never seen her watch a movie without being snuggled up.

"Who do you movie cuddle with at school?" I ask.

"What do you mean?"

"You know what I mean."

She brushes her pink bangs out of her face, though they're closer to her original blond this week than they were last week. "Why? Are you jealous?"

I laugh. "No, Iz. I was just wondering."

"You could be jealous, you know." She swings her leg over my lap. She leans forward and presses her forehead to mine, grins. I slide my hands onto her hips, the familiarity of what comes next taking over.

"I'm not," I say.

"Oh, a challenge. I like it." She leans in and kisses me, and I wait for a beat to see if that little spark of heat will crawl up out of the depths of my chest and respond. But just like earlier, it's gone. I pull back. Izzy looks at me, her brow furrowed.

"What's with you tonight?" she asks, climbing off my lap.

"Izzy. I—I think we should stop hooking up."

"What?" She sits up straight, her feet tucked under her so she's at eye level with me. "But we agreed we'd have fun this summer . . ."

"I know. But . . . I don't know, it was fun last year, and this year—honestly, I'm so tired and busy, I'd rather just watch the movie and talk about that insane CGI. Be friends and not make things . . . overcomplicated."

Izzy won't look at the screen, where Magneto is strapping Rogue into his mutation machine. "This is about Sera, isn't it?" Her voice isn't mad exactly, but she does sound disappointed.

"What? No." I haven't talked to her about Sera at all, not since two summers ago, when I spilled my guts to her at this random party the night Sera turned me down. Back then, Izzy listened and told me it was okay to be upset, but that all romance didn't have to be so serious. I agreed. Less serious seemed better then, but now . . . She deserves someone who *wants* to spend the days with her watching *The X-Files* and making out.

"It is," she insists. "I have eyes, Luke."

"It's not. Plus she's hanging out with that kid from Boston."

Izzy scoffs. "You guys are being so stupid. You're lying to yourselves, and you're lying to each other."

"We're not—we're—"

"Just friends?" she says, smirking.

"Yes."

"Whatever you say, Luke." She hops off the couch. "I feel all sticky from the beach. I'm just going to shower and go to bed. You know the way out, right?"

"Yeah, but, Izzy, I—"

She puts her hand up. "It's fine, Luke. I just—I need some space."

On the drive home, I sift back through all the conversations I've had with Sera since she came back this summer. I'm looking for evidence of any kind to tell me I should let that tiny bit of hope that sprouted up the minute I saw her walk into Lorell's grow at all, or if I'm still just the world's biggest idiot.

It's still light out when I get home. My brothers are at a sleepover, and Mom's in the kitchen, making tea, looking tired and surprised to see me. I hope she wasn't looking forward to a night alone. But I also hope she's got something for me to do to feel useful and keep my mind from wandering next door.

CHAPTER SIXTEEN

Sera

Today's the annual blood drive over at Northport Hospital that our family and the Tisdales always help organize. As usual, we're running late. I throw on my volunteer T-shirt and a pair of shorts, then quickly brush my hair and put it up into a ponytail.

"Do you have all the snacks in the car?" Mom shouts up the stairs as I dig my phone out from under the blankets I kicked off the bed last night.

"Yes!" I reply, taking my charger with me. My phone always dies halfway through the blood drive, and this year I'm going to be prepared. I head down to the kitchen and beeline for the pantry to make sure I really did put all the snacks in the car earlier. I find two boxes of apple juice I'd forgotten. Maddy's bringing cookies before her shift, and Dockside sends pizzas, but we bought everything else with donations from the year before.

I tie my sneakers quickly and run out to Abbi's car.

"Do we have time for coffee?" she asks, yawning. She turns on some music—a rock band I've never heard before.

"I don't think so," I say, buckling and pulling my phone out to fiddle with the response I've been trying to send Luke since Thursday night. He texted me asking to meet up and talk after our boat day ended abruptly, and I haven't responded yet. I should've replied yes right away. Waiting has only made it worse. I still don't know what exactly to say when we do talk. *Thanks for opening up to me, I know it was my turn to explain why I fell off the face of the earth, but it's so embarrassing to admit that I was falling for you and that I was crushed to find you making out with a girl you* still *make out with but say you're not dating? Oh, also I was in heart failure, but I'm fine now.* Too wordy. I try not to think about it. Instead, I send Iris a picture of my first finished application piece. I'm really thrilled with it. The watercolors make the image of my eight-year-old face a little ethereal. She looks invincible. I set it as my lock screen, a good reminder for what today is about.

"I'm stopping at Dunkin'," Abbi says. "There's one right by the hospital, right?"

"Sure, but Mom organized coffee and breakfast for the volunteers." I turn the music down; it's giving me a headache.

"We'll be there on time . . . ish . . . don't worry." Abbi yawns again and turns the music back up. I shake my head. We won't, but that's fine. There's less of a chance of having an uncomfortable encounter with Luke if things are already underway when we arrive.

The blood drive is in a big parking lot next to the hospital. All the volunteers, medical staff and regular people like us, have finished setup by the time Abbi and I pull in at just past eight.

We off-load all the snacks into the tent where people are monitored after they donate. Then I head to the check-in table, where I'm scheduled from eight thirty until noon. Paula is there, but I haven't seen Luke, thank god. I wonder if I can avoid him all day. His name was on the blood draw tent schedule for the morning, so he'll be helping the nurses distribute snacks and juice boxes to the people giving blood. We switch shifts in the afternoon. Simply two ships passing in the night, or the day, whatever. I unbox the flyers on donating blood and find the paperwork for anyone who wants to register as an organ or marrow donor. Paula and Mom are going to be helping with swab kits for those folks, while I'm the face of convincing them to do it.

I play with my *EBE* bracelet and the medical alert ID on my watch while I practice my script in my head. Even though I wasn't here last summer, my speech comes back easily.

I'm only here today because Edith Eichman's parents knew that their daughter's organs could save a lot of lives. Over one hundred thousand people are waiting for an organ donation right now, and only three out of every one thousand registered donors end up being viable as donors. The more people registered, the better chance someone waiting will be helped.

I know the statistics aren't uplifting, but I've always found the combo of personal and specific makes more people willing to sign up. They're already here; they already want to help.

People start showing up before nine, and while it's never

slammed, it's busy. I'm grateful for the caffeine pit stop Abbi and I made. My shift involves signing people in, sending them to the waiting area with info on organ donation to read, selling raffle tickets, and giving stickers to kids. I end up directing quite a few people over to Paula and Mom to get swabbed. It's turning into a really great day, even if my little headache from the morning won't go away. The number of people willing to come out and help others always lifts my spirits. This year, though, it's also reminding me how complicated it will be to get a new heart when I need one in the next few years. Finding a match is rare.

Just as the clock is winding down to my shift change, I look up at the next person in line and . . . it's Jackson.

"Hey," he says with his wide bright smile. "I hear this is where we can come to do some good today."

"Yeah." I can't help but smile back. We haven't made plans to meet up since he came back from Nantucket yesterday. I've been busy. Or confused. But I did tell him to stop by if he wanted to. "Thanks for coming. Have you donated before?"

He nods. "At school this past semester."

"Great." I hand him a clipboard with the paperwork he'll need to fill out and launch into my spiel. "Right now, there's about a ten-minute wait before a nurse will see you. While you're waiting, if you'd like to register as an organ or marrow donor, we can help you with that really quick over there." I point to Mom and Paula. "And we also have some raffle tickets for sale." I pile the small stack of paperwork and pamphlets I give to each person while Jackson scrawls down his information.

The day has really heated up, and I'm sweating beneath the white tent. I hope I don't look too shiny. I pull at my T-shirt to get a little air across my stomach.

"Cool." He hands back the clipboard and I check to make sure it's all filled out. "I'm actually already a registered donor, but how much are raffle tickets?"

"Twenty each." I start looking for the ticket roll.

"I'll grab a few. And then, what are you doing for lunch? Do you get a break?"

"Um, sort of, not really. We have food here. I'm helping in the donation tent starting, well, ten minutes ago." I'm still looking for the big red roll of raffle tickets, which for some reason isn't where I left it last. "Have you seen the tickets?"

I turn to ask the volunteer who's been with me all morning and find Luke instead. He's holding out the roll of tickets, his face oddly expressionless. "Looking for this?"

"Yeah." I take it and turn back to Jackson. "Sorry, how many?"

Jackson pulls out a sleek brown leather wallet with his initials stamped on it and unfolds a wad of cash, peeling off a few hundred-dollar bills.

"Let's do twenty-five."

"Wow . . . thank you," I say, feeling my eyes go wide. "That's really generous." I unroll the tickets and rip off a long strip, then hand Jackson his half.

"Happy to help," Jackson says, running a hand through his golden hair, which somehow falls right back into place. "So, can you hang later? I thought of some new places in Paris to tell you about."

"She's not one of the raffle prizes," Luke snaps, then turns to me. "And you're late. They need you back there." He steps around behind me, hovering a little too close, and starts straightening the clipboards even though they're fine.

"I know," I say, narrowing my eyes at him. Then I turn to Jackson. "I can't today. We're slammed here, but maybe tomorrow?"

"Yeah, that'd be great. I'll pick you up, we can go to the resort in Chatham, take the boat out after."

"Sounds good," I say as I crouch down for my bag and find my water bottle.

"Okay, well, I'll see you back there," Jackson says to me. He gives a nod to Luke, who doesn't return it, then heads over to the waiting area.

"Suck-up," Luke mutters under his breath.

"Sorry, what?" I ask, sure I've heard him wrong.

"Nothing, never mind. Where are the extra pens?"

I push the jar over to him.

"Right here. Did you eat? Are you hangry or something? That was so rude. He just donated a ton of money," I say.

"You don't need to act like my mom, Sera. I'm fine."

"Well, you're acting like a child, so . . ." I say, standing there waiting to see if he'll apologize for being an ass. When he doesn't, I leave the tent, running into Abbi, who is walking around making sure everyone has water.

"You okay?" Abbi asks, looking over my shoulder toward Luke.

"Yup," I say, exasperated.

"I though you two were, like, buddy-buddy again."

"Apparently not."

"Do you need a mediator?"

"God, no. Thank you, but please butt out."

"Don't get snippy with me," she says, handing me a bottle of water.

"I have a water." I hold up my refillable and go to take a sip, but it's empty. I guess I haven't had enough, which is probably why I'm feeling so crappy. I take the one Abbi is still holding out, muttering a thanks.

"You two need to hash it out sooner rather than later," she adds.

"Hash what out?" I ask after chugging the whole bottle and taking a second from her.

Abbi just looks at me, eyebrows raised over her sunglasses, like I'm supposed to know exactly what she's talking about. And of course I do. But I don't feel like dealing with it right now.

"Thanks for the water," I say, emphasizing that that's the only thing that's been helpful in the last thirty seconds.

In the donation tent it's even busier, but it's at least air-conditioned. Everyone donating is relaxing back on their cots. The nurses move among them, checking in and bandaging everyone's arms when they're done. Jackson is hooked up to a blood bag already, looking more relaxed than the older woman next to him. He cracks jokes with her, clearly trying to make her feel more comfortable as the nurse withdraws the needle from her arm. I come over with some of Maddy's cookies. The woman swoons over a story he's telling about his old gig as a lifeguard. I stuff a cookie in my mouth when I pop back to the snack table for more supplies, finally feeling a little more awake. Suddenly one of the nurses rushes past me.

I whirl around. The woman next to Jackson must have stood up too quickly and passed out. The nurse has barely finished wrapping the bright blue tape around Jackson's arm to keep the cotton in place when he gets up to kneel next to the woman. I join him, sticking a straw in a juice box so it's ready.

"You're all right," he says as she blinks her eyes open. "Feels awful, doesn't it? I passed out from heatstroke last summer. You're going to be fine."

When she's ready to stand, we help her over to the seating area. Once we make sure she's okay, I head back to the snack table. But I'm intercepted by Luke.

"Why is he still here? He's not a volunteer. Did he survive some kind of rare medical condition too? Was it his hair? Did it use to be *brown*?"

"Drop it," I say under my breath.

He follows me as I go around the side of the tent and back to the sinks by the restrooms to wash my hands.

"He's not a registered volunteer. We could get in trouble."

"We can use the help, Luke. Don't be an asshole. If Izzy showed up to help, you'd be delighted."

"What does Izzy have to do with it?" he asks.

"Nothing. Just, it's nice to have him here—he's got first aid training, he cares, that's cool of him," I say, pumping soap onto my hands.

"Whatever you say," Luke says, rolling his eyes.

"What's your deal?"

"Nothing, just didn't know you guys were so close."

"What's that supposed to mean?" I ask.

"You told him about Paris," he says.

"Yeah, of course, why wouldn't I?"

"I don't know," he says, frustrated. "I feel like I have to pry information out of you, but you're just, like, sharing everything with some random dude."

My anger builds. "Jackson isn't random."

Luke scoffs. "Sure. Do you even really like him?"

I toss my paper towel into the trash a little aggressively. "Why do you care? This can't be about Jackson. He was a huge help back there. So what is it, Luke? What do you want to say to me?"

Luke opens his mouth, then closes it again.

"Yeah," I say, stepping around him. "That's what I thought."

CHAPTER SEVENTEEN

Sera

That night I can't sleep, even though I'm exhausted from the blood drive and my fight with Luke. Now, at one in the morning, it's all I can think about. I'm lying backward, feet where my head usually goes, trying to trick my body into thinking we haven't already been lying here for over an hour tossing and turning. It cooled off quickly this afternoon and Dad turned off all the AC units, so the house is quiet and a little sticky with humidity. There's a light breeze blowing my curtains around, bringing in the sound of peepers and June bugs humming. I plugged my phone in downstairs so I wouldn't be tempted to doomscroll through Instagram, and I've counted the glow-in-the-dark stars on my ceiling three times. *Forty-two.* I've lost hope that I'll sleep at all when I hear something hit one of my windows. I roll over, assuming it's a moth or a squirrel clambering around the roof, but then there are two more distinct pings against the glass.

I get up and push my curtains to the side. In the thin moonlight I can just make out Luke standing on his back step.

I pull on jeans and throw a sweatshirt over my T-shirt. I haven't snuck out with Luke in ages, but the instinct to go prepared is still there. I grab a light beach towel, just in case, and I put that in my small backpack. Then I creep down my stairs, shoes in hand. The house is dark. Mom, Dad, and Abbi are all asleep. I don't risk going for my phone. I'm wearing my watch anyway, so I can call them if I need to. I ease the sliding door open and shut again, then slip on my sandals. I go around to the driveway and creep under the rhododendron where Luke and I used to hide during neighborhood flashlight tag.

I feel a shy bloom of worry in my stomach when I pop out on the other side.

"Hi," he says, hands deep in the front pocket of his hoodie. "Thanks for coming out."

I straighten up and brush my hair out of my face. "I couldn't sleep," I say, trying to sound light but realizing I'm still feeling bitter.

Luke kicks at a rock, looks at me, then up at the sky. The moon is a bright slice, almost like a smile, taunting us.

"It's been a while since I've snuck out," he admits. "But I had to see you. I feel bad about today." He's nervous, bouncing his weight side to side. "Wanna walk?" He tips his head toward downtown, and I nod. We're quiet as we head down Beach Rose Lane. The peepers are even louder out here, and the tunnel of trees makes it feel like we're inside a terrarium. We leave a little space between us but keep pace, occasionally bumping into each other as we avoid potholes.

I let the silence stay. It feels good just to walk.

We end up at the old marina. There are a few abandoned buildings on this end of town that have always been that way, but one of them should be an ice cream spot with my favorite cherry chocolate chip.

"I'm so bummed Frappie's went out of business," I say, stopping in front of the window. Through a thick layer of dust, I can just make out the painted sundaes that decorate the glass.

"Yeah, it closed just before last summer." He steps back and looks up and down the dilapidated area. "It's sad. It's such an iconic building, it could be something cool."

I look up past the broken *Frappie's* sign to the long, high windows, which are reflecting the stars. "Like what?"

"I don't know," Luke says, but his eyes are following mine, and I can see him thinking, making plans, inventing futures. "This part of town always struggles," he adds. "It feels like things always close, and nothing takes their place. I worry that someone with a lot of money will come in and tear it all down, put up some fancy condos or something."

"Oh, don't say that." I feel a deep, aching sadness that anything in Northport might change. "Sometimes things come back. Or new things come around that honor the old ones."

"Or both," Luke says, smiling sadly at me. "Anyway, somebody should save all these historic buildings."

I get the sense that by *somebody*, he means him. I sigh and shove his shoulder, trying to lighten the mood. He pretends to stumble over, but he's back quickly. He grabs my hand and squeezes it. "I'm really sorry for being such an asshole earlier today at the blood drive." The admission seems to let all the air out of the tension between us. Breathing is suddenly easier. "If you like Jackson, then he's probably cool." He takes a deep breath. "Even though five hundred dollars' worth of raffle tickets was a show-off move."

I laugh a little. He's right about that. "Thanks," I say, squeezing his hand back. "I appreciate it."

"Wanna go in?" Luke says, pulling me to the front door of the closed shop.

I look skeptically at the broken door handle. "Won't it be locked?"

He reaches out with his free hand and pushes. The door swings right in. It creaks loudly, just like it used to, and reminds me of childhood, of the promise of sweets.

"Guess not. Come on."

I follow Luke inside the dark building, and push the door closed behind us. The skeleton of Frappie's sits shrouded in dust. The little two-top tables have been pushed to the left, and the sprinkle-colored chairs are on top of them, leaving the tiled center wide open, almost like a dance floor. Most of the ice cream and maritime decorations have been taken off the walls, so what's left is the sturdy frame of what was probably an old fish market or boat storage. The high casement windows let in the diffused moonlight, and the room glows white and blue like we're underwater. I drop Luke's hand and walk over to the counter. I hop up and swing my feet to the other side. I land in a pile of old empty ice cream cups, then turn to face Luke.

"Welcome to Frappie's, home of the Cape's best homemade sprinkles and hot fudge. What can I get you?"

"Chocolate peanut butter with a cherry dip, please."

"Ew," I say, wrinkling my nose at him. "Unfortunately we don't have that because it's a terrible choice."

"Don't knock it till you've tried it," he says. He looks around the space, taking it all in. "Hey, where do you think that ladder goes?" He points behind me.

I turn around and shrug. "The roof, probably."

Luke hops the counter, too, and tries the low rungs. "Seems sturdy."

"Careful," I say as he quickly climbs to the top.

"There's a door," he calls down. He pushes it until it swings open with a screech. "Whoa," he calls down. "Come up here! The view is great. You can see so many stars."

I look at the ladder and the twenty or so feet I'll need to climb. I've never been afraid of heights, but for some reason this makes me anxious.

"The ladder is wicked sturdy," Luke calls from above. "Don't worry."

I take a deep breath, grab the rungs at eye level, and start climbing. The ladder is indeed very solid, but my hands are sweaty. About halfway up I suddenly wish I'd left my backpack down below because it's feeling very heavy. I pause and take a long, slow breath as my heart skips around a bit from my nerves. I take the last few rungs quickly and heave myself through the door and onto the roof.

I stand up, shake off my weird nerves, and finally look up.

"Wow," I say. The harbor stretches out below us, shadowy boats bobbing gently on the black water.

"I know, right?" Luke is smiling up at the stars.

After a minute, I can finally identify the difference between the water and the sky, and I look for the Big Dipper, the only constellation I can locate with any confidence. I find it spilling itself over the ocean in a tangle of dimmer stars.

Luke lifts his arm and points right where I'm looking. "Big Dipper."

"Hey," I say, pouting, "I saw it first."

Luke laughs, then sits down on the scratchy shingles and lies back. I sit carefully next to him, wondering if the warmth between us will last this time.

"Lie down." He scoots over and pats the space next to him. I tell myself to stop thinking so much and lie back. The wind settles a little once I'm flat, and the sky yawns overhead. Luke moves closer still, his left leg resting flush against my right, his breath hot on my cheek as he points again and calls out Gemini.

"How did you find that?" I'm genuinely impressed. "I can't even see what you're pointing at."

"Here." Luke takes my hand, extends my pointer finger, and draws a line from the bottom right corner of the upside-down Dipper to the top left corner. Then he guides my hand gently, out, out, out, until he stops on one of two brighter stars. "This is Castor, and to the right is Pollux, and they're the twins. Look for this U shape."

"Cool." I trace the shape with my free hand, and move to take my hand back, but he holds it tighter.

"Hold on," he says, pulling my hand to his chest. He splays our hands flat, and I can feel the faint *thump-thump* of his heart. My own is still racing a bit from the climb up the ladder.

I turn to face him. "I wanted to tell you that I talked to Izzy. We *were* sort of together, but we're not anymore."

"So you broke up?"

Luke nods, and I take in his familiar face, the small scar under his left eye. My eyes catch on his bottom lip, which is trapped in his teeth. He releases it and says, "I like someone else."

My stomach sinks. "Oh." I swallow and look away.

Luke lets out a strangled laugh. "Sera. It's you." He says it clear and slow. "I like you, Sera. I have for two years, and I think it was killing me keeping it in."

Beneath me the roof suddenly feels thin, like I might fall through it and then through the floor of Frappie's, all the way to the center of the earth.

"Really?"

"Really," Luke says.

I turn and look at him. He's waiting for a reply like I'm holding the answer to the universe. I repeat what he's said in my head. *Luke LIKES me. LUKE likes me. LUKE likes ME.*

I want to say it back so badly, but a flash of fear makes my chest seize.

I can't just lie there, so I stand up and immediately feel woozy and out of breath. I close my eyes against the swirling spots racing across my vision. I wait for my heart to settle, but it won't. My watch beeps as it registers an irregular heart rhythm. *Crap.* It hasn't done that in months.

"Sera?" Luke's at my side, but I can't look at him. Both because I can't believe this is happening and because EBE can't calm down. She's gasping and struggling and tripping over herself. When my watch beeps three times in a quick succession, I swear out loud. It's called my mom and sent an alert to Dr. Lee.

"Sera? Are you okay?" Luke sounds frantic as he grabs my shoulders, like he's trying to hold me in place, and oh, how I wish that were enough. I want to reassure him. I want to tell him so many things, but I can't find the breath to do it. I open my eyes and find his in front of me. Even in the dark they shine a little green, like the ocean, or a portal out of this dimension. I tip forward into that swirl of green and black, hoping there will be something there to catch me.

CHAPTER EIGHTEEN

Luke

As the EMTs lift Sera into the ambulance, I climb in too. I dial Abbi on my cell and leave a message when she doesn't pick up.

"You're not really supposed to come with us," one of the EMTs says, but she's already closing the door. She attaches an IV to Sera's hand, takes her vitals, and taps notes into a tablet as the siren screams above us and we lurch into motion. I quickly sit on the bench next to the stretcher before I fall over and reach for Sera's hand. She squeezes my trembling fingers, and I try to remember to breathe so I don't pass out next.

At least Sera's awake now, but her eyes are closed, her skin pale and clammy.

It all happened so fast. Sera dropping like a stone into my arms. Her watch beeping and beeping and beeping. Me frantically calling 911 and trying to answer their questions as calmly as I could.

"Does she have any medical conditions?" they asked.

"She had a heart transplant as a baby, but she's been fine, healthy," I sputtered out. The EMTs arrived quickly, but it felt like the longest few minutes of my life, getting her down the ladder once she came to.

"Luke, I'm sorry," Sera whispers now as we careen down the highway.

"You don't have anything to be sorry for," I promise, smoothing her hair out of her eyes. She shakes her head, and the simple motion sends all the alarms connected to her screeching. "Just rest." My voice wobbles. "We'll be there soon," I say, even though I have no idea if that's true.

Thankfully we're there a few minutes later. The staff is waiting for us, and they whisk Sera away. A nurse comes forward and stops me from following.

"Let's let them look at your friend, okay?" She nods to a small waiting room. "You can wait here."

I'm about to sit down when the Watkinses rush through the front door.

"Luke!" Abbi's voice is sharp, panicked. "Where is she?"

I point uselessly at the nurse, who steps forward and takes all three of them down the hall in the direction Sera went. At the last second, I follow. We're taken upstairs to the cardiac unit, my heart clanging in my chest the whole way. The last time I was in a hospital was right after my parents broke up. I hurt my knee during practice. The surgery was quick, the PT torture, but the whole time in the hospital I was itchy, anxious to get out, like my body remembered that time of almost death that Sera and I had lived through together as babies and wanted out.

The nurse puts us in another, smaller waiting room and strides away to get info on where Sera is.

Abbi paces, her arms swinging back and forth.

"Abigail, sweetie." Mrs. Watkins reaches for her, but Abbi shrugs her off, meeting my eyes briefly before looking away again. I know she thinks it's my fault, whatever's happening, and I wish I could say it isn't, but I have a feeling it kind of is.

The nurse comes back. "This way." She turns, and we all follow again, stepping quickly past room after dimly lit room, each with a patient visible through the windows. It doesn't escape me that they're all so much older than us.

At the door to Sera's room, her dad turns and asks me to wait out in the hall. Abbi pushes in first, followed by Sera's parents. Her mom gives my elbow a quick squeeze and then I'm alone. The air is cold and constantly moving. I shiver and hold my arms to stop from shaking.

A doctor goes in, comes out with the nurse, then another nurse goes in with a big machine on wheels. I stand there, frozen in place. Finally there's a moment where the window into her room is clear and I can see her sitting up. She catches my eye and smiles. My heart soars in relief. *She's okay,* I tell myself. I push off the wall to go in just as Abbi opens the door.

"Not now, Luke," she says, her hand on my shoulder, guiding me back across the hall again. I look through the door at Sera, but her dad is blocking my view.

"What's wrong? Is she okay? She seemed fine. We just climbed a ladder to the top of Frappie's, and she was dizzy and . . ."

Abbi looks down at her shoes, then up at me. Her eyes are a

little red, tired. I realize that whatever's going on, it isn't a complete surprise to her.

"Is Sera sick? Is it her heart?"

Abbi nods. "Two years ago, things were . . . not good," she says. "But she had a procedure last fall, and she's on medication now that's been working . . ."

I look back through the window and Sera's looking for me. Our eyes meet, and I can tell she knows I know now. Her eyes flick quickly to Abbi, but then back to me with so much sorrow. She mouths a quick *I'm sorry* before turning her head away.

The floor is still shifting, and I can't stay up anymore. I lean against the wall and slide down it, surprised when Abbi sits quietly next to me.

"Two *summers* ago?" I ask, trying to make it make sense.

"Yeah," she admits. "She passed out at her volleyball tournament. That's why we left a couple days early."

I drop my head onto my knees. I feel nauseous. That's why she didn't meet me that night on the beach. I feel like shit. I didn't know because I was too wrapped up in my own crises that summer—my family falling apart in front of me, my own feelings of rejection—to realize what was wrong.

"She went to find you that night . . ." Abbi says.

I feel my brows furrow, confused. Abbi raises hers at me, and it clicks into place. The party in Dennis. My stomach sinks even deeper.

"How much time does she . . . ?" I can't finish the sentence.

"She's supposed to have a few years before she needs a transplant. She's on the donor list." Abbi sits up, wipes her dry eyes, determination on her face. "Though she's in tier four or five at the moment. She's been stable. But eventually she will need a new heart."

"I'd give her mine." I don't mean to say it out loud, but it's the truth.

Abbi drops her head on my shoulder for a quick moment. "I know." She leans away and stands up, smooths out her wrinkled pajama set. "You should go home, Luke. Sera needs to rest. And if there's something going on between you two . . . something more than friends, please think about whether pursuing that is really what you want, okay? Because I can't let you break her heart again."

I nod, numb, and she disappears back into Sera's room.

CHAPTER NINETEEN

Sera

Like it's a mirror of two years ago, within twenty-four hours I'm released from the hospital with the knowledge that my heart is struggling and instructions to follow up with Dr. Lee in Boston. Before we leave, I ask the doctor if I can go to work tomorrow. I have her repeat to my family that there's no reason I can't, as long as I'm being careful and wearing the new monitor they've stuck to my chest at Dr. Lee's request. Abbi goes to object, and I cut her off.

"She's a doctor, Abigail. I think she knows better than you." I can't have them all turning back to overprotective mode. We don't know how bad it is. I'll probably be fine. I'm supposed to be fine.

The doctor wishes us well but seems happy to be rid of us and the whole stressful situation. I don't blame her.

At home, Mom hands me back my bag, and I grab my phone off the counter.

"I'm going to reheat some lasagna, if you're hungry?" she says.

"Thanks, but I had one of those fancy heart-healthy hospital-approved lunches, so I'm fine." I move toward the stairs. "I just want to go lie down."

When I get upstairs, I take a quick shower to wash the hospital smell off of me and change into clean pj's. I get into bed and find I've missed like ten texts from Maddy and a few from Jackson and Luke, plus a call from each of them. *Shit.* Jackson and I were supposed to get lunch today and it totally slipped my mind. I call Maddy first and ask her if she can come over. She's finishing up a shift at the diner and promises to be by after. I can't think about Luke yet, so I fiddle with texting Jackson but then suck it up and call. He answers right away.

"Hey, are you okay? Didn't seem like you to ghost me."

"Yeah, no, sorry. I . . ." I don't want Jackson to be the first person I talk to about this in detail. I want Luke or Maddy. I keep it simple. "I haven't been feeling well, and I forgot to cancel. I'm sorry."

"It's okay." He says it like he means it. "We can meet up when you're better. I was thinking a day trip to Martha's Vineyard. We could bike around, get dinner at Nancy's."

That should sound exciting and fun. A perfect day with a hot guy who likes me. But it just . . . doesn't. And I'm not going to string Jackson along.

"Um, actually, I don't think I'll be able to," I say.

"Okay . . ." he says, his voice trailing off like he knows there's more.

"You're really nice, Jackson, but I don't see this going anywhere, between us. It's nothing you did. It just doesn't feel . . . right. I'm sorry."

He's quiet for a beat.

"All right," he says finally. I let out a breath. "Thanks for calling to tell me. You're really fucking cool, Sera. I hope I see you around."

I thank him and hang up. Relief washes over me as I snuggle under the covers.

Maddy wakes me from a nap about an hour later.

"Okay, so . . . why are you in bed? Why were you MIA? Why did Abbi tell me not to wake you up? What. Is. Happening?!" She hops onto the foot of my bed and plops down two containers of food. I smell fries, which are probably illegal for me right now, and something tart. I dig myself out of the blankets.

"Fry me first," I say. She hands me two, and I stuff them in my mouth while I think of where to start.

Maddy stares at my chest. I sigh. Guess I'll start there. The monitor is stuck to my skin above my left boob, causing a rectangular blob beneath my T-shirt.

"What's that?" she asks, her voice a little shaky.

"A heart monitor." I eat another fry, and she narrows her eyes in concern at the box. "Temporary," I add, snatching another. "My doctor wants a week's worth of readings for *normal* activity."

"Okay . . . but why are you wearing a heart monitor? What happened?"

I take a deep breath and tell her about the weird fight Luke and I had yesterday, then how we snuck out last night to talk. "We were up on the roof at Frappie's and . . . I stood up too fast and passed out. He called 911. And then my watch called my parents and Dr. Lee—tattletale."

"Romantic," Maddy says. "You're leaving the important stuff out. Don't do that. I can take it."

I look at my friend, her kind eyes and messy hair. I don't want to be the one who makes her sad, but I don't want a lot of things.

"My meds aren't working as well anymore. Or at least they're starting not to. There's some stiff muscle that wasn't stiff before. My ejection fraction fell—not enough blood is pumping out. EBE's timeline might have just gotten cut in half."

"In half . . ." Maddy processes. "So, like, maybe two years instead of five?"

I shake my head. I'm trying not to do the math, because all I can see is a big, blurry image of nothingness in my future. "I don't know. My doctor will tell me more after I see her in Boston." I push the fries away and poke at the other box. Maddy opens it to reveal her famous arugula salad topped with strawberries, watermelon, lemon vinaigrette, goat cheese, and a drizzle of honey.

"I probably won't be able to go to Paris next year," I say quietly. I'm devastated. Maddy had already picked out a pastry course and applied to be there at the same time as me. "Even if

I manage to crawl up to the top of the list and a heart becomes available . . . I don't know if I'll recover in time. I might not ever be able to go." My voice breaks, and I wipe away tears.

Maddy snaps her head up at that. "What? Don't say that. You're going to Paris. Maybe not next summer, sure, but the summer after that, then. And you don't need the fellowship to go. We can just go. When you have your new heart and you're ready. Okay?"

I nod, not trusting myself to talk.

"Good." Maddy plucks a berry from the salad and pops it into her mouth. "Now back up five steps and tell me about what happened with Luke."

I feel my face crack with a smile I can't contain despite the epically shitty news, and Maddy gasps.

"Nothing really happened," I say.

"Bullshit," Maddy deadpans. I laugh.

"Okay . . . he said he likes me, like he has feelings for me."

Maddy squeals and scoots closer to me. "I knew it! What did you say back?"

"Well, nothing . . . That's when I passed out."

"Has he called?"

"Yeah . . ."

"You should talk to him." Maddy prods me in the shoulder.

I pick out a piece of watermelon and make sure to get some of the cheese. "Did you know there's a theory that every heart has a preset number of beats in it?"

Maddy scoffs. "Sounds made-up."

I shrug. "It's just a theory. But do you know what happens when I hang out with Luke?"

"Your heart races," Maddy teases, pretending to swoon across my bed.

"Exactly. I swear, just thinking about him shortens my lifespan."

"That's not fair. To him or to you. If the idea is you only have so many heartbeats, then use them for what matters."

"What if it fizzles out immediately and we ruin our friendship for good? What if it doesn't work out? What if I die and break his heart?" I sigh and fidget with the edge of my comforter. "What if I'm scared he'll break mine?"

"Then be scared, but don't stall your life."

We spend the rest of the afternoon watching TikTok videos as I pry details out of Maddy about Sienna. They bought tickets to a concert together that's not until October, so it must be going well. After Maddy leaves, I pull out my phone to text Luke. What I've learned in the last day is that I don't have time to worry about how things will go between Luke and me. If all I have time for is a long goodbye, I'll take it, if he'll let me. I won't blame him if he wants to go back to just being friends, though. I'll take that too.

Sera

meet me at the studio tomorrow after campers leave? Please? I owe you an explanation . . . good night xo

CHAPTER TWENTY

Sera

After the last campers leave on Monday, I'm still feeling fine, so I go to the open studio as planned and text Luke again to let him know I'll be there for a while. I haven't heard from him, and I'm starting to feel anxious. To take my mind off of it, I prop up my application pieces to look at all three as a whole: one finished, one part, one sketch. But I can't commit to starting anything when I'm turning around at every change in the breeze, hoping it's Luke. Iris texts me back with some advice I asked for, and I turn to my second piece and pull in some yellows, surprised and happy at how well it's working.

Just before five, there's a light knock on the outside wall, and Luke comes in. His hair is a little wet, like he's just come from the beach or the shower. He looks nervous, like when we were fourteen and spent one rainy day sneaking from movie to movie at the theater after only paying for one ticket. We saw *Across the Spider-Verse* three times. I can't help but wonder if he's changed his mind, if maybe I passed out and woke up in a different universe where Luke never liked me at all.

"Hi," I say as he puts his stuff down at the easel next to me and looks at my half-done painting. "There's paper in the storage room." This will be easier if we can work while I talk.

He nods and goes to retrieve a few big sheets of paper for his charcoals. Luke always liked the drier or digital mediums. Pastels were the stickiest he'd get. I used to tease him for it, but I keep the barbs tucked in for later, when he's looking less serious. Luke takes the stool next to me and we settle into a quiet rhythm. With him finally here I feel less distracted, and I make progress on my painting. I make a few notes about how I want to differentiate this piece from the other two, take a photo, and text it to Iris.

I chance a look over at Luke and catch him biting his bottom lip. The three fingers on his left hand are already stained black from the charcoal. He leans back to eye his drawing and frowns at it. Then he pulls it off the easel and crumples it up, tossing it into the huge recycling bin nearest to us. Before I can tell him off for ruining such a good piece, he starts on a new page. I need to stop stalling. I take a deep breath and begin with an apology.

"I'm sorry for not telling you what's been going on with my heart." I swallow and push on. "I should have told you the first time, two years ago, even if things were off between us. I just . . ." I sigh and close my eyes for a second. I listen to the sounds of the birds outside and the air rushing through the open doors and Luke's charcoal dragging on the paper. I open my eyes and turn to him. "I felt like my life was over, and it didn't seem like you wanted or needed me around, so I didn't want to want or need you around."

"It was a weird summer," he says.

I snort, then put my hand over my mouth. "Sorry. That's just . . . an understatement." Thankfully he smiles. My heart liquefies, and instead of fighting it, I lean in. "I was falling for you," I admit. The words are cold in my mouth like I've been sucking on an ice cube. "And I thought it was the same for you."

"It was," Luke jumps in, putting his charcoal down and turning on the stool to face me. "It still is. I meant what I said."

I hold up my hand to stop him. I need to get it all out before he says anything else.

"When we were supposed to meet on the beach that night, I thought you were going to ask me to the end-of-camp dance, and I had this whole plan for saying yes." I laugh a little, remembering the outfit, my rehearsed reply. It's only been two years, but that version of me seems so young, so vulnerable. "And then when I missed meeting you because I was sick, I got scared that everything I was doing was about to be my *last* thing. You were my first *best* friend. Did I want you to be my last first kiss? My last first date? It felt like so much . . ."

"Pressure?" Luke asks, and I nod. I take a moment to think, and he leans closer, taking my hand gently in his.

"Because I knew that if we got together, it would *matter*. You know?" I say. "It would be different than it had been with other boyfriends. Heavier. And I freaked out."

"And you canceled," he says.

I nod. "Yep. Then Abbi caught me crying and made me tell her what was up. She convinced me to go after you."

"What a sap," he jokes as I get a little choked up.

"I know, right." I wipe a half-formed tear away from my eye and keep going. "I went to the beach first, but you weren't there. So I went to find you, at that party in Dennis, to apologize and ask you out myself. I was going to explain about my heart too . . ." I trail off.

"And you saw me with Izzy."

I nod.

Luke wipes a hand over his face. "I'm sorry. I can't imagine how that felt."

I let out a hollow laugh. "It really hurt."

"Sera, I've known Izzy for years. And she was there that night, like she'd been all summer, daring me to pick her." He blinks away a tear. "That day, I'd been ready to ask out the greatest girl in the world. But first, I walked in on my dad cheating, and then, from my perspective, I got stood up. I thought you changed your mind because you didn't like me the way I liked you. And Izzy . . . she was easy to be around. And I needed to get lost in something that wasn't hurting me." He shrugs. "I'm so sorry you saw us. I was upset, and I made a dumb decision. I wanted to tell you about it after, but then you were gone, and I didn't know how."

I squeeze his hand. "It's okay. I'm sorry I wasn't able to be there for you, and I'm glad she was."

"I should have told you how I felt sooner."

"You were dealing with something really big."

He shakes his head. "Still. I'm an idiot."

"Maybe we both are," I say.

"So, can we put all that behind us?" he asks, rubbing his thumb across my wrist, sending little shivers up my arm.

I wish I could just say yes, but I need to be honest with him now.

"Yes." His face lights up. "But about what you said the other night."

"I meant it, Sera. I like you. I don't want to just be friends. I don't want to pretend anymore."

I take a deep breath. "I like you too, Luke, but—"

"No, no *buts*." He moves his stool closer to mine, the metal legs screeching against the concrete flooring. I put my hand on his chest, to keep him back a little, so I can say what I need to say.

"My heart is failing. I have a long road ahead of me. Likely more drug trials, possibly another surgery, and I'll just get worse while I wait to climb the list." I sigh. "It sucks. I could barely get out of bed last year, and I was miserable to be around. I was lucky already. I don't know that I'll get lucky again, and you deserve to be having fun, to be with someone who's going to be able to *do* things with you."

"I don't care. I'm tired of *not* being with you, so can we just . . . can we just try? Can you give us a chance?"

He looks at me with that stubborn expression that tells me I'm going to lose this fight. And that feels like winning. I feel my bottom lip shake and my breath catch.

"I can't promise you anything."

"You don't have to. I want to be with you for as long as we have."

"Are you sure? Because—" But before I can say anything else, Luke stands up and pulls me to him. I wrap my arms around him, pressing my face to his chest, breathing him in. Salt and soap and just . . . *Luke.*

"Of course I'm sure," he whispers into my hair.

My heart soars. "Me too." I've never been more sure of anything. I pull back and look him in the eyes to make sure he can see how much I forgive him—forgive us. "No more secrets between us."

His eyes go watery, and he nods. I lean into him.

"I'm scared," I say. It just comes out. Honest and quiet. "I'm scared one of us is going to get hurt. And . . . I'm terrified of what's going to happen with my heart."

Luke takes my shoulders and holds me away from him, looking into my eyes. "Me too," he says. "But how I feel about you is worth it. *We're* worth it." His eyes drop to my mouth and back up again. There are a thousand ways I can stop this. And one very big reason I should. But I can't push myself out of his orbit anymore. I stand up and capture his top lip with my mouth before I can change my mind. He sucks in a breath as he cups my face in his hands, kissing me back slow and soft. My fingers tangle in his hair as his lips press into mine, steady and sure. He slips his tongue into my mouth, gentle and warm. I feel light as air. I try to memorize the shape of his mouth. His hands travel down to my waist, then up the back of my shirt, and I shiver as he pulls me closer. The contact burns through me, and I feel my toes curl. He tastes like salt and sun and summer. He gives me another small kiss before we take a breath, his forehead hot against mine, like we're sharing a sunburn.

A breeze blows through and startles a wind chime hanging in the corner of the studio, but we don't jump. Something about this isn't startling at all. Nothing has ever felt so perfect and so right.

Luke nuzzles into my neck, then leaves a quick trail of kisses back to my flushed cheeks. "We're good at that," he says, and I grin in agreement and kiss him again.

I forget everything that's happened in the last two years and just live in this moment, where there's no place we aren't connected. Luke pauses and pulls away, looking around. I'm about to complain when he lifts me up and spins me quickly around. I laugh as he puts me down gently on the edge of one of the big drafting tables behind us. He frames me with his arms.

"Sera Watkins," he says, grabbing my hips and holding me to him, "will you go out with me?"

I answer him with another kiss.

"Good," he says against my mouth. "Then this is going to be the best summer of your life. Okay?"

I smile. "Okay."

CHAPTER TWENTY-ONE

Sera

For the first week of this very new situation, we take it slow, or, well, as slow as we can. Luke drives me to work on Wednesday, and we sneak out to the Beach at the End of the Universe that evening. It's sweltering, so we go in the ocean. I stand in the shallows up to my waist, careful to keep my monitor dry, as Luke swims short laps out and back, never straying too far from my side. Things are still tender, but other than that, it's like old times. Except now, when I get the desire to brush his hair out of his eyes, drop a kiss on the corner of his mouth, or lay my hand on his chest—I can. The sun is just beginning to sink toward the canal when I catch him staring, his eyes shining.

"What?" I wade a little deeper and tip my head back carefully so just my hair gets wet. Luke swims in closer.

"I'd like to take you out this weekend."

"We're out now."

"On a real date, Sera. The way you're supposed to."

"I don't think we're *supposed* to do anything," I tease, though I like the idea. "But sounds fun."

"Great. I'll make a plan, you just show up."

"You have to give me some details. I need to know what to wear," I insist.

His eyes drop from my face down my body, half-hidden by the water. I splash a little water at his face.

"Hey, eyes up here, mister."

"But there are so many other good places to look," he says, his hands landing on my hips. I lean in and give him one chaste kiss on the lips, then disentangle myself and start heading back to our towels.

On Saturday, I follow Luke's instructions to dress up and meet him at Nyeman's at closing time. I expect the shop to be quiet, since it's almost five thirty, but it's a hive of activity. Paula is at her desk in the corner with a young couple, the woman bouncing a fussy baby in her arms. They must be interior design clients. There's a line at the register five people deep, and another ten people milling about. I wave hi to Paula but don't interrupt her, instead moving through the store to the back, looking for Luke. I find him helping a couple with a chest of drawers. He looks tired, but when he spots me, he grins and his eyes brighten, like I've turned on a light above him just by showing up. The feeling lights me up in return.

"Hi," I say.

"Hi," he replies, strapping the chest to a dolly. "Give me like ten?"

"Take whatever time you need. I'm early."

The couple follows Luke out of the antiques section, and I trail them, looking around at the furniture and tchotchkes. Luke heads out the door to load the chest into the couple's car, and when he comes back in, he's called over to the register. He helps the new cashier, Sam, replace the receipt paper, then gift wraps the item and hands it off. An older woman comes over asking about carpentry work. He nods and digs under the register for a clipboard. As he's writing down what she needs and looking through his notes, Sam struggles with the next person in line. Luke notices and quickly puts the clipboard down, asking the woman to write down her address and phone number. He gently asks Sam to step aside and rings up the next few people, talking through what he's doing while she watches.

Paula comes up next to me as I'm fiddling with the tassels of an embroidered pillow.

"He's good, isn't he?" she says, turning to look back at Luke. "I don't know what we'd do without him." I agree, but a part of me wonders if she can't see how stressed he is, how unhappy. "Have fun on your date."

"Thanks." I smile, feeling suddenly shy.

She grins and turns toward the back stairs. "I've got to get the boys home."

When the last customers leave and Sam clocks out, Luke locks the door and closes the blinds. I make my way over to him.

"I have to change," he says, "and book that house call, then we can go."

"Okay, but first . . ." I catch his hand to stop him from rushing by and pull him into the kitchenware corner. He almost fights me, but I put a finger on his lips and he stops, that smile from before easing out of him. He backs me up against a shelf of copper pots, careful not to knock anything over. I lace my hands around his neck and pull him in for a kiss. I feel his shoulders relax as his arms loop around my waist.

"Keep that thought," he says, playing with the straps at the back of my dress.

I put my arms down. "I'll be sitting right here when you're ready." I point to one of the chairs in front of Paula's desk. "No rushing."

I take a seat, flipping through one of the old magazines while I wait. Luke comes back in tan slacks and a short-sleeved light blue button-down that perfectly cuffs his biceps. I stand up and smooth out my dress, hoping I didn't wrinkle it.

"Ooh, fancy," I say. "So where are we going?"

"I made a reservation out in Brewster." He's excited and keeps messing up the tie he's trying to put on. I reach out and stop his anxious hands.

"You don't need the tie, Luke."

He looks at me nervously. "It's a nice place, and you look . . ." He casts his eyes down the dress, something Maddy helped me find yesterday since the yellow dress is cute but not right for a nice dinner. It's a silky dark brown slip dress with spaghetti straps. I couldn't wear a bra with it because it's backless. I was nervous about wearing it, but Maddy convinced me. As Luke's cheeks go red, I'm glad I listened to her. I step back and do a little twirl, the asymmetrical hem making a small circle. "Amazing," he finishes.

"Thank you," I reply, planting a kiss on his cheek. "Time to go?"

He nods and we head out back to his truck. He clears a few things off the bench seat and tells me to toss Oliver's skateboard in the back. As I do, I catch sight of a few graphic design books on the seat with sticky notes lining their edges.

At the restaurant, there's no parking, and we have to let the valet take the truck. The first indication that when Luke said *nice,* he meant it. I'm immediately self-conscious of the itchy red patch of skin on my chest from the monitor that I mailed back to Dr. Lee this afternoon. I haven't had any more arrhythmias or dizzy spells. Maybe I won't take a bad turn soon. Maybe I can still have a great summer here and next summer in Paris. I try not to think too hard about it so I don't jinx myself.

Luke rubs his hands on the sides of his slacks, nervous, as he gives the host his name. She tells us it'll just be a few minutes.

"If you'd like to look at today's specials, we have a menu over in the courtyard." She gestures to a small outdoor seating area where there's a little stand with the menus behind glass. We step over and I lean against Luke while we read the menu.

"There are no prices," I say, a little confused.

"Don't worry about it," Luke says, though the wrinkle between his eyes says otherwise. "It's on me."

I keep reading, and everything sounds like something Maddy would love to try, but nothing that I'm comfortable with. A man and a woman come up next to us and we make space for them to read too.

"Oh, look, they have a lobster en papillote with truffles!" the woman exclaims. My Duolingo French is progressing, but I have no idea what she means. Is that a dessert? I shoot Luke a look, and he's just as wide-eyed as I feel. He glances over at the guy, who is indeed wearing a tie.

"Luke," I say, pulling him away from the menu.

"I should've worn—" he starts, reaching to his neck.

"No," I say, drawing his attention back to me. "Can I be honest?"

"Of course."

"This is too fancy. I feel so weird that there aren't prices, and I do not want to eat what sounds like lobster chocolates unless Maddy is forcing me to because her career depends on it."

"But . . ." Luke looks over at the hostess, who's leading two elderly men dressed to the nines inside the dark, candlelit restaurant. "We have a reservation."

"It's fine," I say, sliding my hand into his. "I'm sure someone's waiting, and they'll be over the moon to have us give it up."

"You sure?" Luke asks. He looks down at me and brushes a stray piece of hair out of my eyes.

"Oh my god, yes. I'll eat anywhere with you, but maybe not here, tonight?"

He relaxes and lets out a little laugh. "Thank god," he says, pulling on my hand and guiding me out of the small courtyard. The hostess catches us as we try to sneak away.

"Oh, are you leaving?" she asks. Another couple appears behind us, asking if they can have our place.

"Yes," I say as Luke tugs on my hand, "just remembered I'm allergic to seafood and butter—and ties!" Luke snorts and tugs me farther away. "Sorry for the confusion! Bye!"

We break into a run once we're at the sidewalk and stop at the corner, laughing and catching our breaths. Luke untucks his shirt and undoes one of the top buttons. I take out the clip that's hurting my scalp, and nervously check my watch. My heart rate slows quickly, and I relax.

"Better?" I ask, running my hands through my hair. Luke watches me and then looks back over my shoulder.

"Yes, but we will need the car keys."

"Ah, that."

"I'll be right back."

Luke retrieves his truck, and once we're in the cab I move over on the bench seat and buckle myself in the middle so I can be right next to him.

"So, where to?" he asks.

"How about that seafood shack." I point to a sign that leads to a local beach.

"Picnic on the beach?" he says with a grimace, like it's not special enough.

"Yes." I nod and fiddle with the cassette and the cord that connects to my phone, putting on Cam's band's EP, which has grown on me recently.

"If you're sure," Luke says, taking the right.

"I'm sure."

The beach is emptying out at this time of day, and the sky is promising a truly great sunset. There's a thin scattering of clouds to the west, and it's already a little peachy around the edges. We order a mixed plate from the seafood stand and milkshakes, and when our order is up, I lead the way down to some rocks that offer a flat space for us to sit.

We eat while the food is still hot, and I try not to drink my whole milkshake too fast, though it has nothing on Maddy's peanut butter–chocolate one.

"So, the shop looked pretty busy," I say once we've slowed down.

Luke nods, happy. "Yeah, I'm glad. We need all that summer business because it gets so quiet in the offseason. Mom's got a feature coming up in a local magazine too, for a house she did in Harwich. It's a huge achievement for her, like a dream come true."

"Wow. That's great." I try to find a simple way to ask what I want to ask, which is if he's living *his* dream. "Maybe when things calm down, you'll be able to spend more time on your art?" I say, thinking back to those well-loved art books I saw in his truck.

"Maybe," Luke says with a shrug. "But helping my mom and the town is more important right now."

I look out onto the water. The sky is darkening, the marine layer clouds moving in.

"You okay?" Luke asks, nudging my knee.

I don't want to push him too hard, but I also don't want to let it go. I turn back to him. "Yeah," I say. "I just worry you're letting your passions be overshadowed." At the word *passions*, he shifts closer to me.

"I don't need you to worry about me—you worry about staying healthy." He brushes my hair back over my shoulder.

It's a nice thought, but what's life without worries, particularly over the people who matter?

"I'm going to worry no matter what. It's my right. As your—girlfriend." I try the word out slowly, not wanting to freak either of us out.

"All right," he says, taking the empty fry container out of my hands and putting it to the side. He leans in and cups my cheek, drops his thumb onto my bottom lip. "But say that again."

"Worry," I tease, kissing his thumb. He rubs my bottom lip again and sparks shoot through my toes.

"Girlfriend," he says, coming closer, replacing his thumb with his mouth. He bites on my bottom lip, then pulls away, waiting.

"Girlfriend," I say, breathless. He leans in and kisses me again, his arms framing my hips. I keep myself upright with one arm against the rocks and slip the other under the back of his shirt, wanting to feel his skin.

I guess we're done talking for the night.

CHAPTER TWENTY-TWO

Sera

July rolls on like a dream. It hasn't crossed my mind in the last couple years that I could ever be *this* happy. My heart holds steady, and Luke and I spend almost every day together. On days we both have off, he sweeps me away to the beach or whatever Cape events are happening, of which there are a lot—the pirate festival, carnivals, farmers markets, small concerts at family-friendly breweries. I help him sell raffle tickets at the road race to raise money for the town library renovations. He made a poster for it that looks so professional it reminds me how much more he could do if he could get out of here. I take his brothers to the skate park when he has to work late and try not to call out "Be careful!" constantly. We eat dinner at his house, Paula looking at us with perpetually wet eyes. I want to tell her everything is going to be okay. I'm going to be fine. But I don't know that.

We don't talk about my health much, but Luke is also clearly trying to make every minute of every day feel important. It's the smallest moments between us that mean the most to me, though. Like when we discover a patch of wildflowers along one of the nearby nature trails and he tucks one behind my ear. Or when he notices I'm about to finish my five hundredth reread of book three in *The Soul Druid Chronicles*, my favorite, and leaves the next one in my room so I don't have to go looking for it later that night. I begin to wish for just enough time to make more of these small, sweet memories.

Maddy comes with us when she can. We play mini golf in Sandwich with her and Sienna, who's quiet but super smart. And the four of us go to the Woods Hole Film Festival, where Sienna and Luke get really into an indie science fiction movie for different reasons—he was obsessed with the set designs and she with the score. Abbi tags along too, feeling left out, but ends up in a different theater to watch a documentary. We even go on a couple double dates with her and Cam, no PDA allowed. We spend enough time around her that she sees Luke check in on me and my heart. I think she starts to trust him, just like I have. She also can't be there every minute, so there's plenty of time for all the things Luke and I want to do alone, whether it's arguing over the scientific merit of our universe being one big experiment or learning the new landscapes of each other's bodies.

We hang out at the Beach at the End of the Universe a lot. Sometimes we look for shells or I watch Luke leap from the rock into the water, careful to only swim out a little to meet him. On days where my energy is low, I rest while Luke fills me in on the gossip around town. His voice settles me, grounds me.

One day we're caught off guard by a sudden rainstorm, the

blue sky disappearing behind a shroud of gray in less than a minute. I'm floating in the shallows when the rain starts falling. Fat, cold drops scatter across the ocean surface. Luke's up on the rock. He dives off the end and swims to me.

"We should get out. It might lightning," he says as he brushes his hair out of his eyes.

"No, look." I point over his shoulder to a bright swath of blue already chasing the clouds away. "It'll be gone in just a second." I swim over and put my hands on his shoulders, and though it looks like he wants to argue, his eyes also zero in on me, hot and piercing.

"You are so beautiful." He kisses me slowly, and I ache for more even with him right here. I wrap my arms tighter around him, and he pulls me to his chest. In our swimsuits there's no mistaking he wants to do more too, but he's not rushing, he's never rushing. He acts like we have all the time in the world. I'm the one who's frantic, who's desperate to touch him. His lips travel down my neck. I guide his face to meet mine and we kiss, deeper this time. Above us, the clouds return and the rain comes pouring down. I laugh as Luke grabs my hand and we run out of the water, making our way to the sun tent we set up earlier. I don't bother toweling off, just slip my wet swimsuit top off, watching Luke as his eyes focus with intense precision on the rise and fall of my chest. He traces his hands over my collarbones, my breasts, my breath hitching, holding until I can't wait anymore. I pull him down to our towels and push him to his back, meeting his mouth with mine.

Luke's strong and graceful and slow with me, painfully slow, but he finds the places that make me flush with satisfaction. I've found the places that make him melt into me, and it's in those moments where he feels most like himself to me. When the whole of him comes into focus, the serious oldest son, baseball star, hometown hero, world's greatest big brother, but also the soft, nerdy guy who sees the world with an artist's eye.

"The light, look," he says. I lie next to him, tucked under his arm. "The sun is fighting with the clouds. It looks, like, thicker, right there above the waves." And it does. Rays of sunlight rise out behind the heavy gray clouds. Luke pulls me closer, and we watch the rain fade away.

My phone buzzes. Abbi. Checking in. I groan and pretend to throw it in the ocean.

"Guess we should get back," he says.

"Not yet," I say, kissing his lips.

Abbi's uptick in attention does make it hard to relax, to lean into taking it day by day. I just want to spend time one-on-one with Luke, but she's always insisting on joining us. We have learned, though, that she has little patience for baseball, so we've been going to a lot of the Cape Cod Baseball League games. We cheer on the visiting players playing for Northport, who all know Luke and congratulate him on the high school team's win.

He laughs it off, pretending it's no big deal, and says he's just happy Northport is getting the attention it deserves.

In my time alone, I've finished the first layer on my third

application piece, the future me. Iris showed it to someone in the program and told me my chances of getting in are really high. I haven't mentioned my new complications, though. I'm not sure if I'll get to go, even if I do get in.

Maddy has been working overtime like crazy, but we're going to try and meet up tomorrow. I'm not quite ready to go home and face the inquiries from Mom, Dad, and Abbi about how I'm feeling (tired but fine) and what I've been up to with Luke (none of their business).

"What are your friends up to tonight?" I ask Luke.

"I think they're going to the later game out in Harwich."

"More baseball?" I joke.

"Too much baseball?" He laughs.

"Maybe not too much, but more than I'm used to. I call picking the destination for our next date."

As he merges carefully into the traffic going west, I spot the sign for Provincetown. "What about P-town? There have to be so many new galleries since I was there last. And this artist I follow on Instagram has some work up in a gallery that I'd love to see."

"Remember that drag brunch when your dad got pulled up to the front and they made him dance?" Luke chuckles.

"Oh my god, I totally forgot about that. What a dork."

"How did he *not* know the moves to the Macarena?"

I shake my head as I laugh harder. "I have no idea. Abbi and I definitely went through a line dancing phase."

"Do you think your parents will be okay with us going that far?" he asks, glancing over at me. "It's a long drive, and it gets really backed up in the summer."

"I'll ask them." I slide a little toward him on the bench seat and kiss him on the cheek. He takes one hand off the wheel and places it above my knee, drawing little circles with his thumb.

"Okay, if you're sure you're up for it."

"I'm sure."

CHAPTER TWENTY-THREE

Sera

Mom and Dad said yes to the Provincetown trip last night, but now over breakfast they're second-guessing. Abbi surprises me by coming to the rescue.

"If you haven't noticed," she says, "Sera's heart readings have been steady. I think doing more helps." She fills my coffee mug to the allowed line and pushes it my way. Luke knocks on the sliding glass door and slips in as they discuss the length of leash I should be allowed.

"Morning, Luke," Mom says, giving him a smile to let him know this isn't his fault but also not his place to weigh in. He comes and stands next to me by the counter, and I lean against him. He slips his hand into the back pocket of my shorts, where no one can see. I pinch my lips together to keep my giggle in.

"I don't know," Dad says from his spot at the kitchen table. "You have an appointment in Boston soon. Shouldn't you be resting?"

"I think that's another reason why she should go," Abbi

pushes, snapping open the binder with the records of my check-ins since the incident written in her careful hand. "Who knows what Dr. Lee might say then. What if we have to go back to Brookline?" Even though I've been okay since the night after the blood drive, my entire family has reverted to micromanaging me like they had to last summer. I needed it then. I don't need it now.

"I guess that's true," Mom says before taking a slow sip of her tea.

"I can go with them if you want," Abbi offers, "but Luke is really responsible, and he'll know what to do if Sera feels off at all. Right?"

Luke nods. "Absolutely."

"Sera also knows what to do when Sera feels off," I mutter under my breath. Luke squeezes my hand.

"Okay, then," Mom says, getting up and placing a kiss on the top of my head. "Come home if you're feeling tired at all. But have fun."

When I'm ready to go, Abbi does my vitals and Mom clears me to leave. Luke stands in the corner of the kitchen and watches the whole process with hyperfocus, learning the steps.

"You're sure you're feeling okay?" Abbi asks quietly once Mom is out of earshot.

"Yeah. Promise. Do something for yourself today too, okay?"

Abbi hugs me in response, and I hug her tight, squeezing her until her back pops. She pulls away and laughs, then looks between Luke and me. She leans in to whisper in my ear.

"Just be *careful*. Maybe hold off on any . . . *cardio* . . . until you talk to Dr. Lee about whether it's safe."

"Abbi." I blush. I glance over at Dad, but he's reading something on his phone, oblivious.

Abbi rolls her eyes, winks. "Fine. Have fun."

"Not too much," I promise.

In Provincetown, Luke insists on dropping me off in the center of town before he finds a spot to park. I wander through the bookstore while I wait for him, saying hi to the dog in residence and listening to his owner tell a visiting couple his rescue story. I buy Abbi a book on the history of alternative energy on the Cape as a thank-you, then go meet Luke on the corner. He's holding a bag from the Portuguese bakery. I snap a photo of him waiting for me and text it to Maddy.

Sera

hot boy + hot 🥐 = 🤓

should we bring you back some?

Maddy

yes please! Are you wearing THE DRESS?!

I laugh and take a selfie. I'm wearing a T-shirt and shorts and one of Luke's baseball caps.

Maddy

I demand a date worthy of THE DRESS, and DETAILS!

Sera

I demand unlimited free fries and Sienna details in return!

Maddy

I'll consider it. Meet up tomorrow? Just us?

I send her a thumbs-up and sidle up to Luke.

"Are those for me?"

"Save me a bite," he teases, "but yes. It was a long drive."

We find a bench on the main drag to sit and eat. When we're done, we escape the sun by drifting from shop to shop. As we walk past a little park, we step apart to let a gaggle of brunch-going drag queens pass by.

"I love your hat!" I shout to the queen at the end, who's wearing a giant crocheted shell perched atop her bright red wig.

"Thanks, doll, I love your arm candy!" She gestures to Luke, and he blushes.

The gallery I'm looking for is pretty far up Commercial Street, and Luke holds the door open for me as we step out of the sun into the well-lit, air-conditioned space.

The gallery is run by a local artist, and their current show features work from young up-and-coming artists all over Cape Cod. We wander through for a bit until I find the corner where the artist I'm looking for has their work hanging. The three paintings hanging here are all portraits of people caught in the wind, their hair wild, one guy bald but clearly feeling the wind on his wrinkled skin. The detail is so impressive. I take a selfie and post it to Instagram, tagging the artist and sending them a note.

On our way out, Luke's drawn to an impressive array of mixed-media pieces that are just his style. Graphic and bold, a combination of print design and photography, according to the artist's statement. The central piece is of the ferry to Martha's Vineyard.

"Wow." I'm stunned.

"It's really good," Luke agrees.

"Your work is just as good, Luke. It could fit right beside this piece easily. You should make something to submit."

He shakes his head. "Nah, I don't have time. Plus it's just a hobby. It's relaxing, you know. A distraction."

"Sure." I don't want to let this go for some reason. Worse than him refusing to think about what he wants outside of what his family needs is this insane idea he has that his art isn't worth his time. "But it's still really good."

"Your work will be here, though," he says, deflecting. "Those underwater portraits maybe? They don't just have to be for your application."

"Maybe. I don't know that I'll have enough time to start showing in galleries . . ." I say, trailing off.

"Don't say that," he says, looking hurt.

"Luke . . ."

He scratches the back of his neck. "I just want you to let yourself have hope. Neither of us was supposed to live past two, and look at us now. You can't know what will happen."

He's both wrong and right at the same time. Sure, there are the unknowns that give me hope. But I *know* I'll need a new heart one day. I *know* my body could reject it. I *know* my life will still be shorter than his. It's hard to think past next summer, to pretend we have all the time in the world like I know he wants me to. Am I taking up all the air, not having long-term hopes and dreams for us simply because I think it's too hard to picture them? Summers down on the Cape have always felt like a break from reality, and this one has the same taste of suspended time, but maybe that's not fair. Luke lives here all the time. This is *his* life. I'm just a visitor. In more ways than one.

"You should submit your work to them," Luke says. He marches up to the front desk and takes a pamphlet with information on the gallery. I keep quiet, my head a little fuzzy from all the thinking and the long day.

On the drive home, I let one hand trail out the window while the other rests warm and secure in Luke's hand. My thoughts swing back and forth between this moment and several imagined futures, the bright and impossible kind I haven't been allowing myself to entertain.

Luke calling me while I walk around Paris and me telling him about the light in the city.

Maddy and me tired and grungy on a train to Amsterdam—her rambling about the food we're going to eat while I sketch the view.

There are so many ways my future could look if I have one, each daydream more beautiful than the last.

CHAPTER TWENTY-FOUR

Sera

The next Sunday, Luke takes his brothers fishing and I opt out. Oliver pouts when I tell him I can't come, and Adam asks why, but I just say I have a project to finish instead of the whole truth. I'm zapped, tired, and a little cranky. It's August 8, so I do have to finish my essay before the application is due Wednesday, but the tiredness I'm feeling brings back the ghost of that lonely, sick girl I was last summer. It feels like she's trying to invade my happy, easy, lovely summer with reminders of how little time I could have left. I give in for the day, and I let my family fuss over me. Abbi sets my easel up in the backyard, and Mom carries herbal teas out to me every thirty minutes. I'm trying to do what Luke asked, have hope about the future, and start sketching a new piece of the two of us. But I barely get started before I need to go in and lie down. The humidity is oppressive, a heavy weight on my limbs and lungs. I retreat to my room, close the shades, and blast the old shaky AC unit until I'm freezing and can snuggle under my blankets in Luke's red baseball hoodie. I sleep most of the day, hoping that'll make me feel better.

When Monday rolls around, I'm a lot better, but Luke doesn't drop me at work. Instead, he hangs around while the kids are checking in and quickly becomes too engrossed to leave.

"You don't have to stay," I say as Rose and another girl from the softball team pull him over to the clay bucket. They're begging him to scoop huge pieces for them like he did for a couple other kids. We're doing slab pottery this week. They'll make their pieces today, then glaze them on Wednesday so I can fire them before they do presentations on Friday.

"I want to," he says, his hands smeared with rusty wet slip. "I like being back here. It makes me want to work on my own stuff more, which you keep telling me to do."

I almost call him out. He's been so resistant to working on anything for longer than one session. I'm getting tired of sneaking his crumpled-up work out of the garbage and stealing his posters off the window at the shop before they get taken down. I know he just wants to hang around and watch me because I'm looking off, and because Abbi told him yesterday was a bad day. There wasn't enough cold water on the Cape to make the purple bags under my eyes go away this morning, so it wasn't like I could say she was making it up. I want to tell him to go. Go hang out with Maddy, who actually has the day off, or his teammates before they're all off to school or their full-time jobs. But I also selfishly want as much time with him as I can get. I reach out and wipe a streak of clay off his cheek.

"Okay," I say with a shrug, "you can stay." Rose, who's been pretending not to listen, jumps and claps her hands once so loud with excitement that everyone jumps. I have to laugh. "I guess that's a consensus, then. Okay, everyone. Mr. Luke is joining us today." A swell of cheers goes up. "If you need help getting clay from the big bucket, please ask him. And please treat him like we treat all teachers here at Blue Honeybee."

There's an adorable chorus of "Yes, Miss Sera" that makes my heart swell before they get back to work.

With Luke there, the day flies by. There are some tears at checkout, so I have to promise he'll be there for a little bit on Friday, too, before Rose will leave with her mom, who's trying not to laugh.

"She has a little crush," she admits to me as Luke bends down and promises Rose he'll be back. "We're all glad to have you teaching this summer, Sera. And it's been so wonderful to see Luke have some fun again." I look at her, a little surprised, and she gently taps my elbow. "Rose is in Oliver's class, and Paula and I are close. She worries about him." She gives me a knowing smile and pulls Rose away.

"Bye, Miss Sera! Bye, Coach Luke!" Rose says, eyes still red but her worries forgotten, as she skips off ahead of her mom, already asking if they can go for ice cream.

I'm still thinking about what Rose's mom said when Luke comes over and asks if I want to stay and do some painting. Am I any good for Luke, long-term? Who knows what's going to happen with my health, and I don't want to become another thing he feels responsible for, like his family.

I turn the problem over carefully, keeping it at arm's length in my mind, as we walk over to the open studio. It's just stopped raining, and as the sun comes back out, steam radiates off the warm ground. Luke takes my hand and I think how loved I feel, how held, with such a simple touch.

In the studio, we set up at our usual spots. I pull out my third self-portrait and Luke sets up another fresh sheet of paper. We fall into silence and light chatter as we work. I'm starting to think that this one might finally almost be done, so I pull out the other two finished ones and stare at them all together. They're feeling really strong, cohesive, as Iris would say. I take a photo and send it to her, then roll my stiff neck. I go stand behind Luke to see what he's doing.

I'm floored by his drawing. A lean heron stepping one foot out of the marsh, like it's about to run and take flight. Its shiny dark eyes look to the sky.

"I want that as a tattoo," I say, leaning my chin on Luke's shoulder and taking in the depth of detail he's pulled out.

"We're not supposed to get tattoos," he reminds me.

"I think this is worth the risk of infection." I kiss his cheek.

"It's just a bird," he says, shrugging, "and not a good one." Still, he reaches out and adds some shading to the bill. The bird suddenly looks like it has quite a lot to say, if you can win its trust.

"It's fantastic," I breathe.

His hand stops, and he puts the charcoal down.

"You're distracting me." His eyes glint with trouble. "You ready to go?" he asks. He turns on the spinning stool and pulls me closer with the backs of his heels until I'm trapped between his legs. I lean forward and give him a quick kiss that I can't quite break off.

He murmurs something unintelligible into my mouth and then leans back.

"Hmm?" I ask, playing innocently with the hem of his shirt. I let the thrill and heat of want tingle down my spine. Luke lets out a small groan when my fingers brush his stomach.

"Or we could stop by the Beach at the End of the Universe." He sounds guilty asking, but he also kisses me again, slipping one of his hands up the back of my shirt, where it settles warm against my skin.

"Yes," I whisper, moving away to pack up quickly. He cleans up too, carefully moving my paintings to the drying rack for me. As I'm grabbing my bag, Luke tosses his heron drawing into the trash can between us. When he turns away, I rescue it from the bin and fold it carefully before hiding it in my bag.

Maddy comes over Tuesday night when I'm too tired to meet her at the diner like we planned. She brings homemade granola bars, a list of YouTube clips on European backpacking we *must* watch, and very detailed stories about the chaos of summer people who eat at the restaurant. As she launches into another story about an annoying tourist, I try to keep up, but my brain just wants to shut off for the night. I wish tomorrow were Friday so the kids would have presentations and I wouldn't have to do much. Just three more days, then it'll be the weekend, and I can rest with Luke at the beach.

"Why so sleepy, sleeping beauty?" Maddy nudges me as I

shut my eyes for a second, and for the first time this summer, I hear a real tinge of sadness in her voice. My stomach sinks at the sound of it, but I recover quickly.

"Oh, you know," I tease, rolling onto my side and propping up my head, "just falling in love. It's exhausting." I wink.

Maddy squeals, and Abbi comes to check on us, padding down the hall from her room and pushing her way in without knocking. She's got gold under-eye masks on, so it's hard to take the stern look on her face seriously.

"All good in here?" she asks, hovering.

Maddy assures her we're fine and invites her to sit with us for the next video, but she leaves us alone.

"She always like that?" Maddy asks. I sigh dramatically.

"Lately, yes. It's gotten a lot worse. She's threatening to take another semester off this fall, but I don't want her to do that. Dad worries it'll reflect badly on her and she might get kicked out."

"Shit." Maddy grabs a pen and starts doodling on my ankle.

"Yeah. And she LOVES school and learning and everything. It's so weird. I wish she'd just, like, get over it."

"Get over what?" I look down at the heart Maddy's drawing and laugh.

"Me dying."

"Oh, Sera. I don't think any of us are going to get over that, *if* that's what's coming," she admits, drawing a sad face next to the little heart with Luke's and my initials in it.

"I know," I say, because I do, and yet I don't because it's different to be the one who might be leaving. My sadness and anger have a tentative end date, and theirs have to just go on as long as they do.

Thankfully Maddy pivots. "So . . . I have to ask . . ."

"Ask what?"

Maddy raises her brows. "Have you and Luke . . . you know?"

"Have we what?" I say, playing dumb, but I can't keep a straight face.

"Out with it!" Maddy says.

"No," I say. "We haven't . . . yet."

Maddy squeals again, and I reach for a pillow and pretend to smother her. "But soon!" she says, her voice muffled from beneath the pillow. She wrenches it free. "I hear Luke's an experienced . . . lover." She draws out the last word so loud I shush her.

"My windows are open, Maddy. He could hear you," I whisper-yell.

"LUKE'S WHAT?!" she shouts. I scream and wrestle the pillow back to smack her with it.

Abbi comes back in.

"Sera," she says as Maddy and I hiccup through our giggles, "I don't think you should be getting so worked up."

As if agreeing with her, EBE coughs through an irregular beat and my watch beeps once. Maddy pales a little and apologizes.

"Oh, don't apologize for making me laugh, Mads. God, Abbi, come on, learn to have some fun," I say, tossing the pillow her way. It smacks against her shins and falls to the floor. She doesn't smile.

"Take it easy," she says, like a warning. I sit up and flash her a look.

"Or what, Abbi?"

She opens her mouth, closes it, and then pivots and leaves, slamming my door behind her.

CHAPTER TWENTY-FIVE

Sera

I'm feeling fine in the morning, but Abbi insists on coming with me to work. When I say that Luke will probably join me later in the day, so she doesn't need to, she goes over to Paula's to confirm. She comes back, head all high, and tells me that Luke has a commitment all day (like I'm not aware he's taking his brothers to see his dad) and she'll take me. I guess I shouldn't have lied, but her worrying is getting under my skin. At least she and Cam are going away to Maine for a couple weeks. She leaves right after she takes me to my appointment in Boston tomorrow, and I think we could both use the break.

The kids at camp like Abbi, though not as much as they like Luke—a feeling I can relate to these days. Since it's an easy day, with the kids glazing their slab pieces before moving on to a free-choice project, she's clearly bored. I keep catching her picking up her phone and putting it down as she paces around the room. When Jayda comes to get the kids for their beach time, she swoops in to help. When I say I'm fine to do it, she looks at me incredulous, annoyed that I'd be so silly as to consider taking a three-minute walk in the heat.

I use the ten or so minutes of silence to sit and watch the wind playing with the seagrass atop the dunes. The camp cat comes and finds me, an orange flash of personality who gets renamed every year. He's showing some age, a little whiter around his chin than I remember, but he's just as lithe and feisty, playing with my smock strings like he's a kitten. I lean down and scratch his head.

"You're going to outlive me *and* the universe, aren't you?" He meows in agreement and then trots off as Abbi returns.

"How are you?" she asks, reaching for my watch. I pull my arm away from her.

"Leave it, Abbi. You just checked after lunch. I'm feeling the same."

"I just want to look. You need to stay healthy to be ready for a transplant."

Suddenly I'm furious, the rage boiling up in my chest and spilling over, and I'm surprised by how much I've been holding in.

"Will you just fucking leave me alone?" I snap. "Jesus." I drop my head into my hands and groan, trying not to simply scream at her to leave.

"You have a headache, don't you?" Abbi doesn't even pause for me to answer. She just marches back into the barn. I follow at her heels as she goes to the cubbies, where my things are stored, and starts packing my bag up.

"What are you doing?" I go over and wrench my bag from her hands.

"Sera!" I've broken one of her fingernails, and she prods at it before shaking it off. She opens her palms toward me like I'm a rabid skunk. "Take a breath; you'll cause an incident."

"I can't keep my cool when you act like this, Abbi. Why can't you just let me make my own decisions?"

"Because you're not being careful enough," she says, her voice rising.

"Who *cares*? What does it matter? I'm not going to spend my last several months tiptoeing around pretending death isn't sitting in the corner counting down the seconds."

"Maybe it wouldn't be only *months* if you slowed down a bit," she snaps.

Her phone pings with another text. It's face up on the table next to us, and I read it. It's Cam, saying he understands if she wants to cancel their trip.

"What is this?" I ask, grabbing her phone and waving it in her face like it's proof of some great treason.

"Nothing. Butt out of my life." Abbi reaches for it, but I step back, still holding it.

"Go on the goddamn trip, Abbi."

"Watch your mouth—there are kids around." Abbi looks quickly side to side and tries to grab her phone again. I take a few quick steps back, putting a table between us. My heart beats fast with the effort, the anger and upset. My watch pings, and Abbi's eyes widen in panic.

"No. I won't watch my mouth, because I saw you put your entire life on hold last year. And now you're doing it again, sitting here acting like things will work out if we're careful and boring. All you're really doing is keeping me from living my life while I still have it. And I'm sick of it. I'm sick of you acting like you know best, like you know *everything*. You're not the one dying, Abbi. I am! You're just avoiding anything good because you *like* feeling depressed."

"Stop it, Sera." She starts to cry, but I can't stop. All I see is red; all I see is the last few weeks of her circling around me like a vulture just like she did all last summer and fall. I can't stand her hopeful anxiety anymore.

"No! You stop it! You actually *have* a future, so stop fucking wasting it on me!"

"You don't get to tell me how I spend my time." She lowers her voice in response to my shouting. I scoff at her hypocrisy, but she barrels on. "And aside from right this minute, I'd like to spend as much time with my little sister as I can."

"Well, too bad, because I don't want to spend any more time with you. Mom can take over Sera watch. I don't want to see your face hovering around me anymore."

"Mom's tired too, Sera, don't you get that? Don't you see how this is killing all of us? Don't you notice what we've given up?"

"And I didn't ask for any of it!" I shout.

This shuts her up, but now we're both crying, and my heart is struggling to keep up with my breathing. My watch pings again, and I sit down on a stool and toss Abbi's phone back at her. She just barely catches it. She shoves it in her pocket, then wipes the tears from her eyes. She's spent so much time helping me get through the last year, and I love her, but in this moment, I hate her too.

"Maybe we need a break," Abbi whispers.

"No shit," I snap, willing my tears to stop and taking a few long, slow breaths.

Abbi stares at me a beat longer, then turns and walks out the door. "I'll send Dad to pick you up," she says. "Find someone else to take you to your appointment tomorrow."

In the morning, all heart failures avoided, my gut sour from our fight, I finally feel bad for yelling at Abbi. I go knock on her door. I have every intention of trying to make up without letting things go back to how they've been. I just don't think I can take it if she doesn't give me a little space to breathe.

There's no reply.

"Abbi?" I ask, knocking again. "Abigail?" I push the door open, hovering in the doorway as it reveals her empty room.

She probably left early for her trip to avoid me. I stand there as a calm, uncomfortable silence settles into the house.

I sigh and walk into her room, looking around.

Abbi's room smells like lavender and the incense she likes to burn. There's a pile of ash in the ceramic tray on the bedside table next to an empty space where she usually keeps the stack of books she's reading. She's got a big desk with two overflowing bookshelves on either side and a cozy armchair we found at Nyeman's two years ago. My eyes catch on a line of shells decorating a couple of shelves in the corner. I recognize them. Treasures I found as a kid and gave to her. Mixed in with them are small pieces of art I've made and photos of the two of us.

My old volleyball jersey I thought was missing sits folded on the lowest shelf. Maybe she didn't mean it, but the way everything is laid out, the shells stretched out in lines across the edges of the shelves, guarding all these mementos of our life together—it looks like a shrine.

"I'm not gone yet," I whisper to the room.

CHAPTER TWENTY-SIX

Luke

Sera doesn't want to talk about her fight with Abbi. I don't want to press her, but I do want to help, so when she asks me to take her to her doctor's appointment in Boston, I say yes.

The waiting room is full of older people, spouses waiting for their partners, some people my parents' age flipping anxiously through stacks of paperwork. Sera leaves me with a sketchbook, because she's thoughtful like that. I sit and doodle while I think about the awkward visit with my dad yesterday. The boys wanted me to go, so I said yes, but there was a woman over. Someone new. She was young, pretty, and shocked to see me.

"No need to tell your mother about her yet, okay, boys?" he said to Adam and Oliver, giving me a nervous look over their heads as the woman slipped on her shoes and left. She was clearly shaken by the fact that my dad has an eighteen-year-old.

"We don't lie to Mom," I said, trying to keep my voice light. Dad just changed the subject.

"Do you boys want to go out on the new boat?"

The whole thing had sat heavy on my chest since, reminding me of how fleeting love can be. *Sera and I won't be like that,* I tell myself.

Sera's gone about an hour, which she told me to expect, so I hope that means things are good. But when she steps back into the waiting room, the look on her face tells me the appointment hasn't gone well. Her eyes are red, her cheeks splotchy.

I jump up and hug her, breathing in the sugar-lemon smell of her and holding her slightly trembling body tight. If I could hug the sadness and the worry and the sickness right out of her, I would. She nestles her forehead into my chest, like she can hear my thoughts.

"Not good, huh?" I say, my throat thick.

"No." Her voice is small. "Not good. I have to come back next week."

"Do you want to tell me?" I ask.

"Ejection fraction is still low." She swallows. "They're submitting my name to be moved up the list."

My stomach sinks. "Let's get out of here." I reluctantly let her go and loop my arm around her waist, hoping she's up for the plan I threw into place while waiting.

She leans into me and we head for the door.

Sera is quiet the whole way to the garage. In my truck, I grab her hand across the bench seat and kiss each of her knuckles, like she's been in a fight, which she has and still is. She leans across the bench and gives me a butterfly-light kiss on the lips, whispers a thank-you, and then settles in against the window. I hope she's not too tired for her surprise.

It takes her about ten minutes to realize we're not going home.

"Wait." She stirs and sits up, swinging her head to look around the part of the city I'm taking us through. "Where are we going?" She looks at me with curious anticipation, and I know I've chosen right. I try to keep a lock on my grin, but she pulls it out of me.

"A surprise," I say, making sure she can't see the directions I've put up on my phone, which is resting against the dash by my always-a-little-off speedometer.

Fifteen minutes later, I'm walking a slack-jawed Sera into the blissfully air-conditioned lobby of the Isabella Stewart Gardner Museum. I pull the tickets up on my phone, purchased in the waiting room of the hospital, and then tug Sera into the building.

"I've never been here," she manages to say as we're directed past the gift shop to the long glass hallway that leads to what our ticket taker says is officially called "The Palace."

"Me neither, but it's supposed to be cool." I grab a map and then we step into a moody and dark European-looking entryway. I look at the pamphlet. "So, she built this entire building as a museum to house her personal art collection. She even collected a lot of the architecture, like the pillars and some of the ceilings, not just the paintings and statues and stuff."

"That's awesome," Sera says.

As we move out of the entryway, the sun reappears, beaming through intricate pillars surrounding a lush courtyard. I lean over the rope keeping us off the beautiful mosaic floor and squint up at a massive skylight. It doesn't look that big, but there are people at every open window and balcony on the first three floors. It's bustling with tourists trying to get out of the oppressive heat.

"This is the place that was robbed, right?" Sera asks as we head into an area labeled *The Spanish Cloister* to get away from the crowd around the courtyard.

"Yeah"—I flip through the pamphlet—"in 1990. They still haven't found any of it. The empty frames are upstairs."

"They left the frames? That's . . . a statement." We fall quiet as we continue deeper into the museum. Directly ahead is a huge painting, and it brings us both to a halt.

"Wow." The painting is taller than me and probably ten feet wide. It features a woman dancing in front of a group of guitar players in a sparse room. The movement of the piece is incredible; I can almost feel the ruffles of her skirts whipping around her. There are a couple of women who must be friends of hers watching with delight from the right.

"What's going on with her hand?" I ask, finding the limb twisted in a way that looks uncomfortable.

"She's dancing. No, reaching for something," Sera says, a little breathless. There's a twang in my chest, the thrill of sharing her artistic interpretation. "Beckoning."

"She looks so . . . focused," I say quietly.

We observe her for a while longer, as other guests come up and take photos and look at the strange collection of pottery and stools that decorate the space in which the painting hangs.

"She's absorbed," Sera decides. "Her hand *is* interesting, though. It looks like it's about to move, like we've just caught her in this one strange position by chance. It reminds me of the heron you drew. Like it was about to take off, like we'd caught him unaware."

I startle at the comparison. Sera's always too nice to me about my work. But I try to humor her, gazing back at the painting and its moody lighting. "Really? This is so much more skilled."

"It's the motion, or the promise of it. I feel like you see that really well." She shrugs. "Should we keep looking?" she asks, turning around and pointing to a small line into another room behind us.

I agree, and we join the flow of people moving through a contemporary gallery into a yellow wallpapered room smaller than my bedroom in Northport and crammed with art. Sera lets out a chuckle of disbelief.

"I bet it doesn't feel like this in Paris," she says, standing inches from a painting of a ballerina.

"Like what?" I ask as I'm drawn to a painting in the corner that looks like nothing more than a black rectangle.

Sera follows me, gesturing at the small space. "So personal."

"You think?"

"I'll ask Iris, but all the photos of Paris she's sending look like you're in these huge rooms with tons of tourists." She glances around again. "Not in a tiny room with only six other people." She sighs. "Maybe this is better, and Paris would just be disappointing. Maybe it's good I won't be able to do the fellowship."

I wince and bite down on the instinct to beg her to take it back. What happened at her appointment is fresh. She can feel however she feels, but I also want her to know I'm not going anywhere. I slip my arm around her and hold her to my side, continuing to stare at the dark rectangle in its gilded frame until it begins to reveal its secrets. Slowly, details start to emerge as my eyes get used to the black, and then it's not black but gray, silver, blue.

"It's a foggy ocean." Sera gasps. "Like the Beach at the End of the Universe at night." She sidles closer.

I nod, pointing out two small lights. "I can see two boats now."

"And those lights, in the distance, maybe a lighthouse, or another ship?"

"Wow." I'm floored, almost giddy with how impressed I feel from this one small painting. I shake my head. "I mean, I know there's a lot of great art here, but wow. I could stare at this for hours. I bet you'd see something new every few minutes."

"We could steal it," Sera whispers, and I laugh too loud. All the other people in the room whip their heads at us.

"Sorry, sorry," Sera says, laughing with me as we leave.

We weave our way back out into the courtyard and into the next set of rooms. Sera's immediately drawn to a painting hanging in the far left corner of a woman with long, curly red hair. She drops my hand and moves to look closer. I can tell she's thinking about Abbi.

"Have you talked since she left?"

She shakes her head. "I should text her." She sighs. "Apologize . . . but not today."

"Whenever you're ready, she'll understand."

"Maybe."

*

Over the next hour we make our way up through the building's three available floors and then back down. The top two floors are much quieter and more open, with a lot of high ceilings, including a painted one. There's so much gilt and gold, and so many little trinkets and letters. We talk about how we know we're missing things as we move along, but you have to keep moving so you don't get overwhelmed. You see what you can see, and you appreciate it before you're swept up in the next thing.

I snap a selfie of us in one of the open balcony windows and text it to her. She turns quick and presses a kiss to my cheek, just shy of the corner of my mouth, and I take another.

"This is my new background," I say, quickly making it so. Sera kisses me again and then asks if I'm hungry.

"Wicked, actually," I admit, thinking of the last bite of eggs I managed to get before Oliver and Adam ate them all this morning.

We go down to the café and order giant iced teas, two sandwiches, and a few desserts. Sera sends a photo to Maddy.

"This might be the best date I've ever been on," she says, reaching across the table and poking the back of my hand with her fork like I'm on the menu. "Are you having fun too?" she asks, taking another bite of the coconut cake.

"Yes. I wish it didn't have to end." I keep my hand in hers, Sera's heartbeat in my fingertips.

"I saw a studio out there." She tips her head toward the main hall. "I think anyone can use it. We could draw for a while?"

I take a bite of cake, then nod. "I'd love that."

We settle into the studio with our sketchbooks. The quiet hum of visitors passing by the room reminds me of being in the open studio at Blue Honeybee, and it's easy to fall into our normal rhythm of working and glancing over at what the other person is doing.

I'm sketching the courtyard, a woman standing in the shadows, thinking about the way the light moves playfully around the plants. We both lose ourselves in the task for a while, until a tour group goes by, and I see Sera flinch at the rise in chatter.

"We can go," I say, closing my sketchbook. "I'm just going to use the bathroom first."

"Okay." Sera smiles. "I do feel the beginning of a headache coming on. I'll just finish this and wait for you here."

When I'm back, Sera has packed up everything and is watching a group of kids shuffling down the hall, following behind their camp counselor. Two at the back are giggling and poking each other.

"They remind me of Oliver and Adam." She nods in their direction just as the counselor comes over and separates them, moving one to the middle of the line.

"Yeah, but probably less annoying," I joke, taking her hand.

As we exit back into the hot sun, a sign on a building to our right catches her attention.

"Oh, look. It's MassArt. I think they have a small design museum. Do you want to go look?" She's pointing across the long green lawn outside the museum, to a gray and modern building with the words *Massachusetts College of Art and Design* across a long window wall.

"Maybe another time?" I suggest. I don't want to look inside a school I would've been applying to before everything with my dad went down. And Sera has a headache anyway.

"Really? You'll come back and go with me?"

"Of course."

Sera's eyes light up even as she takes her bottom lip between her teeth. I reach up and free it, rub my thumb across her soft pink lip, then leave a small kiss there. I want her to be gentle with herself, so I'll be gentle, even though I immediately want to get us back in the truck with fewer people around. I take a slow, deep breath and push the desire back as Sera licks her lips and looks at me like she knows exactly how naked I'm picturing her right now. Then she pulls away and moves toward where we parked the truck.

"Whoa, slow up," I say as she drags me down the sidewalk.

"Nope. Come on. I want to make out with my boyfriend in his truck."

CHAPTER TWENTY-SEVEN

Sera

Friday morning, I wake up early and go for a walk on the beach before my parents are up. It's my last day teaching camp. Iris is back on Monday. I collect rocks for each of the kids as thank-yous and then come back home and make a pot of coffee. The spitting of the machine is the only sound in the house. Even though Abbi is still in Maine, I can feel the tension between us. I'm sitting with my allotted share of caffeine on the porch with the fan blowing the humid air around as best it can when Mom comes down and joins me.

"You were up early." She swats at my feet until I move them, then sits on the other end of the love seat and puts my feet in her lap.

"Feeling good today," I admit, even though doing that makes me nervous, like I'm going to jinx it.

Mom squeezes my knee, her eyes sad. "I'm glad. Can I take you to camp today?"

"Sure." I lift my mug up to cheers with hers and she smiles, then tucks a strand of hair behind my ear. I watch the sun catch on the freckles across her nose, so much like Abbi's, and wonder if I'll get to keep any memories when I die. We're not religious, and when pressed about their beliefs my parents shrug, atheists to their core. Abbi is spiritual, but I don't think any of us expect there's going to be anything more than their memories of me when I'm gone. And it does now feel like *when* is soon. Funnily, I thought I'd be angrier, but I'm just wildly grateful for whatever time I have left. I push the sad thought away and pull my phone out to show Mom the new pictures Iris sent me from Paris until we have to go.

It's my last day, but not the kids', so I have a schedule for them to do presentations of their weekly projects in the morning and then free art in the afternoon. I don't know what Iris will want to pick up with them next week, and they haven't had a free day in a while.

Maddy shows up right when Jayda picks the kids up for their time down at the beach.

"Lunch in town?" she asks, giving me a quick hug and taking a turn around the room, admiring the kids' work. "I remember making these at school." She's looking at one of the self-portrait outlines that haven't been taken home yet. "Was it fun? Teaching?"

"Yeah. I'm going to miss it," I admit, grabbing my bag and following her to her car. "Though not as much as your milkshakes."

Maddy sighs dramatically. "Are you talking about when you're dead? Stop it. You only got the news about moving up the list yesterday. You don't know what's going to happen. You could get a heart this year. Plus it's still summer. Let's enjoy it. Your application was due this week, right? You turned it in?"

"I did."

"Good. Your birthday is coming up, and there are still beach days to enjoy. Let's make the most of it."

I smile. Maddy's reminders are a helpful distraction from the occasional arrythmias that have me scrambling for a breath a couple times a week. I tap at my watch to check its battery level.

"You're not sick of me yet?" I ask.

"Definitely not. I only wish you were better at sharing the details of what's going down with Luke. Like how good of a kisser is he, really?" she asks.

I roll my eyes. "How's Sienna?" I ask in return.

"Top-notch kisser," Maddy says, beaming. "So, Luke?"

I zip my lips and toss the fake key out the window.

"That bad, huh?" Maddy shakes her head, and I make a face to show her just how wrong she is. "God, you're a tease!" Maddy shouts, laughing, cranking her radio up for the end of the song as we pull up in front of Earl's Sandwich Shop.

After lunch, Maddy drives me back to camp. I'm surprised to find the big garage door to the studio closed—it's never closed.

"I'll get it!" Maddy steps forward and heaves open the door. The kids burst out at me, shouting "Surprise," their little limbs fighting toward me all at once. Iris waves from the back of the room, and I do a double take. As I field a hug from each of my students, I finally manage to put together that they've made me a gift.

"It was Miss Iris's idea," Rose tells me. "Do you like it?"

I'm holding a thick paste paper book full of their drawings and thank-you letters. I hug it to my chest even though part of it is still a little sticky.

"I love it," I say. "I have something for each of you too."

Once I've given the rocks out to each kid, it's time for free art, which Iris and I co-monitor. Then it's pickup, and the studio is empty and quiet. I walk around, tidying here and there and taking in the smell of crusty paint and old clay. I'm going to miss coming here.

Iris asks if I'd like to come over for dinner as a thank-you for filling in.

"Bring your pieces. And I want to tell you all about Paris."

I text my parents and Luke to let them know, and ride with Iris to her place.

She lives in one of the tiny one-bedroom cottages close to Northport Beach, but she's expanded it by adding a personal studio off the kitchen. She even has a fancy air filtration system so she can work in the winter when it's too cold to open the windows. The front of the house is practically drowning in wildflowers, and she's got a little garden where tomatoes and squash are starting to come in. We go in the front door, and I kick my shoes off, following her through the tidy blue living room/dining room and out the back of the tiny kitchen to her studio.

"Wow." I admire the pieces she's been working on in Paris

as she unpacks them. She has me help her set them up. She'll be using them to apply to a couple gallery shows in the fall and winter. Iris is a fan of oils, which have that distinct tacky smell. Just like her pieces from the winter show I saw in February, these paintings are close-ups. Put together, though, they form one image of two people, one sitting, the other standing, staring out a window in a beautifully sparse bedroom. Each piece is a slice of their bodies in relationship to each other, all from different angles. I stop and stare at one of a hand hovering over a bare shoulder. The tension in it makes me shiver. The hesitation is heavy and worrying, which conflicts with the bright and colorful brushstrokes.

"It's . . ." Iris waits. I know she wants to see what I'll say before she tells me anything. "It's like snapshots of their whole relationship over time," I decide. "Here"—I point to where a hand grips an elbow, the other hand over it gently—"the person sitting needs comfort and is grateful the other is there. But here"—I point to the one that chilled me—"the second person is hesitating, like they might not be welcome. Like they're fighting."

"You have a good eye, Sera." Iris is smiling. "That's the goal. That one moment doesn't just hold the present but the past and the future too."

"Are they a couple?" I ask, turning to the next, a cheek pressed against a stomach in a thin blue dress. There's an intimacy, but it doesn't feel like love, like the way I feel pulled toward Luke even when he's miles away.

Iris brings me a cup of tea and stands next to me, looking over her pieces. "Sisters," she says quietly. She gestures to the gold velvet sofa across the room, and we sit. "Now, tell me about what I've missed."

I tell her about the kids and their amazing creations. I fill her in about Luke a little, and she cheers. I blush and change the subject to our trip to Boston, and the painting Luke loved at the Isabella Stewart Gardner Museum. "He always did like a darker palette," she says.

"I've been getting him to do a little more artwork, but he's not very serious about it."

Iris shrugs. "Art doesn't have to be serious."

I think about that for a minute, looking past her paintings to the waving grasses between the marshes outside the window. Everything has become serious in the last couple years for me. Art in particular. It was all I had left that made me feel like I still had control in my life. But I guess it's silly to expect every minute of your life to be important.

"Those are very cool," I say again, pointing at her paintings.

She smiles. "It was just such a treasure to go. I'm so grateful. And I'm so glad to see you enjoyed your time too. The kids really took to you. I was looking at some of their work. You did a great job. I'm so proud of you."

"Thanks, Iris," I say, smiling at her.

She puts her mug of tea on the coffee table and claps her hands together. "All right, time to eat!"

For dinner, she's prepped a tarte she learned to make in her French cooking course, and we eat our way through quite a few of the cheeses she brought back.

"Okay, this one smells like an old dirty sock"—I laugh—"but it tastes like . . . I don't know what—but it's delicious," I say, scooping up another piece of the offending goop with some baguette. "Maddy's going to love stuff like this."

"That seems to be the trick—the stinkier, the better," Iris says. "You'll be well prepared to find the good stuff when you go." She winks. "Your application is in, right?"

I sigh and feel the tears rise up. I let them. Iris scoots her chair closer to me at the kitchen table, a concerned look in her eyes. "It is, and I do want to go," I start, wiping my eyes, "but—"

"You'll get in! I know it. I've already submitted my reference and showed the photos of your work to one of the directors, and she loved it." She reaches across the table and squeezes my hand, and I place my other one on top of hers, steadying us both as I finally tell her the truth.

"It's not that," I say. "Iris . . . I'm sick. My donated heart is failing, and my treatment options have run out. All that's left is a new heart, which . . . well, it can take years to get off the heart transplant list. I probably won't be able to go next year. If I'm even still around."

Iris tries to hold it together, but like everyone in my life she's shocked, heartbroken, and all the things I feel too but am perhaps just used to. I let her dissolve into tears for a few minutes. I hug her and assure her how grateful I am for the job, her mentorship, and the great memories she helped me make this summer. When she gets ahold of herself, I ask her if she'll critique my application paintings in person.

"Might make you feel better," I say, with a sad smile.

"Looking at your art always makes me feel better," she says. "Show me." She blots the last of her tears away with her cloth napkin.

I get my pieces and set them up on easels she brings in from her studio.

"This one is my favorite at the moment." I put the future me painting in the center.

"It's beautiful, Sera. The underwater theme is so interesting to look at. You have such a good eye. And your technique has really improved. Maybe you can defer if you get in but can't go next year."

I nod, wiping my own tears away, and we switch to talking about the kids and who might have some real talent and should stick with it.

"I always saw it in you, and Luke too, when you were younger. There was something advanced about the way you both saw things. I thought it might be because you went through something so big when you were infants, that it maybe gave you a broader perspective, an ability most of us have to wait a lifetime to access. Now I'm sure that's true."

"I don't want my art to be seen as good or more valuable just because I might die young," I say slowly. "And Luke's work blows me away and he doesn't even practice much. I hope he picks it up again."

"Tell him," Iris says. "Sometimes it just takes someone we love telling us what they see in us for us to take a chance on ourselves."

CHAPTER TWENTY-EIGHT

Sera

On Monday, Luke asks if I want to go out to his soon-to-be part-time campus with him. He needs to drop off some paper-work he finally got back from his dad, and he says he wants me to see it.

"I know you're mad at me for not reaching," he says as we drive, "but it's a great school, really."

"I'm not mad at you," I insist. "I just wish you would admit you have real talent that's worth exploring." Thinking about what Iris said, I add, "I think you could be an amazing artist *and* whatever else you want. You don't have to be one or the other."

"That sounds like a lot," he admits as he pulls off the highway.

"And baseball, work, your family, school, friends, and *girls* weren't?" I tease.

He blushes and laughs a little. "I guess you have a point."

"Of course I do." I poke him in the shoulder. "I know you." I gently poke him in the ribs and he smiles his gorgeous unfiltered smile. He parks the car in a very empty parking lot, then unbuckles and slides to the middle of the bench seat, reaching for me. I'm in his lap in seconds, unable to keep my hands to myself. He hasn't shaved in a couple days, and his cheeks are a little scratchy, his chin chafing mine as I capture his mouth in a kiss. His hands make their way across all the sharp points of me, shoulder blades, elbows, wrists, and then he pulls me closer, his tongue moving over mine, liquid and slow. I'm instantly flushed with want.

"You do know me," he murmurs as he takes a breath. I groan a little too loud as his hands tense against my hips when I shift against him. He takes another long, slow breath, holding me still. "We shouldn't. Not here." But he doesn't let go right away, and I take the chance to press my chest to his and kiss him one more time before I ease off his lap.

"Serious business to attend to," I joke, once my heart rate is calm and my skin has stopped buzzing. I sneak a sip of his mostly melted iced coffee. "Shall we?"

Luke grabs his backpack, and we head to the main building. The campus is nice. Green and open, even if it is small. Luke drops his paperwork off in the administration office, and they hand him a thick folder and tell him he can start registering for classes as soon as today.

"Can we walk around?" I ask, and the secretary nods, sliding visitor badges over.

"You can't get into locked buildings with these," she says, "but the main building is open. You're welcome to come to orientation even as a part-time student, so anything you can't see today you can request to see that weekend before classes start the following week."

It all feels so soon. I'll be nineteen by then, and I feel a small thrill at knowing I've made it further into adulthood. It's the little achievements that matter.

"Let's go see where you'll be going to class and stuff," I say to Luke once we're back in the hall. "Maybe check out the library for a good study spot?" I wink.

"Sure." He takes my hand in his, rubbing his thumb across my knuckles.

"And for the day, can we just pretend that my heart transplant is scheduled and happening and there's nothing to be anxious about in the next few months other than eight a.m. classes and staying in touch while you're here and I'm in Boston?"

Luke's lips quirk up. "I can do that."

"Yeah?"

"Yeah."

I lean up and kiss him on the cheek and then pull him down the hall.

We wander for a while, poking our heads into large, empty lecture halls dark with wooden paneling, and long, bright computer labs. The library doesn't have many secret corners, sadly, but it has some cozy study rooms along one side and a beautiful view of the quad.

"The business finance professors are this way." Luke points down a sad-looking hallway and starts down it. "I wonder if the guy I interviewed with is here. He's from Northport too." Luke seems excited, and I try to feel the same. But it sounds so boring compared to who he actually is, even though I know what he ends up doing for work won't define him or change him.

The offices are all closed and quiet.

"They're probably getting the last few student-free days of summer vacation in. My dad's always grumbling about kids showing up at his office before classes even start at Emerson," I say. As we pass the next hallway, I notice a splash of colorful art hanging on the wall. "What's this way?"

Luke shrugs, and we go to check out what turns out to be the art wing. Student artwork decorates the hall. Most of the studios are closed, but we find one propped open by a paint can. I raise my eyebrows at Luke and pull the door open. The room has a high ceiling and long, clear windows against the far wall that let in beautiful light. There are four sections, one in each corner, that look like they belong to artists of different mediums. A sculptor, two potters, and what must be a screen printer, whose desk is littered with small tins of paint, carved wooden print blocks, and a stack of silk screens.

We wander toward the window and look out. The early clouds have cleared off, and the sky is blue and brilliant.

"Can I help you?" a voice says from the doorway, and we both jump.

"S-sorry," Luke stammers, "the door was open."

"He's starting here in a few weeks," I add. "I wanted him to check out the studios."

"Ah, okay. Welcome," the young woman says as she makes her way to what must be her corner, the desk with all the printmaking supplies.

"These are great," Luke says, gesturing to the drying rack next to her station. "Are you combining screen printing with linocuts?"

The woman nods and launches into a description of her project. She lights up as she talks, and I can't help but picture Luke and her making prints together, getting dinner after class, dancing at parties, maybe even dating. The idea of it hurts, but I'm not going to kid myself. Even though we agreed to pretend today, that's a more likely future for him. Maybe not *this* girl, but someone like her.

As we say goodbye and head back into the hall, I can't help but get excited for him again.

"I can't wait to visit you here," I say, taking his hand again and sticking to our pretending-everything-is-fine plan. "I could sit in on your business classes and then come model for your art homework."

Luke gives me a half-hearted smile.

"Wait, is it uncool to have your pre-college girlfriend come visit? I don't want to cramp your style." It's a joke, but it's also got some truth in it. "Abbi broke up with her boyfriend before Thanksgiving freshman year. She said it was too much."

"No." Luke stops, turning to me. He takes my hands. "I mean, yes, you should come visit. You're not too much. I don't want anyone but you."

I don't bother to say that he might feel that now, but hopefully won't always, because he actually sounds upset.

"Okay." I slip out of his grip and wrap my arms around him. "Then you're stuck with me."

"Happily," he whispers into my hair.

"You'll have to take me to try the terrible cafeteria lunches and talk about philosophy or psychology or whatever other classes you're taking." I laugh, pulling away from him and heading toward the door. We step back into the August heat.

"Or"—Luke swings his backpack around to his front and fishes out a couple containers of food and a bag from Lorell's—"we could eat on the quad."

"Sounds amazing."

He lays out a beach towel on the grass in the shade of a big oak tree. He's packed drinks, sandwiches, fruit, and pastries. We keep playing the *what-if* game, spinning imaginary scenarios of us together here or him visiting me in Brookline, or even in Paris next summer, now that my application is fully submitted. Something about having plans in place makes it easier to invent dreams about the future, even if they probably won't come true.

"Maybe we could do our own study abroad together. After I go to Paris with Maddy, I'll know my way around, and we can see the art and soak up the culture."

"If by *culture* you mean *cheese*, I'm in," Luke says, grinning. The sun reflects the strands of copper in his hair. I reach out and play with it, and he closes his eyes.

"I want to go so badly." I whisper it, in case the universe can hear and is keeping tally on my wishes.

"You will," Luke says, opening his eyes.

"Maybe." It's as much as I'm willing to admit for now.

Luke is itching to sign up for classes, so while I polish off my sandwich, he creates his student account on his phone with the paperwork he was given and starts picking courses.

"Does this sound like too much?" he asks, passing his phone over. "They say to start with three classes if you're doing part-time like I am, but that feels like so little."

"I'm not sure," I admit. "Abbi would know. Or you could ask Izzy." He nods and goes fishing for the last pastry before I get my hands on it. I scroll through the list and frown. It's all basics and business classes, nothing art, nothing literature, nothing that I know will interest that curious, visual part of his mind. I find the course lists and look through them quickly.

"You should take this Graphic Design 101 class." I show him the screen. "It fits with the days you're here, and it's only a pass/fail."

Luke's face falls a little. "I don't know, Sera. I don't really have the time . . ."

"Do it for me?" I finally ask, pushing past the silliness of our fake game to the reality ahead of us. "Take it for me. Just the one class. And if you like it, take another, but if you don't, then you don't have to. I just . . . I just don't want you to miss out on a great opportunity. And *I* might not be able to take classes like that, so maybe it's selfish, but if not this first semester, at least in the first year? Promise? Just try?"

Luke watches me rambling. His green eyes are sad, like there's a shadow over them. He takes his phone back and adds the class to his schedule.

"I'll let you know how it goes," he says as he pulls me into his arms and kisses me. This kiss is small and simple, not hot and desperate like earlier. This kiss feels like the kind we'd have ten or twenty years from now, comfortable and accepting, honest and real.

CHAPTER TWENTY-NINE

Sera

At my next appointment with Dr. Lee, my parents and I learn that nothing has changed. Like always, I have my vitals, EKG, echo, and all the regular tests first. I change into the papery hospital top and slip on my headphones and listen to the podcast Maddy sent me about ultraviolet light's effect on vegetables. At some point I switch to an audiobook about the intersection of art and the environment that Abbi has been bothering me to read so we'll have something to talk about the next time I see her. She's still up in Maine with Cam. She's sent a few pictures to the family group chat that I responded to, but other than that, we haven't talked.

The nurses and techs are quiet and quick. In less than an hour I'm back in my clothes, my chest still a little sticky from the ultrasound gel, sitting in Dr. Lee's corner office, hearing the same info all over again. None of this is new, and yet the wound is made fresh again. My heart is failing. My name is too far down the list for real hope, but we all claw at it anyway. My parents ask Dr. Lee to repeat things, but I never need any of the bad news repeated. It sticks in my mind after one utterance, like useless lyrics to a generic pop song. I have time to look around her office and spy on the shelves of books and the photos and knickknacks from all the patients she's had over the years. Time to wonder what I'll give her if I get another heart, what my family might send if she tries but can't save me.

If I stay stable, my next visit will be in three months. In the meantime, because things could move fast if I don't, I'm given a bunch of paperwork to do and numbers to call, along with a binder to fill out with my end-of-life wishes.

"It'll feel good to be prepared," Dr. Lee says.

I flip through the binder in the back seat as we drive home and start a section for each person I want to leave instructions or notes for: Mom, Dad, Abbi, Maddy, and Luke.

My hand shakes a little as I write his name. The papers suggest I write whatever I want to, not to worry about how the other person might take it or interpret it. Still, it's hard not to imagine everyone's reactions, particularly Luke's. It feels like I could have a lifetime to say goodbye to him and it still wouldn't be enough.

When we cross over the Sagamore Bridge, the sun is out and reflecting off the canal in bright flashes of white gold. I roll my window all the way down, breathing in the salty air. It's weird to think about whether I want a death doula or if I want to be cremated or turned into a tree when I feel so alive. All I know for sure is that I don't want to be plugged in and hospital-bound for long stretches of time. For some reason, that's easy to know, and I write it quickly on the first page before putting the binder aside.

Without work, I fill the days with painting new pieces. Mostly I paint by myself but sometimes with Luke. I play games and watch movies with Mom and Dad, hang out at the beach with Maddy and Luke. I go to a few bonfires with the whole crowd of Northport kids, but don't stay long. Most of the town has gotten wise to my situation, and it feels like I'm a sad sort of celebrity. Everyone is a tad too nice. They get quiet about their joys when I join around the fire, even though I tell them it's fine. They give me free pizza at Dockside, and the clerks at Lorell's put aside the best muffins for me. It's nice, but it's also a lot. I no longer feel like it's just me and my family waiting for my heart to give out. It feels like all of Northport is holding its breath too.

When someone from my health insurance calls to ask if I want a home visit to evaluate home care options in Northport, I say yes, because it seems like the smart thing to do. But we're all left a little worn out after their visit, even though it's barely past noon. To get through the day, Mom suggests we make a big, complicated dinner, taking out a recipe for homemade tacos that involves a lot of different marinades and salsas and giving everyone a task. I miss Abbi when it's time to slice the peppers and Mom makes me wear two layers of gloves and an old pair of her giant sunglasses.

"I'm not allergic to spicy peppers, Mom. This is ridiculous." The glasses are heavy and stretch way up past my eyebrows.

"Trust me, those things will make you cry buckets," she

says, so I leave it, and crack old-timey movie star jokes until I'm done.

Dad makes margaritas and pours me one with a small splash of tequila so I can "understand the experience better." We're finishing up the last of the tacos when there's a knock on the front door.

"What's for dessert?" I ask as Mom jumps up.

"I didn't make anything, sweetie."

Before I can complain about the lack of sugar, she opens the door and Maddy steps inside.

"Thanks, Mrs. Watkins. Hey, Sera!" She sweeps in and pulls me up out of my chair before I can ask why she's knocking at the door like a weirdo instead of just coming in like usual.

"I'm here on official fairy god . . . friend duties," she says, pushing me toward the stairs. "I've been instructed to kidnap you for the evening. Let's go." She nudges me up the first step.

"What?" I protest, and she keeps pushing.

"God, you're slow! Let's *go*. You're putting on that yellow dress and we'll brush your hair, then you're coming with me."

"What's going on?" I look back at my parents, who are giggling at the table. I know it must be something with Luke if Maddy is set on me wearing the dress, but Mom just shrugs and Dad waves, clearly in on whatever is happening.

In my room, Maddy digs out the dress and makes me put it on.

"Wow, it looks better than it did before. Okay, spin, spin."

I do, to please her, and find it doesn't make me dizzy, so I do it again.

"Okay, you have to tell me what's up, Maddy—please?"

"Nope, Luke swore me to secrecy, and that's all you need to know!" She digs around on my vanity, looking through jewelry. She selects a dangly pair of earrings Abbi got me that I never wear, and demands I take off the art teacher necklace. Then she slips an unfamiliar oval locket around my neck. I crack it open. There's a tiny picture of my family on one side and one of me, Maddy, and Luke on the other.

"That's from me," Maddy states, "just so we're clear."

I hug her. "I'll take it to my grave," I say, dead serious.

"That's the point," she says, a tiny wobble in her voice before she lets me go. "Okay, let's see: dress, jewelry, now hair . . . let's just brush it out, leave it long. Or, wait . . . can I give you bangs?"

"Ummm . . ."

She pulls out haircutting scissors.

"Do you just carry those around?" I ask as she sits me down in front of the mirror.

"How else do you think I keep my hair so fresh?" She tousles her bobbed hair, which has remained very sleek for the whole summer, now that I think about it.

She goes to the bathroom and comes back with a wet towel, dampens the front of my hair, and then pauses. "Ready?"

"I trust you." I smile, then close my eyes as she combs out the wet hair and snips. I feel the strands falling into my lap and try not to panic.

"Okay, wait, I just need to . . ." She snips a little more, and I hear the sound of my blow-dryer being dug out, and after some drying and last snips, she finally tells me I can open my eyes.

"Wow." I'm grateful I trusted her. The bangs are more subtle than it sounded like they were going to be, soft and light, and they make me look a little older. I play with them a bit and then laugh. "Thanks, Mads."

"Perfect, I know. You don't need to tell me. Time to go!"

She tells me to get a light sweater and meet her downstairs. I hear her whispering with my parents as I find my bag and some shoes as well as a sweater and take a last look at myself in the mirror.

I give us a minute. Me and my reflection. To remind us that we're here, alive. I turn my wrists and look at the thin, pulsing veins in my forearms. I pinch my cheeks lightly until they're a little red. My hair is a little frizzy at the ends, but the swoopy bangs are staying in place. I run a hand through them, fluffing out the sides, and everything falls back into place. My scar peeks out from behind the chain of the locket.

I try to forget the watch on my wrist tracking my every move. I push away the tiredness that seeps from the center of my back out to my limbs, which are sometimes too much to lift these days, but are feeling good tonight. I erase the diagnosis, and the list, and my unfinished binder from my mind. I focus on being a girl who's going out to meet her boyfriend for a surprise.

I stop by the bathroom to brush my teeth and take one of Abbi's prepared "safety bags" from the lower cabinet. It's just an old makeup pouch with tampons, liners, and painkillers, but also condoms, lube, and single-pack wet wipes.

Once I'm downstairs, Maddy rushes me into her car and takes off, blasting some new artist rapping in French. She tells me Sienna is helping her prepare for our trip musically as well.

Apparently Berlin will require clubbing. She's immune to my piercing looks, refusing to share more details about tonight. When we hit Main Street, she turns left down the alley past the bookshop, then left again onto Harborside Main, slowing as we hit the abandoned end. She stops in front of the ghost of Frappie's, puts the car in park, and announces that we've arrived. Through the dusty, dark windows of the shop, I can see the soft orange glow of flickering lights. My heart flips. I take a slow, stuttering breath.

"You okay?" Maddy asks.

"Yeah." I lean over and hug her. "Thank you."

"You don't even know what's up." Maddy laughs.

"But I know you helped, so thank you." I let her go and get out, waving as she turns around and drives away.

The night is warm, but the breeze off the ocean is cool and fresh. It pushes me toward the door to Frappie's, where I find a sign in Luke's hand that mimics a Paris metro sign, only it says my name. I trace the edges with my finger, then open the door and step into a dream.

String lights by the dozen dangle and weave through the rafters overhead, giving the whole room a warm, golden glow. Against the counter leans a model of the Eiffel Tower, and the arched doorway into the kitchen has the Arc de Triomphe framing it. The center of the room has been swept clear, and there are several layers of cushions and blankets around a small, low table covered in pastries and cheese. The bare wall to the left is lit up with a projector, paused on the opening shot of *Amélie*.

Luke stands at the corner of the lounge area he's set up,

dressed in a nice pair of jeans and a button-up, but thankfully no tie. He's tamed his hair some, though it's already rebelling as he runs a hand through it, nervous.

"I thought, in case you can't go to Paris yourself next year, I could bring Paris to you." He's twisting the stem of a flower in his hand, and I take it from him, sticking it behind his ear. Then I drape my arms over his shoulders and lean up to capture his lips with mine. He smiles, and our teeth click. Then he wraps his arms around my waist and twirls me once, carefully.

"Do you like it?" he asks.

"I love it."

I kiss him again, hard and quick, and he slides a hand up into my hair, holding me to him.

"Iris lent me a series of photos from her museum visits too," he says, finally taking a breath of space from kissing me. "I thought we could look through those first, then watch the movie?"

I nod and we settle into the pillows. I select a blue macaron and take a bite as he starts the slide show. It tastes slightly floral and isn't too sweet.

"Did Maddy make these?" I ask, and Luke nods. "Wow, she's going to go places." It's gone in seconds, and I move on to a tiny pain au chocolat. We go through the photos, getting to the Musée d'Orsay last. I ask him to pause it on one of the large water lily photos, standing and brushing the croissant crumbs from my fingers. Up close, the colors blur and pixilate. I stand there and squint my eyes and breathe in and imagine I'm really there—the dappled sunlight streaming in from skylights, the long, curved benches behind me empty. Luke's shadow joins mine, his chin coming to rest on my shoulder, his arms around me. My stomach flutters.

"It's beautiful," I mutter.

"You're beautiful," he says into my hair, his lips trailing down the side of my neck. My body heats, and the butterflies in my stomach travel lower. He pulls me back toward the blankets and puts on the movie, dims some of the twinkle lights, plays with the volume so it's not too loud, then sits behind me. I take a sip of my lemonade and then settle back into his arms.

I've seen the movie before. Amélie's parents think she has a heart defect, so she lives a safe, quiet, and lonely childhood, but finds small joys in the oddest things. I cringe when her mother is crushed outside Notre-Dame. I always start to enjoy the movie when she finds the hidden box in her apartment and finally starts living.

I take in the scenes of the city as she bikes around Paris on her mission, but I'm distracted by the heat of Luke's whole body pressed against mine. I trace the lines of his veins down his arms, line up the pads of my fingers against his, and follow the crosshatches and wrinkles in his palm. Soon Amélie's mission to push her father to travel and her coworkers to fall in love is a background to the desperate need in my chest as it radiates through me. I turn in Luke's arms and push him back against the pillows. He wraps his hands around my waist under my dress as I straddle him. He whispers my name, playing with the edge of my underwear, and I feel no embarrassment at the heat I know he must feel pulsing from between my legs. I lean forward and kiss him slow at first, then faster. I pull away and work at the buttons on his shirt, revealing more of his scar as it leads to the muscles of his stomach. I put my lips to that wrinkle where he was opened, where a part of me will always live, then sit up and pull the dress over my head.

Luke's eyes go wide and he pulls me closer. I lean away for just a second to reach the pouch in my bag, unzip it, and pull out a condom.

"Sera." Luke swallows, and I kiss the rise and fall of his Adam's apple. His strong arms tense as he holds me at a distance, and I can feel him beneath me. "We don't have to do anything you're not—"

I interrupt him with my tongue, grinding my hips closer to his so I can feel him rub against me. "I'm ready," I say against his mouth, pulling back and looking him in the eyes. "I want you, Luke." Just saying those words out loud sends a thrill through me. Luke groans and rolls us over. Suddenly I feel nervous, like I want to rush through the next few steps. I start to shimmy my underwear off, and Luke stops me.

"Wait," he says, trailing his mouth down my neck, past my bra, to my hip. He lowers himself until he's resting his chin on my thigh, looking up for permission, with his hands gripping my hips. "Let me?"

"Yes." My voice is dry, desperate. His fingers leave a burning trail of goose bumps down my legs as he removes my underwear without breaking eye contact. I suck in a breath as he dips his head between my legs. I flutter my eyes open as he stops and looks up at me, worried at first, then grinning, before leaning back down. In just a few minutes, with the firm press of his focused mouth paired with the flick of his tongue, my whole body is alive and tingling with release.

He sits back on his heels, and I push up on my elbows to take him in. He's breathing low and fast, his chest rising and falling in time with mine, his eyes a dark, stormy ocean unable to look away from me. He stands up and discards his clothes until he's naked. I gape for a moment, heat rushing to my already warm cheeks. He kneels and I reach for him. His skin is hot, tacky, his fingertips wandering my body, unable to let go. My bra comes off, and the condom wrapper slips in my shaky fingers. I laugh again. Luke smiles, kisses me, and takes it, opens it with ease. I snatch it back, wanting to slide it on him myself. His whole body tenses, muscles pushing against his skin as I put it on. When I let go and lie back, he relaxes, breathes out slow and controlled, shaking his hair out of his eyes.

"Come here," I say.

He leans over me, blocking out the light from the movie flickering against the wall. I run my hands through his hair, kiss him as he lies against me. I slip one leg over his back, and we fumble for a moment as he reaches down and finds his way into me. The pressure is tight at first, but he moves slow, and the pain is sharp but quickly over, dulling into a pleasant throb.

"Are you okay?" he asks.

"Yes." I kiss him quick. "Let's just go slow?" I ask. "I want to remember this." I trace his brow, his cheek. He nods and breathes slow, drops his head, and taps my nose with his.

"Me too."

I take a deep breath and reach my other leg around his thigh to pull him closer. He snatches a breath in, and I let out a low moan as the pressure builds again.

"Sera." His voice is deep with pleasure.

"Luke," I whisper into his ear.

After, Luke stays on top of me, showering my face with kisses until I can't stop giggling. Then he pulls away, rolling over onto his back, panting like he's just sprinted the bases after hitting a home run. I look over at him, my heart racing but holding strong. He laces his fingers through mine. The light from the movie flickers over us. I rest my head on Luke's chest and listen to his heartbeat, a familiar, steady rhythm, like the ocean pulling away and rejoining the shore.

CHAPTER THIRTY

Luke

I hadn't meant for us to have sex, though I'd be lying if I said it hadn't been in the back of my mind as I set up Frappie's. Mostly I just want to see Sera happy, like she is right now, tucked next to me beneath the blanket, going on and on about the colors in the film and wondering what Paris would look like in the rain. Her skin is cool to the touch but heating me up all the same.

When the movie ends, Amélie getting her own love story after helping everyone else, I reach for my phone and start another one. *Jeux d'enfants*. All I know is that it's about childhood friends falling in love. It's all in French again, and I wasn't able to find the subtitles, so we're a little lost. Neither Sera nor I are really paying attention, though. Her hands are wandering across my chest, sending little shocks of electricity coursing through me. I turn on my side and trace her cheek, her nose, her eyebrows as she wiggles them at me and laughs. I dip my hand lower and follow her collarbone, the thin line of her scar, where she was opened up and gifted me my life. I press my palm to her chest and feel her heart beat as though everything is fine, keeping the secret of her time left from us. I'd call EBE a traitor, but Sera wouldn't like that.

"She's gotten us this far, hasn't she?" she asks, like she's reading my mind.

I kiss her chest and whisper a thank-you and silently beg her to hold out because I don't think I'll be able to handle it if she doesn't.

We ignore the movie and mold ourselves together again. I feel the nostalgia creeping in over everything. Her diagnosis is like a high-pitched ringing in my ears, always there, always threatening to drown all the goodness out. I try to just stay present with her eyes holding mine, her lips on my ear telling me that everything is perfect.

And I believe it when she says it, sure that nothing has ever felt so good, so right in the universe as it does right now. Desperate for her to stay, for it all to stay just like this, like one long, perfect kiss.

CHAPTER THIRTY-ONE

Sera

August begins to slip away. The summer crowd thins and the heat peaks. Maddy and I plan a big beach party for my birthday. It's the night before Luke goes to his orientation, but that morning I wake up feeling nauseous and slow. The idea of trekking out to Thirds for the whole afternoon and evening is too daunting. I text Maddy to cancel while I nibble on some dry toast in my room, brought up on a tray by my dad, who hovers and fusses. I lean back into my pillows and sigh. The last few days have been like this.

"I'm sorry, sweetie," Dad says, sitting on the edge of my bed. "Maybe we could do something small here at the house? Just a few people? I'll make my famous grilled pizza?"

"That sounds great, Dad. Thanks."

He stands up again and comes to kiss me on the top of my head.

"It won't be the same here without you. If—if we don't find you a new heart." His voice is clear, and I'm glad. We've been working on this, saying what we feel when we feel it. My therapist agreed it would be good for everyone, but especially me, to know how much I'm loved but also to have support in the choices I've made.

"I'll work on haunting the place, but only if it comes to that," I say. He laughs.

"I'll go over and tell Luke and his family about pizza night. I'm sure the boys would like to come too."

I thank him and text Maddy the plan, asking her not to bring anyone else. I spend the day napping and wake up to the sounds of someone in my room. I open my eyes and find Luke on the window bench, sketch pad in his lap.

"Are you drawing me?" I ask, both delighted and embarrassed. He looks up at me, caught. I managed to shower earlier before I climbed back into bed, so I don't smell, but I can't look pretty.

"Getting you back for the boat portraits," he says with a shrug, then puts the pad down and slides into my bed with me. I snuggle into his chest and press my ear to his heart. The cold I've been feeling in my bones ebbs away. I listen to the strong regular beats, and with each one I make a wish for him: to make friends at school, to draw more, to save Harborside, to help his brothers through those awkward teen years, to find love again and again, to travel and see the world, to be a husband and a father and an uncle, and to grow old and cranky and silver with knowledge and time. I want him to share how he sees the world with as many people as he can—they'll all be better for it. I weave myself into these imagined moments and hope he'll always feel me with him when his heart races with joy. The pieces of me stitched into him, holding him here in the universe for as long as it takes to live a good, long life.

"What are you thinking about?" he asks, playing with my bangs.

"Your future."

He swallows, and his heart picks up.

"Our future," I lie, like it's a spell to break his sadness.

Adam and Oliver are sent up to get us a few minutes later. Adam catapults himself onto the foot of my bed.

"Wake up! Time for pizza!" he shouts, somehow getting tangled in the blankets.

"Guys," Luke admonishes, sitting up and helping Adam out of the nest he's gotten himself into. "You're supposed to knock."

"And you're supposed to keep the door open," Oliver sings, "like Mom said! Six inches!"

Luke stammers, and I dissolve into laughter. We got caught on his bed last week, and I thought Paula's head was going to explode. She came up with the six-inches rule on the spot, which was actually pretty impressive.

Downstairs, Mom and Paula are working with Maddy to decorate the patio a little. Maddy bounces over and gives me a hug.

"Happy birthday, Sera."

"Do you have the thing?" Paula asks her.

"Oh! I forgot it in the car!"

She turns and disappears around the corner of the house, and I catch Mom's eye. She's grinning, but she shrugs.

"Wasn't me."

Maddy comes back with a small box even though I asked for no gifts.

"From everyone who wanted to be here," Maddy says, handing it to me. I'm just opening the edge when the porch door creaks open. I turn around and find Abbi hovering there, Cam just behind her. She barely has time to say hello before I'm out of my chair and crushing her in a hug.

"Hi." She laugh-cries into my shoulder.

"Hi," I say, getting a curl of her hair stuck in my mouth. I let her go and say hi to Cam too, taking the box of cookies he's holding out for me. They join us at the table, and soon everyone's laughing at stories about their hiking mishaps in Maine.

When we're done with pizza, Abbi goes in for cake plates, and I follow. She pulls out the nice china plates that we never use, and shrugs when I ask if that's okay.

"It seems like a thing to celebrate," she says. "We weren't sure you'd make it here, right?"

"Yeah, nineteen." I smile. "Maybe I'll finally get into that smoking habit I've been dying to try."

"Sera!"

"What?!" I cross my arms, but she knows I'm joking. She looks at me for a beat, and suddenly her eyes fill with tears. I tell her about the new rule: Say what you're thinking and feeling no matter what.

"I thought I might miss it," she whispers.

"My death?"

"No, well. Maybe a little, but no, you growing up." She hiccups, and I pull her into a hug again.

"Sorry I didn't call," I say.

"It's okay. I think we needed that fight."

I nod and tip my head back to the porch. "So you and Cam aren't sick of each other after being stuck in a tent?"

She laughs. "We're great. We're actually getting a place together for next semester."

"Really?! You're not going to take any more time off school?"

She shakes her head. I hug her again.

"I'm so glad. I can't wait for you to get way too smart for your own good and write a wordy dissertation I won't understand."

"I wish." She swallows, tries again. "I hope you'll be there for it."

"Me too." I hug her again, and we stay there for a few minutes, just two sisters sorry for hurting each other's feelings. Then we wipe our tears and go outside for cake.

After cake, I open my gift as we all relax in the yard and watch the bats start to swoop overhead. Oliver and Adam do cartwheels in the grass. Mom fills her and Paula's glasses again, and Dad is asking Cam about the apartment he and Abbi are planning to rent. Maddy scooches over as she sees me reach for the stack of papers inside the box. They're handwritten requests from every shop on Main Street.

"What is this?" I ask, flipping through a few. Maddy and Paula share a look and explain.

"We know you didn't want gifts, but everyone in Northport wanted to show you how much they love you."

"They're commissions," Paula jumps in. "We want you to make some art for the town."

"It's a job?" I laugh, incredulous.

"Yep!" Maddy hugs me. "Don't think you were getting out that easy."

I pass the box to Mom, who bursts into tears and has to be led back inside by Paula and Abbi. Dad takes it from her and shakes his head.

"Window art designs for every shop on Main Street. Do you think you'll be up for it?" Maddy asks.

I nod. "I'll make the time. But I'll need help."

Luke comes and sits on the arm of my chair, reading through the papers from each shop owner, his eyes glassy.

"This is a great idea," he tells Maddy. "I'll help."

"Us too," Oliver says, butting his head between us. I tousle his hair, and he darts away. Luke slides an arm around me and squeezes. It's a perfect present. Something that means I'll leave part of myself in Northport whether I'm in Paris next summer or . . . not.

I head upstairs after saying good night to everyone and take a few minutes at my desk, coming up with ideas for the commissions. Outside my window I see Luke's light turn on, and I go over to my window and crack it open. He opens his too, turns his music on, and cranks it up just enough so I can hear it. He disappears and comes back without his shirt on, getting ready for bed. Through my tiredness I wish I could sneak over and spend the night in his bed, but he has to leave early tomorrow.

My phone pings three times suddenly, and I dig it out of my

pocket. It's a health chart alert, a text, and an email from Dr. Lee. Each one has the same message.

> Happy birthday, Sera. We received the news today that you've been moved up and are now second in line for your match type. Please call me in the morning to discuss.

I look back up for Luke, but his light is off.

"Second," I whisper down to EBE with disbelief. I'm so grateful for her, and I've asked her for so much over the years, but I finally ask the thing I've been avoiding. "Think you can hold out for me?" She beats strong and steady in reply, and I let myself picture it: The transplant and all those future moments with Luke becoming a reality. Paris and school and love and family and a life in Northport. I shut off my light and settle into the window bench, watching the stars as they grow brighter, shining a miracle down on me.

CHAPTER THIRTY-TWO

Sera

I wake to a pounding headache and a stuffy nose. My luck. Just as things seem to be looking up, I get hit with a summer cold. I'm glad that Luke is off to his orientation for the weekend and Maddy's got work so I can focus on resting. Luke texts me from the sad, gray-looking dorm he's been put up in and asks if I want to help him with plans for the Northport Labor Day picnic when he's back on Monday.

Sera

of course, maybe we can sneak away and spend the night at the beach at the end of the universe? . . . I miss you

Luke

I miss you too—my roommate for the weekend is trying to get me to help him pick up girls at a party tonight . . .

Sera

you should go! Maybe dance on a table and come back with a good story!

Luke

No way

Sera

fine deprive me of my entertainment

btw, I've got some really really good news to share. I'll tell you in person when you're back!

Luke

❤ news?! I can't wait that long! Talk later?

Sera

tomorrow—enjoy your night! 😉

Mom comes up with soup and crackers. She takes my temperature and checks my vitals. Everything seems fine, the temp is low, and there are no erratic beats from my heart in the hour we sit together. I'm just tired.

"It's just a cold, Mom. Also, look." I show her the messages from Dr. Lee. Mom stares in disbelief for a moment while I grin, her lawyer eyes skimming the text to confirm meaning. "It's real," I say.

"Oh my god, honey!" She wraps me in a tight hug and won't let go.

"Mom, you're suffocating me," I say, laughing. She pulls away reluctantly and a new email notification pops up on my screen. It's from the fellowship in Paris.

"Oh—the fellowship just emailed me."

"What does it say?"

I sit up and run a hand through my tangled hair. "This is not how I pictured getting *good* news," I say, looking down at the pj's I'm still in.

"It doesn't matter," Mom says. "Open it!"

I open it.

> Dear Mlle Watkins,
>
> We are thrilled to welcome you to the 2028 Paris Artist Cohort! Your work shows great promise. You are exactly the kind of artist we like to nurture and support here at Le Jeanne Fontaine Collaboratif. The details of your acceptance and the timeline for your stay with us are attached. Please let us know your acceptance or your regrets by October 1.

"I'm going to Paris! I'm going to get a new heart and go to Paris!" This all feels so unreal in my stuffy head but no less delightful, even though having to decide by October seems impossible. I have to tell Iris. I have to tell Luke! And Maddy! I pull my mom into a crushing hug and start dialing Maddy before I remember she's at work and text her instead. I text Luke too, a quick notice of more good news, asking him to call me. Maybe I can get him to come visit next summer too.

However, instead of all this good news calming my mom, it makes her a little more anxious.

"I wish you'd let me take you to the ER, just to make sure," she says, smoothing my sticky hair off my forehead.

"I'm okay. Really. I don't want to be in the hospital for no reason. It'll make me worse. I just need to rest. Thanks for the soup, though."

She leaves me alone, and when she comes back for my dishes later, I ask her to stay. We pull up old movies on my laptop and I fall asleep on her shoulder, the smell of her perfume in my dreams, the sounds of old Hollywood accents in my ear.

When I wake up, it's dark and my phone is buzzing. Luke's calling. I answer in the middle of a yawn and hit the video button.

"Hey," he says. He's outside somewhere, sitting against a brick wall. His hair is getting too long and keeps falling in his eyes.

"Hi." I climb out of my bed. "Give me a second." It's almost midnight. I start digging around on the floor for more clothes.

"Where are you going?" he asks as I almost drop my phone while pulling on his baseball hoodie and heading downstairs.

"To the tree house. I've been inside all day." He looks worried, and I tell him to stop. The latest dose of cold medicine kicked in hours ago, and I feel good right now. "I'm fine, it's just a little cold. And I don't want to wake anyone up. I can make it to the tree house just fine."

Outside it's humid and hot, the air heavy and still. I'm grateful Luke helped Adam and Oliver restore the regular ladder to the tree house so I don't have to use the rope one. I heave myself into the small structure. They've redecorated a little, but it's still the space Luke and I made our own, with a scratched-up painting of the night sky on the roof. I can see the ghosts of our kid selves snuggling up underneath it and talking about all the adventures we'd go on as we grew up. Always together.

"You there?" Luke asks. I pull him out from the pocket of

the hoodie and prop him against one wall, leaning back against another.

"Yeah, I made it. It's *tiny*."

"We were tiny," he says.

"Minuscule," I joke.

"Sera, you're keeping me hanging here. What's the news?!"

"Oh, right. Sorry. Well, it's twofold. First, I got into the fellowship!"

Luke grins, looking proud but not surprised. "I knew you would."

"I have to reply by October if I'm going." Luke's face falls. We've been avoiding all reminders of my ticking clock, and talking about specific dates in the future always brings it up. "But I heard from my doctor last night, and I've moved up the list. It might not be by October, but there's a better chance now." My heart flutters with nerves.

"Really?" Luke says. The hope in his voice brings tears to my eyes.

"Yes. Really." I suddenly want to hug him so badly. I wrap my arms around myself, the smell of his hoodie enough for now. "I wish you were here."

"I'll be back soon."

"Maybe, when I'm better, we can go to one of those fancy Airbnb tree houses," I say.

"That'd be fun." He yawns.

"You're tired. How was the party?"

He shrugs. "Fine, same as all parties. Though I wasn't the only one not drinking, which was a nice change."

"Hey, I never drink."

He laughs. "Yeah, but you don't like those parties anyway."

"True. Bad music."

"Don't let Cam hear you say that. I think he played a house party in Falmouth last night."

"Oops." I laugh.

"Are our oaths still there?" Luke asks, leaning forward so more of his face takes up the screen.

"Our oaths?"

"Yeah, in the back corner, closest to the trunk."

I shuffle over and move the beanbag Oliver and Adam have stored up here and find the scratched-in words Luke is talking about.

"I forgot about these." My voice is a whisper.

I run my finger over the words there and read them aloud.

I, Luke Tisdale,
will always be there for Sera Watkins,
who saved my life.

I, Sera Watkins,
will always be there for Luke Tisdale,
a part of my heart.

"What saps," I say, wiping my eyes.

"It's still true, you know," Luke says.

"I didn't save your life," I argue.

"You did. You and EBE together. And this summer, well,

you've reminded me that it is *my* life. You're the best thing that's ever happened to me, Sera."

I let the tears welling in my eyes fall and say the first thing that comes to mind.

"I love you, Luke."

The words float out of my mouth and through the screen. Luke smiles the widest smile I've ever seen.

"I love you too, Sera."

CHAPTER THIRTY-THREE

Sera

I feel a little better in the morning and go for a short walk with Dad to Northport Beach to get some fresh air, but I quickly need to head home. The walk back is agony, my muscles cramping, my head pounding. My stupid immune system is having a rough time. I collapse into bed and sleep until dinner, then take my box of tissues and retreat again to sleep.

When I wake up in the middle of the night, I don't know where I am. The blankets feel unfamiliar under my stiff and swollen hands. Everything is foggy, distant. My body feels like it's vibrating out of reality. Time jumps. I'm in bed. I'm in the bathroom. I'm in bed again without the sheets, looking toward the windows and the dark rectangles of Luke's room. Suddenly Mom and Dad are there. I think I called them, but I can't be sure. My mouth is cottony. I ask for water, and Dad lifts a straw to my mouth while Mom retakes my temperature.

"Too high," Mom says.

"I'm calling." Dad pulls the straw away and thunders downstairs. His steps shake the whole house.

"Sera." Mom says it like it's not the first time she's tried to get my attention. I move my slow, sandpapery eyeballs toward her, wincing the whole way. She's outlined in purple light. Protected.

"You're shining." I smile at her, but she's not happy at the news.

"You have a fever, baby. We're going to the hospital."

I don't want to go to the hospital. We haven't finished all my death decisions; the binder is only half filled out. The text from Dr. Lee and the words in my fellowship acceptance letter float out of my head and spin around the room. *Second. Paris. Second.* It's dizzying.

Dad comes in with strangers. Giants with voices that don't make sense. They take me out of my bed, and I start to shiver, but they won't put the blanket back—they have their own. I'm moved to a spine board and floated out the door. The stairs chirp like birds as I'm carried down them. Mom's purple light bobs in my periphery. All the other lights are too bright, piercing through my eyes like knives. My body trembles with the erratic beat of my heart.

My heart.

EBE is crying, she's hurting, she's so sorry, she's tried so hard, but it's time for her to go.

It's time for us to go.

Outside, thunder rumbles loud and ominous. It chases some of the fog in my head away.

"My phone," I say as I'm lifted into the ambulance. Someone presses it into my hand. The EMT on my left attaches some monitors to my chest, puts cool compresses on my head, my arms, and my chest, and then starts a line of fluids. I feel a cold liquid rush into my arm. It shocks me back into reality. I understand him as he shouts instructions to the driver, tells my parents I'll be airlifted to Boston.

I lift my phone and it's calling Luke, thank god. I wasn't sure I'd be able to do it with my fingers turned to sausages. It rings and rings and rings. Then his voice fills my ear, his smooth, deep voice. I smile, but it's not really him, just voicemail. I listen to him ask me to leave a message or text if it's about fall softball league. There's a loud beep, and for a moment I don't know what to say.

"Luke," I say, struggling to get the words out. "You're the brightest light I've ever known. We'll always be part of each other—for us that's true." I pause, wait to see if more words want to make their way out of the tangle of my mind. "I love you, Luke." It feels so simple. It feels like there could never be enough. It has to be enough. I hang up and squeeze my phone in my hand as the ambulance screams through the night.

CHAPTER THIRTY-FOUR

Sera

My confusion doesn't abate. I'm at the hospital, but sometimes I blink away into sleep and come back to a new universe, no swimming in the ocean needed. But no, wait, I *am* in the ocean, off at sea, rocking in the waves of a storm. The sounds are so clear, the spray of rain against the hull, the flash of lightning illuminating my torn sail. I gasp for air, and I crawl my way across the deck and pull myself into consciousness.

I'm in a hospital bed, monitors sticky on my chest. The window curtains are drawn back to show a black city night, rain lashing the windows. Mom, Dad, and Abbi are in the room. I say something, and they all come to me, talking at once, like seagulls squawking overhead. I wince and they quiet. Mom talks first, then Dad. Abbi says something, and I ask her to repeat it.

"Luke is on his way."

"It's okay." My voice is tight, every word too much effort. "I love you."

There's another flash of lightning, and the rain intensifies against the windows. I slip into sleep again and wake with the monitors gone. Free of obligation. Free to die if I am ready.

Am I ready?

Mom is in bed with me, her hair tickling my cheek. I feel Dad's hand on my shoulder, Abbi sitting at my feet, her hand in mine. She's reading from book three of *The Soul Druid Chronicles*, which means she got the binder and my half-written wishes, which means this really is the end. I'm so sorry for leaving, but I'm so glad they're here. Time moves slowly. I sleep, and I wake to find myself surrounded by my family, though their positions have changed. Dad holding my feet. Mom brushing my hair. Abbi tucked in next to me, still reading. Her voice quiet and calming over the chaos outside. I'm too tired to talk, so I just stay, exist in the space between them for as long as I can.

EBE strains and sputters, and I tell her it's okay. She can let go.

I sink deeper into the ocean of light around me. The crashing waves are loud, but I hear the faint sound of my name.

"Sera!"

I shoot up out of the water, looking for whoever is calling me. Luke is up on the spaceship rock. He's wearing the new swimsuit his mom got him, the outer space one with the matching goggles we patched back together after a bully snapped them at camp yesterday. He waves a long, skinny arm at me, hurrying me along. I don't remember the number I shouted, but I swim as fast as I can toward the shore. In between strokes I see him running to meet me. I rush out of the waves, shells digging into my feet, my heart pounding with effort. Each one of those beats done and gone and given.

"Did I do it?" I gasp.

"So close." He grabs my hand, and we run together back to the rock, climbing up and leaving damp hand- and footprints behind, which evaporate into the blistering sun. At the top, he reaches down to help me, and he's no longer ten but thirteen. His braces are blue and pink, and he has a row of acne like a constellation along his chin. I grab his hand, let him help me up even though I can do it myself.

"Where should we go?" I ask. "Somewhere really far? The other side of the universe?"

"No, let's just try the closest galaxy. I want to see what Northport looks like from there."

"You won't be able to see Northport, silly. Just the Milky Way, *maybe* the sun."

"I'll know it." He shrugs and offers me his hand again. I slide mine into his and take a second to look at how we're linked. I look up to tell him I'm glad we've been thrown together, that I don't think there's anyone else I'd want to travel the universe with, but he's jumped ahead of me again. He's eighteen, handsome, tall. My heart races for a different reason.

Luke smiles down at me, strong and confident and kind. He looks out over the ocean at the gathering clouds.

"We should go, before the rain comes."

"I love you, Luke Tisdale," I say over the wind.

He turns back to me and grins wider, scoops me up and spins me around.

"I love you, Sera Watkins. And I've got you," he says, voice clear and deep in my ear. I relax. I breathe. "I'll keep you here," he promises as he puts me down and places a hand against his chest where the pieces of our hearts sit entwined. His scar lights up, and I trace the line of it. He moves his hand from his chest to mine. "And you'll keep me here, no matter where you go."

"Let's go together?" I ask, taking his hand again and turning to the ocean. It's choppy and wild, waves coming from all directions capped with frothy white foam. The water is a dark blue-green, almost like Luke's eyes as he meets my gaze and squeezes my hand tight in his.

"Together."

We sprint off the edge of the rock and plummet into the ocean. It's ice-cold and it tugs me down. I start to panic and pull on Luke's hand, my anchor, my home, my last line to the surface. There's a sudden light in the darkness, like someone's set a firework off underwater. For a second, I can see us both suspended there in the dark, surrounded by bubbles and seaweed and specks of sand that glint like dust in the sun, making the sea look like outer space. Luke is smiling. I reach for his face and the light fades.

Then so do I.

CHAPTER THIRTY-FIVE

Luke

The rain is coming down in sheets, and I'm soaked by the time I reach my truck. I told my roommate to let the organizers know I'd be gone, but not why. I couldn't repeat the words Abbi had said through the phone when I called her after listening to Sera's voicemail.

"We're in Boston. Sera's fighting, but . . . I think you should come."

It's a Sunday, so the traffic on Route 6 is frustratingly thick. I sit in the cab of my truck with the rain pounding overhead like the sky is dumping the whole ocean on us. I inch along with the other cars over the Sagamore. Finally we pick up speed as two lanes become three and people spill off until it's just me and the other idiots on Route 3 to Boston.

I remember the drive we took earlier this month to the doctor. The smell of the hospital waiting room. The moment I caught Sera sitting in a pool of light at the museum. The way she glowed around the edges. I can't imagine her light going out. I can't imagine living without her.

A car speeds onto the highway and cuts in front of me. I press on the brakes and slow down to avoid it, honking as long and loud as I can like I'm letting out a scream of rage. The driver doesn't even have their lights on. My frantic heart calms as the car speeds away. I move out of the lane, not wanting to be behind them, and I slow to five miles under the speed limit.

"I'm coming, Sera. I'm coming. Just hold on for me."

There's less traffic moving toward the bright blob of light that is Boston. Through the rain, still unyielding, my wipers on high, my body tense. I flex my fingers against the wheel and crack my neck. I feel my heartbeat and imagine Sera's breath on my ear with every pump of blood. Twenty minutes and I'll be there. I know she'll wait for me.

There's a crack of thunder as a flash of lightning hits a building to my left. It lights up the sky, sending sparks into the rain. I spare it a glance, immediately thinking I'll have to draw it for Sera, to show her the way the fire briefly touched each drop, like a nebula, spinning new stars into existence. I feel flooded with purpose.

It's Sera I'm thinking about when there's another flash right beside the road. It's so close I have to squint as it fills the car with light.

CHAPTER THIRTY-SIX

Sera

The light returns, and I fight it, pain in my chest, in my hands, in my head. So much pain I want to scream. I gasp awake, taking in air like I've never really had to breathe before. The pain is still there, and it sharpens me to awareness. So many wires run from my body to the machinery around me. The heavy fact of them ignoring my wishes makes tears spring to my eyes. This isn't what I wanted. Why is this all here? The pain narrows into rage. I fumble for the sticky tabs on my shoulder first, even though it hurts to move, and I peel one off, then another.

The machinery rats me out, alerting everyone within a five-mile radius that I'm disturbing its watch, but it can fuck off, because I won't be plugged in like a bad science fair project.

A nurse comes rushing in, my parents and Abbi right behind them. In my anger I narrow my gaze at them.

"How could you?" I mutter, my lips cracked and dry. "How

could you? I don't want to be plugged in to wait." I'm on the verge of tears, the anger is so powerful, but I don't care—let the anger take me, let it explode my fragile heart. I listen for EBE's frantic scrabbling, but there's an unfamiliar feeling, a long-ago-remembered sound in my chest instead.

"Sera, calm down," Mom says, helping the nurse maneuver the electrodes back onto me, interrupting my objections. "You've had a transplant. You're only one day out of surgery. Please."

I hear the words, but they don't really register because I'm listening instead to my body, that steady, strong *thump-thump-thump* echoing in my chest. I place my fingers on my wrist, and even there, the beats are regular. I count them like I've been taught to, and they don't skip dramatically. The beats keep a calm rhythm, going from a slightly high ninety beats per minute to a gentle, regular sixty-three.

"A transplant?" I look between the nurse and my parents, and my anger ebbs away. I look at Abbi's red eyes. She nods and tears start streaming down her face. She wipes them away with her sleeve, and Dad pulls her into a hug at his side. The pain is still sharp, and I realize I should tell them. "Something hurts," I admit. The nurse fusses and reviews things on my chart, then tells me she's giving me some pain meds and they'll probably make me sleepy, so I should rest. She gives my family a careful look as she backs out of the room.

"I'd wait until the doctor comes around to share anything else," she says as she exits.

In the silence of her departure, I breathe through the pain and listen to that miraculous heartbeat. EBE is gone, but someone new is in her place. I want to know their name. I want to say thank you until my voice is raw. I'm going to live.

"Who?" I swallow. "Who saved me this time?"

"Rest, Sera," Mom says, pulling a chair up next to me and offering me a sip of icy water. But there's a nagging feeling in my gut that I can't shake.

"Wait, how is this possible? I was only second on the list."

Mom's face pinches, and she chokes out her next words. "I'm so sorry, my love, but not now."

I tense. "What? What happened? Please tell me." Mom goes fuzzy as the drugs sweep away the pain and start to tug on my consciousness. "Please?" But she shakes her head and looks away. I turn to Abbi.

"Tell me," I demand.

Abbi opens her mouth, and my parents protest. "No," she tells them. "It's not kinder to wait." She steps closer, rests a hand on my shin. "There was a heart . . ."

And with her beautiful, smart, storytelling voice, my sister goes on to tell me the worst thing I've ever had to hear.

"I'm so sorry, Sera," she says. "Luke was in an accident . . . the rain. He was close by. And he was a match."

I lift my hands to my ears as she speaks, as if with the right pressure on my skull I could turn back time so I'll never have to live with what I've lost.

A sob finally escapes me, and I turn onto my side. I curl my knees up to my newly cut-open chest and form a hollow around my center. I take a ragged breath in. The sound I'm hearing is the sound of Luke's heart in my chest, *our* heart, keeping me here, but only because he's gone.

CHAPTER THIRTY-SEVEN

Sera

I meet with Dr. Lee and the surgeons who ruined my death and have now ruined my life. I know, logically, it's not their fault that Luke is dead, but all I can feel is anger, a new kind of rage at the thought that I have to be alive without him here.

"I know this is hard, Sera," Dr. Lee says, standing beside my bed as I glare out the window at the brilliant August sky. "But we don't choose our fates. You were lucky."

I laugh, harsh, bitter.

"No one ever said luck was always a happy thing," she admits, and I finally turn to look at her.

"What am I supposed to do now?" I ask, honestly wondering if there's anything I'll ever be able to do again. Every heartbeat is a reminder that he's gone. And I have to spend my life being grateful for that? I feel sick.

"Live your life," she says, shutting her iPad cover and giving me a sharp look. "There's no reason to think your new heart won't take, but you have a long road ahead of you. You'll need cardiac rehab to recover from this surgery, then a valve replacement procedure in five to ten years. If it's easier to just think one or two steps ahead, do that. But then, yes, you should think about the rest of your life." She packs up her stuff and then turns back with one last thing to say. She must be an older sister, I think. "What would Luke do?"

I don't respond. Instead, I look back to the window, facing the perfect blue sky, which I will continue cursing until it agrees to turn gray.

What would Luke do? I know what he'd do for himself—we talked so much about it—but I've taken all that. Taken everything. More than I deserve. I don't know how to live with this, the unfairness of it all. My bones feel achy and heavy with grief. My eyes are so tired of crying but then continue to do it. Only my heart, Luke's heart, our heart, feels light and effortless. Behind it, my soul is bruised and battered, tired and fed up, wanting only rest.

Abbi is back in school, like she promised, so my days are taken up with Mom sitting there in the room like there's nothing more to say. Like I'm just supposed to heal and move on. Paula wants to visit, but my stomach cramps with anxiety at the thought of seeing her. And the thought of Oliver and Adam sends me back into tears.

"It would've been better to let me die too," I sob when

Mom mentions Paula and the boys. "How will they ever forgive me?"

"Don't say that, Sera. Luke wouldn't want you to say that." She tries to take my hand, and I push her off. My heartbeat races to keep up with me. The unfamiliar rush of blood makes me feel flush and warm.

"How do you know? How could you let them do this? I don't want it!" I scratch at my arm where the IV is. "I don't want it. Please take it out!" I cry as I reach for the bandage on my chest. Mom grabs my arms, holds them down. When I finally settle, she pulls me toward her.

I collapse into her arms and dissolve into tears. There's no getting away from that sound, the beat of Luke's heart, keeping me alive and aware and away from him. A nurse comes in, gives me something to make me sleep.

I wake up with my face still wet. Hurting all over. Blissfully alone. Whatever they've given me has dulled all my edges and dimmed the world around me. The sky has listened, finally, and a gray drizzle greets me through the window. I'm allowed to get up to pee, so I pull my headphones over my ears, put on something loud to drown out my heartbeat. Using my walker, I slowly take myself to the bathroom. Above the sink there's no mirror; they probably don't want anyone seeing how truly messed up they look after surgery. I manage to splash my face and brush my teeth. I don't know what's going on with my hair, but I'm sure I don't care. When I leave the bathroom, I'm no longer alone. Maddy and my mom are chatting by my bed. I ignore them. I just want to go back to sleep.

"Look who's here, Sera!" Mom is overly cheery, and I shoot her a look.

"Hi, Sera." Maddy puts her heavy tote on the ground. I can't imagine why she's brought so much stuff, and I'm pretty sure she's supposed to be at the diner, but I've also lost track of days.

"Shouldn't you be at work?" I say as I sit back on my bed. Mom lifts my feet to help me back in, then makes up some excuse about needing coffee and leaves us alone.

"I took the day off. I wanted to come see you."

"I don't really want to be seen. Sorry to disappoint." I push the button to make the bed rise, and the noise cuts through the tense silence. Maddy isn't deterred, though—she's annoyingly persistent, like usual.

"I brought some of your art supplies over from the studio. Iris thought you might like to paint." She smiles and plops down in the chair my mom keeps vigil in.

"You don't have to stay," I say, strained. "I don't really feel like painting . . . or talking."

Maddy nods. She looks around the room, then back at me. "This whole thing . . . it's fucked, isn't it?" she says point-blank, and though she's blunt, I see sadness in her eyes. They're puffy behind her glasses. Luke was her friend too.

I squeeze my eyes shut against the flow of tears, the anger beating at my rib cage. I can't handle other people's grief. It's too much. I'm still shoveling through mine to no end.

"You should go," I whisper.

"Nah. I don't have anything going on today except researching French culinary courses. Wanna hear about the differences between the grandes sauces?" Maddy pulls her iPad out of her bag and clicks around. "Some of it's in French, so keep up if you can."

She dives into the most boring reading I've ever been subjected to. I let her voice wash over me until I fall asleep again.

CHAPTER THIRTY-EIGHT

Sera

Two weeks later I'm back at home in Northport. Dad is back to teaching, so he's staying in Brookline but coming down to the Cape when he can. I just feel closer to Luke here. I keep to my room, my bed a rather ripe-smelling cocoon even though the visiting rehab nurse, a gentle middle-aged woman named Kathy, washes the sheets every three days. She's the only one who seems to understand how much I just want to be left alone. We exchange no more than five words every visit. She doesn't attempt to make me smile or see the bright side. She just does her job, and I exist, and it's the saddest, most perfect thing.

Daily, Mom comes up and insists I walk on the treadmill if I won't go outside so I don't end up back in the hospital. Eventually Paula comes by and we sit, and we cry, and I forget all the words she says to me as soon as she says them. I can't hold them. I can't bear any of it. I don't understand how she can even look at me. *I* can't look at me. I've thrown blankets over the two mirrors in my room. The French braid a nurse at the hospital did before I left is still in, loose and greasy, until Kathy wordlessly guides me to the bathroom one day and washes it out. I don't want to shower. I sponge where it's necessary. I don't see the point to anything. I watch mindless reality TV that Maddy texts me about, and I walk on the stupid treadmill, and I cry and I sleep and I think about Luke. This is enough of an existence for me. This is all I deserve.

Abbi comes down for a day and tries to bully me into seeing reason, but she's missing vital evidence—anything that shows I'm worthy of taking Luke's future. He's the one who had plans to revitalize his town, to be there for his brothers, to give a seemingly unending amount of love to the people close to him. The only thing I've prepared for is my stupid little paintings and my death. And it's been denied me.

My next visitor is Iris. She smells like paint and has two easels with her. A standing one for her, and a portable one that fits on the bed for me.

"I thought we could paint together," she says calmly, like I'm a sick kitten she's trying to coax into a carrier to be taken to the vet.

"No thanks." I can't imagine making anything new, anything vibrant.

She stays, hovering, a paintbrush twirling between her fingers. "Okay. Can I tell you a story, then?"

I shrug. Everyone has been trying this too. I think it makes them feel better.

"When I was fourteen, my twin sister, Ivy, died of leukemia."

I feel a deep twinge of guilt and sadness for Iris. "I'm sorry."

"It's okay. Well, no, it's not, but I'm okay now."

"You weren't before," I agree. That makes sense.

"No. It seemed like a cruel twist of fate—a mistake—that we'd be born together and she'd get so little time. She was my best friend. She was funny and kind and had an amazing singing voice. I was totally lost without her. And for a long time, I was convinced I wanted to die too."

Iris goes quiet, playing with the long sleeves of her linen tunic.

"I'm not considering that," I admit, "even if I *feel* dead already."

She nods, clears her throat, and keeps talking. "My parents put me in an outpatient program. One week we had a professional artist come and run a workshop on oil painting." She smiles, thinking back on the memory. "Picking up the brush and combining colors gave me the same feeling I used to get listening to Ivy sing. I was young, so I called it a sign. But now I think that artist was just the right person there at the right time. She gave me the tool I needed to pull myself back into my own life."

"I don't have a life," I mutter.

"Life is for the living, Sera. I had to learn it, and you will too. I had to learn that my sister loved me as much as I loved her, and that she wouldn't want me not to live just because she wasn't with me. I wouldn't have wanted her to waste her life, her talent. Why wouldn't she feel the same toward me? Just because it was hard didn't mean it wasn't worth trying."

She sounds like Luke, upset with me for not imagining our

future simply because I wasn't sure I'd get one. Challenging me to live while I could instead of just planning for it all to end. Tears prick the corners of my eyes as I nod.

Iris stands up. "I'll leave all this with you. Maybe there's a tool here that will help, but maybe you'll find that somewhere else. Just be open to it, when it comes."

I finally find my voice through my tears. "How am I supposed to take the life that was his?"

"Oh, Sera. I don't think he'd begrudge you that. I don't think he'd know the difference between your happiness and his." Iris is wistful, her eyes drying. She gestures toward the easel she brought me. "I'll go. But think about it. Okay?"

When she's gone, I let the tears out until I'm drained and find a kind of calm. I don't want to work on my own art, but I do want to see Luke's. I crawl out of bed and, from underneath it, pull out a bin where I've been keeping things from the summer. Rocks and shells and the gifts from the kids, but also all the drawings Luke was throwing away and all the posters he'd designed for events that I found around town. I smooth them out gently, line them up in a circle until I'm surrounded by the bold text and sharp black lines of his beautiful work.

The way he captured the world, always in motion, always moving, shifting, changing. *Living,* a tired but reawoken part of my mind whispers.

I shuffle through the sketches. The seagulls, herons, and crows. A small bird I think might be a finch. A drawing of his brothers and his mom; one of me, half-finished, asleep; another where I'm standing by the edge of the water at our beach. One of a teammate halfway through a swing. A few close-ups of shells, their insides swirling with history. My window from his room, which sits dark and quiet across from me now. The waiting room in Boston, the museum, the sea and the sea and the sea.

There are more of the harbor than I remember. The abandoned buildings on Harborside Main tucked into each other for support, but not lifeless. Never lifeless. I pick up one of Frappie's, and the first bloom of an idea takes root like a seed in my heart.

CHAPTER THIRTY-NINE

Sera

Nine Months Later

Abbi is taking too long to get ready, fussing with the waves she's put in my newly cut hair.

"Can you be done, please? I need to get there early to help finish setting up and rehearse my speech." I clench the notebook with all the details for tonight's event. It's already curved from my sweaty palms handling it over the last few months. It's been a busy year.

"Okay, okay, yes, I'm done. You can put this on now."

I turn and Abbi is holding up the yellow dress, the one I bought with Maddy last summer. I blush a little, thinking about the last time I wore it, but I have to keep some memories for myself. I put the dress on, and Abbi zips me up, plays with the way my hair is falling for a minute until I brush her off gently.

"Can you make sure Mom and Paula have what they need from Maddy for the catering?"

"Yep." Abbi flounces to the door, her own black dress swirling at her ankles. She stops and turns back to me. "And, just in case there isn't time later, I'm really proud of you, Sera. The gallery is a huge achievement, and Luke would be so pleased to see you doing your work *and* helping Northport and his family."

I feel my eyes well up. "Shit. I should've worn waterproof mascara," I say into her neck as I hug her tight. "Thank you."

She leaves, and I scan my room to make sure I haven't forgotten anything. It's a total mess, the closet half-empty and my suitcase on the bed still barely packed, but there's nothing I can do now. I have a gallery opening to run.

Down on Harborside Main, big string lights have been hung through the abandoned end, which isn't as abandoned anymore. Frappie's is lit up like a lighthouse when I pull up and park out front. And the two buildings next to it show signs of fresh paint and new windows. When I won the grant to turn the building into a collaborative art gallery, I promised not to tear anything down. The bones of the building were good—those tall windows let in so much light, now that they're clear of dust and paint. We mostly did some fixing up inside so the layout worked better. My dad found a new love of saws and blueprints and built a beautiful wood-and-glass display case to hold smaller pieces. I have the last handful of pieces in the back of my car, part of the dedication exhibit, and I carry them in carefully, thanking Izzy when she grabs the door for me.

"Oh, are these them?" she asks, excited, though her eyes are damp with a sadness I know well. Izzy and I have become closer in the last year. She helped with a lot of the gallery plans, showing up in overalls ready to paint and hammer and hang. It's nice to be able to talk to someone who cared so much about Luke too.

"Yep. Left wall. Help me hang them?"

Izzy takes the top three off my hands and we go to work, only two hours until opening.

As she unwraps the first piece, she slows and stares, her pink hair falling across the canvas.

"They're beautiful, Sera." She wipes a tear off her cheek, and I lean into her, looking down at the piece. I've been getting all of Luke's salvaged work framed. Iris helped me pick out the mats and frame styles. Izzy holds the heron, its long neck regal and strong. The one on my lap is of his brothers reeling in a fish off the end of the dock.

Designing this exhibit took me all year, working out the layout and making a new piece of my own to fit with them.

There are twelve in all. I'm hanging them on the wall like a clock around a mixed-media piece I made out of Luke's smaller abandoned drawings. In the center is a photo I took of him and his brothers out on the boat, the three of them facing west, where we'd seen the spout of a whale. I enlarged it so the sky above them could fit multiple scans of the seabirds Luke drew by the dozen. Terns and gulls, even a lone heron. The composition took me forever, but I'm happy with how it turned out.

"Let's get them hung," I say, giving Izzy a quick hug.

The two hours fly by as I remind volunteers of their jobs, fix a display I decide last minute needs to be rearranged, and help Maddy, Mom, and Paula with the food. When we open the doors at seven, the sky is still bright, and the gallery is filled with light. I'm floored by how many people come through. The place is practically packed by seven thirty. I have to ask one of Luke's old teammates to man the door and only let more people in as others leave. Then I rush to the little presentation area we've staged by the front.

I clear my throat and step up to the mic Cam is letting us borrow.

"Good evening, everyone." My voice crackles through the space.

The crowd lowers its chatter, moves closer. I look down at my curled notebook one last time, then put it on the stool next to me.

"Thank you so much for coming to the opening of Northport's newest gallery, Harborside View." There's a whistle from one corner, and I tamp down my smile. Maddy, of course. "After months of hard work, I'm so happy we're open to show the world what Northport has to offer. The proceeds from all purchases you make tonight, and fifteen percent of all purchases at Harborside View in the future, will be put into the Luke Tisdale Scholarship Fund, which will be awarded annually to a Northport graduating senior looking to study art. Let's have a round of applause for our local businesses and volunteers who were able to make this all possible."

I clap with everyone else, the sound rising into the old wooden rafters and out into the warm June night.

"If a piece is stickered with a little star, it's been purchased, so move quick," I joke. "Also, please don't forget to check out our dedication exhibit on the east wall"—I wave my arm toward Luke's work—"and consider making any additional donations to the organ match program. A reminder, however, that unfortunately none of those pieces are for sale. They're part of our permanent collection." Paula and I agreed we couldn't let any of the work go, no matter the price.

With the details out of the way, all that's left is the scribble in my head of all the things I want to say but know can't be covered in one rushed speech. But I don't have to say it all now, I remind myself. There's plenty of time. I take a breath and say what's needed.

"There's nothing like the pressure of a shorter life expectancy to make you make hard choices."

My voice rings out into the gallery like a bell. I catch the eyes of some of Luke's other organ recipients around the room. My heart thumps, proud and sad at the same time. I place my palm over it and take a slow breath before continuing.

"Some people would crack under that. I have." I try to lighten my voice, and a couple of laughs break the tension. Paula smiles at me encouragingly. A few steps to my right I see Mom squeeze Abbi to her side, hard enough to hurt.

"But I was lucky to know someone who encouraged me to keep living." I swallow. My throat feels thick, and my eyes well with tears. I let them run but somehow keep my voice steady. "Luke Tisdale had so much life in him, and he just wanted to share it. He made Northport vibrant and fun. He brought me back to life long before this." I pat my chest. The flat sound echoes out. "He saw beauty in the world all around him, and his work shows that. I'm so happy that we can share that with you tonight and share in his dream of reviving Northport together."

There's another round of applause, and I smile proudly before stepping away. Maddy meets me in the corner with tissues.

"Way to make me look like a crybaby," she says.

I laugh and hug her, then I'm pulled away by someone interested in some of the art.

A couple of hours later, the room is still buzzing with people even though most of the art has been purchased. I've chatted with everyone, and my job is done for now. I hover in a corner and watch for a bit until my phone alarm buzzes me out of my reverie.

I find Paula and the boys and give them all quick hugs. Maddy and I leave for Paris in the morning, and I need to finish packing. I give the keys to Abbi and Cam and walk home in the cool blue night. The sounds of the Cape blanket me. The bats fly overhead, there's a breeze blowing through the scraggly oaks, and the peepers revel in the humid night. And beyond all that, I can hear the soft crash of the ocean against the sand, as steady and as even as my heartbeat.

AUTHOR'S NOTE

Curiosity about science and medicine often lies at the center of my writing. *Last Kiss of Summer* was inspired by real stories of domino surgery, but I was also interested in what it means to fall in love with someone you're so intrinsically tied to.

For the medical side of things, I pored through information from hospitals like Massachusetts General, Children's Hospital of Philadelphia, Cleveland Clinic, and University of Pittsburgh Medical Center; read articles from the *American Journal of Transplantation* and organizations like the American Heart Association, the Mayo Clinic, and the National Institutes of Health's National Library of Medicine; and scoured data from the National Social Security Administration, the Health Resources and Services Administration Organ Procurement and Transplantation Network (HRSA/OPTN), and the United Network for Organ Sharing (UNOS). I also spoke to a couple of medical professionals. A huge thank-you to Shirlene Obuobi, MD, and Molly Rojee, RN, for their guidance. Their expertise was so helpful; the departures from fact in order to better serve this novel are my own.

What I learned as I researched and wrote this book was that every individual patient's story is unique, like every individual love story is unique. As I got to know and love Sera and Luke, I knew I would need to take some liberties with the medical facts of their heart conditions and treatments so they could have the best summer of their lives. For instance, in the real world, Sera wouldn't have as much freedom to be up and about as much as she is, and the heart transplant at the end wouldn't be a viable option for her because of the previous surgery, but it felt right for their fictional story to make these choices.

If you're curious to learn more about organ donation, please check out UNOS at UNOS.org.

ACKNOWLEDGMENTS

No book is ever the solo work of just the author. I'm so thankful for the community around me that made this not only possible but truly fun. Thank you to:

Jess Regel at Helm Literary for believing without hesitation in my ability to write this book. I'm so grateful to have you as my agent and even more grateful to call you my friend.

Jen Klonsky and Simone Roberts-Payne for your great editorial guidance, and everyone else at Penguin Young Readers and Penguin Random House who touched this book before it reached readers, including but not limited to Nicole Rheingans, Miranda Shulman, Natalie Vielkind, Cindy Howle, Misha Kydd, Janet Rosenberg, and Christine Ma.

Jessica Harriton and the team at Alloy, particularly Lanie Davis and Romy Golan, for your whip-smart ideas and for making sure I never felt alone with the harder parts of this book.

Jessica Jenkins for the beautifully perfect cover.

The Rights People team for finding such great international homes for Sera and Luke.

Mom and Dad for always letting me walk around with my head in the sky or in a book, and for telling me I could do this way before I believed it myself. Dan for being there every step of the way through this and for always reminding me that I do know what I'm doing when I start to worry I don't. Matt and Lauren for listening and sharing in my excitement.

Bubba for taking every book I've ever handed you and asking if it's mine—this one is!

JR, Shel, Finn, and Piper for being a home I can come to whenever I need and for reading so much I have no choice but to try and keep up.

My best friends, Claire, Zuri, Kate, and Al, for all the advice so I never had to make decisions alone, and for making life in general full and fantastic.

My YA writing group, Al, KC, Holly, and Rachel, for your enthusiasm, shared woes, and incredible, unblinking support. You're next!

Libraries! Particularly the Sudbury Goodnow Library, as well as the Sandwich Public Library, for letting me in and for all you do for readers of all ages.

My clients—your genius is an inspiration every day, and I can only hope to weather my author experiences as gracefully as you have.

Sara DeNobrega, Deidre Smerillo, Jennifer Lyons, and all my publishing colleagues for your support of me as an agent and now as an author.

Arthur Flowers, Bruce Bauman, and Steve Erickson, who put me on the road to writing for more than just myself. And to all the other writers and mentors who have read my work and supported this crazy dream.

My *best*-best friend, Lauren Schoen, for taking me with you to Martha's Vineyard for our teenage summers and for always being so accepting of my high need for your approval and opinions, which I value more than the peanut butter sauce at Mad Martha's.

Darlene and Steve for always letting me overstay my welcome on the Vineyard, where I wrote the first draft of this book. I'll be back for the next one.

And Tako. Every writer needs a grouchy, cuddly emotional support mascot to remind us to feed them, and thus ourselves.